What
Florida Writers Association Collection, Volume 9

Featuring Person of Renown author

E. J. Wenstrom

Published by Black Oyster Publishing Company, Inc.

For inquiries write to:

Black Oyster Publishing, 806 Dogwood Drive

Casselberry, Florida 32707

ISBN: 978-1546992097

ACKNOWLEDGMENTS

One-hundred-eighty-five entries poured in from one-hundred-sixty-two FWA members, twenty-three of whom submitted two stories. Entries were posted without author names to a specially designed website accessible only by judges. Our judges read and scored the entries. FWA is deeply indebted to them, and thanks each for their time, dedication, and expertise.

Each entry is presented as submitted, with only minor editing, if mistakes like missing quote marks, misspelled words, or forgotten periods happen to be caught during the audit stage. Many of the entrants took advantage of either attending one of FWA's many Critique Groups across the state or using FWA's editing service, which offered special pricing. The quality of entries reflects the professionalism of our members. Thank you, Bobbie Christmas, for managing that special editing service.

Thank you to Christine Holmes and WhiteRabbitGraphix.com for the design of the cover for *Florida Writers Association Collection, Volume 9, What a Character!*

It is with heartfelt gratitude that FWA acknowledges E. J. Wenstrom's contribution to this publication. She had perhaps the hardest job of all – picking only ten to be her favorites out of sixty truly exciting winning stories.

The fourth annual Youth Writers Collection Contest, created to provide our youth members an opportunity to become published authors, produced twelve winners, three of whom submitted two entries. FWA acknowledges and thanks our Youth Writers Groups, their Group Leaders and especially Serena Schreiber and Kristen Stieffel for their efforts to accomplish this goal.

Our sincere thanks from FWA's Board of Directors to Tom Swartz of Black Oyster Publishing for being our official Collections publisher, and for graciously donating all publishing costs. His patience and expertise throughout all aspects of production were invaluable.

Su Gerheim
Collection Contests Coordinator, 2017

Table of Contents

***What a Character,* Florida Writers Association Youth Collection, Volume 4**

Age Group 9-13

Age Group 14-17

INTRODUCTION

What a Character!

Florida Writers Association Collection, Volume 9

This phrase—the theme of this year's Florida Writers Association Collection—is one that is often thrown around in a tongue-in-cheek manner. Even if we mean it in a friendly way, when we throw out this phrase about someone, the phrase tends to have a tinge to it … *she is a bit odd, there is something a little off, he doesn't quite fit in, in some way.*

But as authors, that thing that turns a person just a few degrees off kilter is exactly what we live for. It is the thing that makes us human, rounds out our characters, and brings stories to life. A character's *character-ness* is to be celebrated.

Of course, this is not the only way we talk about "character." There are also the tried and true, the loyal, the ones willing to stand by their principles no matter how dark the circumstances nor how dire the consequences. This type of character makes for some of our world's most remarkable stories, too—and some of its most important.

Ultimately, both of these types of "character" tend to lie in each of us, to varying degrees and facets. There are eccentricities in each of us. And, we all have the grit to fight for those things most important to us.

Being in touch with both of these sides of "character" makes us better authors. And, in turn it makes us better people.

In the stories that follow, you will find a celebration of characters of both types, and from all across the spectrum. I'll leave it to you to determine which characters are which types.

E. J. Wenstrom
2017

New York Rain

The back door opens and a figure crawls into my cab.

"West forty-five and ninth." His words are stiff, like he's trying to hide an accent.

"Sure." It's only a few blocks. But it's raining tonight.

New York in July. The locals hate it. Where I'm from, it's always this hot. Hotter, even. Where I'm from, the rain burns like acid. So here, it doesn't bother me. Rain means it's safe out for us Logians. That the Petulians have to stay in.

And more fares, too—New Yorkers, you'd think the rain burned *their* skin, the way they run from it. Not that I'm in this for the money. Just my cover. I drive the field agents a few blocks. Get their reports. Call it in. It's a low key gig. But the locals' food is pretty good, so I like keeping USDs around.

I peer into the rearview mirror. The guy's face is hidden under a wide-brimmed hat. Despite the heat, he's in long pants, and a long raincoat with sleeves that are wrapped up into gloved fists. It's odd, sure, but who isn't, in this city.

We drive in silence. I pull up to the curb.

"Thank you."

I reach my arm back and take the folded bills from him. "Stay dry out there." Not that he'll have any trouble, all bundled up like that.

He slams the door on my words, and he's running across the middle of the street, hunched under an umbrella, never mind the traffic.

I shake my head with a snicker. Then I look down to sort the cash. But there are no bills in the folded mass he passed me—just ripped papers, folded into a bill-shape.

I leap from the cab, the AC rushing out around me.

"Hey! This ain't how we pay around here!" I yell.

But he's already disappeared into the street-light glare.

"Aaaugh!" I kick the side of the cab before getting back in. I'm smarter than that. But something about the rain, it's taking me back home, and I forget how the locals can't be trusted.

I blame the timing. Ezm's spawn must be due any day now. Makes a guy homesick.

They warn you about planet-fever, how the mind can get antsy trapped on a single globe so long, when we're used to rocketing through the stars. Just no one ever thinks it'll be them.

I plop back into the cab and toss the papers into the passenger seat. Try to remind myself it's not about the cash. The mission. That's what really matters.

I just hate being played for a damn fool. Maybe I've been here too long. Maybe it's time I raised a flag to HQ and went home. To Ezm and the spawn.

I squint and pick the papers back up—there's something scrawled on them: "NO DEAL."

A chill runs down my neck with the dripping water, and I drop the paper. That was no human. It was a Petulian. Here in my own cab.

And me, with my guard completely down. My hearts race, pounding out of sync. We gave them a procedure to respond to the truce agreement. Looks like they ignored it.

How was a Petulian even out on a night like this? No wonder he was covered head to toe. He practically gave himself away with that getup, how did I not see it? I'm getting too comfortable in this world.

We were going to make it easy on them. But now it's going to be a full-out war, this time. By the time it's over, there won't be anything left to mine for either of us.

I come back to myself with a jolt.

I pick up my telecomm: "Mothership."

While it works to connect, I pull a U-ie and head after that Petulian bastard.

The rain is getting worse, pounding on the roof and making it harder to make out the figures on the sidewalk. Maybe it's doing me a favor and melting that Petulian shit right now.

The automessage picks up.

"Greetings. We are unable to assist your hemisphere at this moment. The Chief on duty will respond when we receive your signal."

"It's Xzan. You're not going to believe this. Call me right now, damnit."

I disconnect. Hell.

When I look back up from the telecomm, there he is, huddled under an awning, clutching that dumb wide-brimmed hat tight over his face.

That bastard.

I swerve up against the curb and leap out onto the sidewalk.

"Hey!" I shout.

He jolts when he sees me, makes like he's going to run, but then jumps back again when he reaches the slate of water leaking off the awning's edge.

"Didn't think I'd look for you, didjya?"

He calls back to me, though between the roll of thunder and his Petulian accent, all I catch is something about *protocols.*

He has a point—ground agents aren't supposed to take matters into our own hands. We follow directives and we report back. Who ordered me to chase a Petulian down in the street? No one.

But if I follow protocol, I know exactly what happens. Their message goes up the Logian flagpole, and after a message like this one, nothing gets relayed back down. One button and poof, the planet disintegrates, along with all of us on it. And I got a spawn to get back to. So forget protocol.

It's his own fault. If the Petulians had followed protocol in the first place, the Council would go on with negotiations for ages.

"Protocol?" I say, edging up on him. "Protocol's *gone*."

I knock off his hat and shove him out into the rain, then wrestle him out of the raincoat.

As the drops land on his head and soak through his shirt, his skin begins to sizzle. He cries out. I step back, and a grim satisfaction swells within me. Soon all that's left is a pile of clothes and yellow ooze.

Then I drop his note next to him. It settles into the wet sidewalk and the ink blots. Soon it is completely illegible.

As I head back to my cab, my telecomm buzzes.

"Xzan here."

"What's going on?" It's Admiral Vuuz. The reception is crackly through the cloud cover.

"False alarm," I say. "Thought a Petulain was tailing me. In this weather, it gave me the willies. But it's fine. Just a rainy night playing tricks on me."

"A Petulian? In the rain? You've been planet-side too long."

"Tell me about it. In fact," I start. "I was thinking. How about a station back home for a while?"

The line goes quiet as Vuuz considers.

All tonight bought me was time. But as long as I'm out of here before the Petulains hand off another message, I don't care what happens next.

"Yeah, we could do that," Vuuz says. "Give me a few days to look into it."

I grab a newspaper out of a case and use it to wipe off the goop sticking to my fingers.

"Great, great. The sooner the better. I'm a father now, you know. Or about to be."

E. J. Wenstrom

E. J. Wenstrom is a fantasy and science fiction author, lover of monsters, consumer of stories, and coffee addict. Her ongoing *Chronicles of the Third Realm Wars* series starts with her FWA Book of the Year-winning debut, ***Mud***. Join her email list at ejwenstrom.com for a free prequel novella.

Mr. Redden

I saw him out our pool hall picture windows, walking along busy Harvard Boulevard with a careful gait, clutching a skinny case to his side like it contained diamonds. He held himself erect, moving slow, eyes forward. I figured him for a hundred, hundred and ten years old. I knew immediately he was going to be trouble.

Dad confirmed it the moment the geezer came in.

"Hello, sir. Fine day for pool," my father said. "Meeting someone or—?"

"Table for one I'm afraid," the old man spoke in a quiet, firm voice. "Straight not snooker."

"It's your lucky day, Mr.—?"

"Redden," the man extended his hand. "John Redden."

"Mr. Redden, we have a special going on—" Dad looked my way as he shook the man's hand. "Kind of a house rule...."

No Dad, no, for the love of God....

"Play with my boy and you play for free."

And there it was, my sentence for the afternoon.

"Well, sir, I would be honored," the old guy bowed slightly in my direction, "if the boy doesn't mind."

"But Dad, I've got—."

"Your *cue* under the *counter*." Dad pinned me with his eyes like a bug on a board. "Chalk it up." He smiled at the old geeze. "Pick any open table. My son Mark will bring the balls."

My first life lesson began that day as I watched the old dude flip the latches on his battered case and pull a work of art from its faded gold velvet lining. The two-piece cue had a polished white ash front with a dark stained mahogany butt. Carved and inlaid with mother-of-pearl along the handle and a tiny ring of red gemstones top and bottom, the stick glinted in his hands as he screwed its two halves together.

"Wow," was all I could think to say.

"Here," he held it out to me, "want to try her?"

"No, I'm good," I said. "I'd probably break it or something."

"It's called a Portuguese Fancy. Won her off a sailor a long time ago in a place not near as nice as this."

He plucked a chalk off the table rail and proceeded to dab at his cue tip. Not casual and cool like the high school kids. He took his time—I'd find out later he did that with everything—and covered every sliver of exposed tip with blue chalk.

I shifted from foot to foot.

He looked up as if just seeing me. "You break," he said.

Watch this, Methuselah.

CRACK.

I blasted the triangle of balls hard enough to scatter all fifteen across the blue felt, dropping the 11 and 14 in the process. I stole a glance at Mr. Redden and received a nod and a tiny smile.

"Looks like I'm stripes," I said. *And two balls ahead.*

My next shot was toast. The white cue ball hugged the cushion, trapped behind two solids. I banged it hard as I could and watched the balls slam around.

Then Mr. Redden went to work.

He stalked the table like a jungle cat, checking angles, sightlines, pondering shot order—*the dude took forever*—until finally, he bent to the shot. Arthritic fingers shrugged off crooked stiffness and curled to a shape they must have formed a million times. Thumb and forefinger encircled the cue, three remaining fingers splayed wide and pressed to the felt.

Mr. Redden stroked the cue stick smoothly once, twice, and tapped the cue ball just hard enough to slide the green 6 into the side pocket and stop the white ball behind the red 3 halfway up the table. He took that straight-in corner shot and caromed the cue ball off a cushion to leave it with an easy angle on the maroon 7. He stroked that one into the opposite side pocket—and stopped to examine his cue tip for chalk.

Are you kidding me?

I bounced the butt end of my cue on the floor, rocking the stick hand to hand. "Nice shooting, sir."

He looked at me, removed his wire-frame old-person glasses and polished them with a handkerchief he pulled from his shirt pocket. "I appreciate that, young Master Mark. And I want to thank you for indulging an old man with your company."

He put his glasses back on and studied me a beat then bent and shot quick. CLACK! The cue ball shot the length of the table to the yellow 1-ball camped in front of the corner pocket—a slam dunker. The 1 bounced in and out and rolled to the middle of the table.

"Ooh, tough luck man," I couldn't help grinning. I had a bead on my 10-ball and rushed to blast it into the corner. It sank with a satisfying CLUNK!

I looked over and he smiled at me and picked up the chalk.

Now it's my turn, sucker.

My 13-ball ticked the edge of the cushion and slid on by the side pocket.

"Shi—*oot!*" I slammed the cue butt on the floor.

"MARK!" My dad called from the far counter.

And so it went.

I spent a summer's worth of Saturdays with Mr. Redden. After the first few I actually looked forward to them. I learned to shoot a much better stick, in spite of myself. I learned to plan my shots. *"Think. Where's that cue ball going to end up after you take the easy shot?"* I developed a work ethic. *"Your dad must be real proud of you, the way you take care of these tables."* Most important, I started forming a life philosophy, though I didn't know it at the time. *"Any fool can slam-bang balls around and hope, Mark. The smart man uses just enough to get the job done and controls his outcome."*

Then came that Saturday morning in August.

Mr. Redden was late, which never happened. I busied myself brushing tables, eyes scanning the sidewalk every thirty seconds. I saw a bag lady approaching slowly, but paid her no mind until the bell dinged as she opened the pool hall front door.

She stopped at the front counter and spoke to my dad. I noticed the pool case in her hands only when she slid it across the counter. He looked up and motioned me over. I shook my head and stayed rooted in place.

No way. Huh uh. No. I couldn't swallow.

"Come here, son," my dad said. "I'd like you to meet someone."

When I refused, the old lady walked over. She changed from bag lady to sweet old grandmother the closer she got—one with a sad smile and shiny green eyes.

"You're the young man my John carried on about." She held out her hand and in reflex, I took it. She pressed my hand between both of hers. "He was so proud of you, said you shoot a mean stick, when you try."

I yanked my hand away. "Where's Mr. Redden?"

"I brought you something he wanted you to have."

"Give it back. Tell him he can give it to me himself."

"I'm sorry, honey." The old lady's sparkling eyes dripped tears. "I wish I could, I really wish I could."

Mark McWaters

Mark McWaters has an MFA in Creative Writing from the University of North Carolina and is an award-winning 25+ years advertising veteran. Creative Director/copywriter stints at several national advertising agencies kept his writing wheels greased. He is a Writers Group Leader, past RPLA *Collections,* Short Fiction and YA Novel winner.

Vignettes

They were scuffed, scraped shoes
skinned of all their original sheen,
shoes so worn they resembled
the cracked, brown earth of the Mojave.
Bag lady shoes.

Shoes as soft as butter
with the patina of Italian leather
slid across the scarred stage floor
in pirouettes and smooth jetes.
Ballerina shoes.

The pungent odor of rain-wet shoes,
the damp-dog smell of drying shoes
left a distinct reminder in the air
of closeted rooms on cold winter days.
Little boy shoes.

The click-clack of high heels
echoed in the halls.
The staccato sound of footsteps,
like Nazis on parade.
Headmistress shoes.

Standing two stories tall,
the lucite-encased display of brown and black shoes
is filled with tiny high tops and grown-up heels,
worn-through work boots and dangling laces.
Holocaust shoes.

Elise Zarli

Elise Zarli is a retired nurse and a member of the Arcadia Writers' Group. She has published two books of fiction and is currently working on her latest one. She writes, paints, and maintains a botanical garden that she shares with her husband and pets.

Just Your Average Hero

You'd think wearing skintight spandex and a red cape in broad daylight would get a guy noticed. I haven't had an Oreo in over three months so my super suit looks extra spiffy stretched out against my four-pack abs and what will one day be my bulging biceps.

But no. Every other cosplaying, wannabe, police academy reject is hitting the streets looking for Corporal Chaos. Amateurs. They have no idea that he's holed up in an abandoned warehouse on the edge of town, the kind of neighborhood where the sun sets an hour early and the city buses don't run.

I found that last part out the hard way when the driver made me get off the bus seventeen blocks away.

"Moron. Read the map at the stop," he snarled. "You people are freaks."

I think he was talking about the couple that had gotten off a few stops earlier. They were dressed in canary yellow jumpsuits with real feather wings sewn on, but they told me that it was just for show and they couldn't actually fly.

Yet, I told them. Can't fly *yet*. They seemed confused.

The walk made me pretty sweaty so my super suit had big, matching, armpit stains, but I felt good overall, considering that I had the inside information that Chaos would be alone in his lair.

I found him in his hideout, which was like an office, except more evil. He had a bunch of maps on the wall with pins in them.

"Picking your next target, Corporal? Not on my watch!"

The look on his face when I launched myself at him was priceless. I should have waited for backup, but heroes never wait for backup. We cross the line and live on the edge. It's in our blood.

"Gah! What are you doing? What the hell's wrong with you?" he yelled, putting his arms up to block the beam from my wrist-mounted laser.

"Don't swear, Chaos. I won't tolerate profanity," I told him.

He must have had some kind of invisible laser repellent because he threw me off pretty easily. I'd bulked up to 108 pounds, but even so, his evil strength was too much for me. He kind of trussed me up and tossed me in a broom closet. I tried to improvise an explosive device to blow the door off and re-engage, but all I could find was some Lemon Pledge and a damp mop that smelled like barf. I have to admit, I was a little scared. Even good guys lose a fight sometimes, but it was getting way after dark and mom was super strict about my curfew. She had no idea how hard it was to keep the town safe when you have a nine o'clock bedtime.

Chaos obviously had the cops on his payroll, because they totally took his side and didn't search his lair. They wouldn't even look through his desk for evidence of evil plans before they drove me home. But I got in the last zinger, like heroes always do.

"Don't worry Corporal. Maybe you'll get promoted to Sergeant some day," I taunted him.

"My name is Russell, you weirdo."

So now I knew Corporal Chaos's secret identity. Pretty clever, huh? Mom wasn't too happy but she'd gotten used to the crooked cops bringing me home from my missions.

"Where was he?" she asked the crooked cop in charge.

"Water Plant. No damage this time."

She shooed me upstairs and called Dr. Braverman's answering service.

Dr. Braverman was one of Chaos's minions. I knew it; I just couldn't prove it.

The next day most of the wannabe heroes were gone. Just like that. I scoffed at how easily they'd given up. Probably moved on to try their hand at slaying vampires or werewolves. Dummies. Like vampires or werewolves even existed. At least with them gone, I could do my thing without worrying about collateral damage. I rinsed out the armpits of my super suit and headed out as soon as mom went to work. My anonymous source had messaged me that Chaos had undergone major reconstructive surgery overnight and was now posing as the manager at Walgreens.

No one turns a beloved neighborhood drugstore evil on my watch.

This is the part where the lawyer says I have to stop talking because it could hurt my case when I go to court next month. It's like in the movies where they try to shut the hero up and frame him for stuff. They even got to mom, which is a real setback because she pays for my bus pass and now I don't have any transportation.

"He was doing fine until that comic book convention came to town. Next thing you know, the suit came out again," I overheard her saying to the lawyer.

So now I'm a lone wolf. Abandoned by everyone. No family. No friends. They even took my super suit. The lawyer says I can't get it back and that I definitely can't wear it to court. He doesn't understand that a hero never shows his real face to the world. Taking my suit is like handing Superman a big old bag of kryptonite.

What they don't know is that they only took *one* of my super suits. Heroes always have a back up plan, an exit strategy, a clean uniform hidden under the mattress. I knew the day would come when it would just be me against the world. And dum-dum Dr. Braverman has an office on the first floor with windows that open. Amateur.

I hate leaving. But my anonymous source just sent me another urgent message on my secret, non-traceable, phone that I got from the dentist's office prize box.

Chaos is back.

My source says that I have to head right over to the Dairy Queen on Oak Street. It's mission critical to leave now. Heroes don't have time for goodbyes and

CAT scans and mandatory court appearances. Even an average hero like me knows that when duty calls, you answer. With my super suit on, I'm invincible. And after I finally defeat Corporal Chaos, I'll have an Oreo Blizzard with extra whipped cream and then call mom for a ride home.

I hope I don't get grounded again.

K.C. Bonner

K. C. Bonner is a Florida native. She lives in southwest Florida and has an assortment of farm animals and rescue pets Although she generally prefers the company of goats and chickens to humans, she makes allowances for her family.

The Leg

I didn't want to scare my son once I saw him at the airport. My leg bounced. The back of my head sunk against the seat's rest and the 737's constant hum burrowing into my brain. I recalled two years ago waving my wife Claire goodbye as she stood alone with our little boy Kevin Junior– I called him Kev. Time flashed by and still I'm filled with fear, but this time for Kev.

He was four when I deployed to Afghanistan. Though I knew little boys changed a lot in two years, I knew some things never changed. Kev always scared easily. I recalled one year when I dressed up as Santa. I came in the front door. He screamed and cowered behind the Christmas tree, refusing to emerge until I disrobed and eased him out with a calming tone. "It's me. It's only Daddy."

I opened my eyes. A Southwest Airline flight attendant floated down the dark aisle, her eyes scanning the rows of sleepy passengers. She appeared too peppy for being at the tail end of a trans-Atlantic flight.

I felt the twitchy burn below my left knee. Instinctively, I reached to scratch. Clink. I hit my metal prosthetic and I was again reminded of the mine that blew off my lower leg. I rubbed my thigh. I could picture Kev screaming at the sight of my robotic leg, and then running for the closet. The thought saddened me deeper than I ever imagined. My son, my Kev, scared of me.

I was the one who held him seconds after he was born. He was the one I rocked in my arms, pacing next to his crib trying to settle him. He awoke a tenderness inside me I never knew existed. I'd lie on my side on the floor and play peek-a-boo with his stuffed Mickey Mouse while Claire cleaned and powdered his rashy bottom. His smile was the best thrill in the world.

I reached into my jacket pocket and pulled out the fist-sized stuffed puffin he handed me when I deployed. "She'll protect you," he told me. The Afghan desert winds and sun had bleached the puffin's furry mat, but holding it to my face, I still smelled Kev. One whiff and I felt Kev's chubby arms wrapped around my neck, giggling as he rubbed his nose against mine.

But none of this mattered if he darted away from me and my crippled body. I couldn't hold him, play with him, and make him laugh.

My entire time in rehab as I healed and learned to walk on this metal leg, I thought about Kev. I'd grunt and strain on my walker and remembered the times I tried to man up Kev. I'd take him outside, run him around, and toss a ball with him. I'd show him how to shoot a rubber band at targets. I'd kid around with him and pop up beside his bed to give him a playful fright. I'd even show him creepy movies, talking about them with excitement and thrill. But he hated all of it. He liked low-key excitement. Stories with happy endings. Playing with stuffed animals. Claire reinforced these behaviors, feeding him nerdy things like tame cartoon episodes of Star Wars. In the hospital, I'd smile at the nurses and fake bravery as I'd learned as a kid. Kev never hid his fear. He hid from it.

And now, at six, I knew Kev wasn't ready to see this thing.

"Sir?" A pretty, blonde attendant smiled at me. She whispered, "Do you want another?" She pointed to the empty mini-bottle of liquor resting on my tray.

"Uh…" I wanted one. But I already downed a few Guinesses at Heathrow during my layover and a pair of these little bottles in flight. Any more and I'd be stumbling all over this metal leg of mine, likely scaring Kev even more. "No thanks." I smiled weakly.

She took my empty bottle and shuffled off.

I jammed the stuffed puffin back into my jacket pocket.

The plane shuttered.

I gasped and gripped the armrest. Behind closed eyes, bursting flashes of gunfire rushed through me like a nightmare in fast forward. And then, gone.

"Sir," the attendant whispered. "You okay?"

I faked a smile. "Yeah. Fine."

She nodded and pointed. "Your tray table. We'll be landing shortly."

I clicked the tray table up and straightened the seat's incline. Shifting, I felt a slight pinch of the metal leg's strappings against my lower thigh. I grabbed the sides of my fake leg and repositioned.

The landing was rough. Every bounce and jolt shifted my leg, the prosthetic pinching my skin.

At last on the ground, the plane rolled to the terminal. Lights came on and people stood and groaned as they retrieved their luggage from overhead bins. My injured leg throbbed. I favored the real leg so much I practically dragged the metal one down the aisle.

As usual, I felt the stares and hushed whispers, especially from children, gawking at this thing emerging from the bottom of my shorts. I gripped my bag and tried to ignore the attention. Unfortunately, doing this made me think about what bothered me the most – seeing my son. Or more accurately, him seeing me. Every wobbled step brought me closer to the inevitable shocked face, possibly a yelp, and him running away. I had already missed a third of his life. Though anxious to see him, I dreaded his reaction.

The security checkpoint lay a hundred yards ahead. I breathed and hobbled forward, resisting the urge toward the airport lounge on my right. Just one more drink. Maybe two. – *No.* – I continued on. This walk felt longer than the ten-mile hikes through the Afghan desert.

The elderly security guard nodded from his stool.

The hall narrowed. My leg ached. My breathing rattled.

I turned the corner and gasped.

Before me stood something I never expected. A dozen kindergarteners faced me, all dressed in Star Wars C3PO robot costumes. At the center of the crowd was Kev with the biggest smile I'd ever seen.

"Daddy!" He rushed me, his plastic costume rustling. He wrapped his arms around both legs, real and fake.

I patted him, this robot character, my son, but held my breath, waiting for him to notice.

He backed, his eyes focused on my metal leg. His smile never faded. He looked up, pointed at his legs, and said, "Look, Daddy. I got metal legs too."

I dropped my bag. Tears poured.

In Afghanistan, bullets flew at me. Grenades. IEDs. Explosions. Nothing compared to the power of this boy.

I grunted and knelt onto my remaining knee.

Kev lost some of his glow. "Why you sad?"

I hugged him. "I'm not." I wiped my face. "C'mon." I stood and picked him up.

The remaining miniature C3POs surrounded us, some waving plastic light sabers, others holding Welcome Home signs.

Claire smiled a few feet ahead, trembling hands barely holding her camera and eyes too glassy to see through the lens. She rushed to me.

I squeezed her hard and whispered, "Thank you."

John Hope

John Hope is an award-winning short story, children's book, middle grade, young adult, and nonfiction writer. His work appears in paperback, hardback, audiobook, and multiple short story collections. Mr. Hope, a native Floridian, gives informational and inspirational presentations to schools, conferences, and is a board member of FWA.

Casey's Angels

I smelled the angels again. Their sweet scent mingled with odors of freshly cut grass, the fried chicken restaurant around the corner and the musky odor of the Miller's Siamese cat, Cleo.

The fragrance hung heaviest around my owner. Old Henry turned eighty-eight this month. We shared the indignities of aging—cataracts, incontinence and hip pain—Henry's from a fall and mine from advanced hip displaysia.

I pushed myself into a sitting position and poked my nose in the air as Henry petted my head. The heavenly fragrance was good and bad. I never doubted my master was anything but heaven-bound, but the strong smell indicated Henry's departure loomed nearer.

Perhaps the angels came for me. It was hard to know for sure, since they had hovered near me ever since I was a puppy.

My front legs slid forward, my hip creaked and I laid at Henry's feet. Sixteen years I'd lived with him, and his wife, Carol. The angels took her last year. For a Golden Retriever, sixteen was ancient. Though the angels might take us soon, me and Henry would look after each other, until one of us no longer could.

A sharp odor stung my nostrils. I lifted my head and growled. "Hush now, Casey," Henry said. "You always loved children."

True, but I smelled demons as well as angels and the boy across the street stunk of sulfur and brimstone.

He always had, even as a baby wrapped in a blanket in his mother's arms.

Old Henry's hand cupped the back of my neck as I struggled to sit up.

"Now you wanna play with Josh? You're too old to play, Casey. Lay down, boy."

Across the street, Josh sat on his porch steps. My ears twitched each time he stabbed a pocket knife into the old painted wood.

I always obeyed Henry, but instead of laying down I leaned against his leg and watched the demon. Blue eyes, cold as river ice peered at us from beneath silky, yellow bangs. He looked like an angel, but smelled like a monster. I worried Josh might hurt Henry. I worried more about my limitations to protect him.

Josh meandered across his front lawn and disappeared into the woods bordering his yard.

As a younger dog I'd followed six year old Josh into those woods. That day the boy's scent contained an ominous odor of lighter fluid. Josh held the Miller's Siamese kitten and wrapped a length of rope around its neck. I startled the boy with my barks and the kitten seized the opportunity to squirm out of the rope and bolt off into the woods. Ever since, Henry and the Millers both marveled when Cleo scampered over and rubbed her sinewy body against me on our daily walks.

I limped down our porch steps to the end of the front path. My eyes blurred but I finally made out Cleo's slinky shape, safe, inside the Miller's front window.

Sighing, I turned at Henry's call. The old man gripped an aluminum walker and pushed himself upright. "Dinner time, ol' boy."

I followed the thump-creak of the walker and shuffle of his footsteps into the house.

***

The yellow puddle spread on the kitchen floor along with my shame. Henry worked an old bath towel with his foot and sopped up my urine from the linoleum.

"Don't fret now, Casey. It's my fault for dozing off."

While that may be true, the indignity of not being able to hold my water anymore was beyond humiliating. I'd rather the angels take me than have poor Henry slip in one of my puddles and break another brittle hip. His first fall had ended our beloved fishingtrips.

"C'mon, boy." Henry held open the back door. The ramp his daughter had installed formed a gentle decline to the patio. Henry abandoned his walker for a wrought iron chair, pulled a pipe from his sweater pocket and lit it with a shaky hand. I limped to the grass, surprised I had more water to pass. A smoky aroma different from Henry's pipe alerted me. I forced my legs to trot and investigated the dark swatch of lawn between our house and the Miller's hedge.

Josh crouched in the darkness, a flash of fire illuminated his twisted grin.

Barking, I ignored the searing jolts of pain that ran from my hips and down my back legs and bolted toward the demon.

Josh scrambled to his feet. A can clattered against the side of the house and a whoosh of fire leapt into the air. Adrenaline surged and I jumped through the flames. My front paws hit the boy's chest, my weight knocked him to the ground. I stood on top of him. The demon punched and kicked, his boot heels jabbed into my soft belly and aching legs. It hurt so bad, I sunk my teeth into his arm to make him stop.

Josh screamed.

"Casey!" Henry maneuvered his walker across the bumpy grass. "Casey, no!"

Footsteps slapped on the driveway next door. A blast of icy water hit me. I released Josh's arm but held him down and growled.

"Henry, call your dog off." Mr. Miller aimed a hose, dousing the flames climbing up the wooden siding. "What the hell happened?" Henry's fingers fumbled to get a grasp on my wet collar.

"Look's like Josh set another fire. And Casey bit him." The neighbor twisted the nozzle off and pulled a cellphone from his pocket. "I'll call the cops."

***

The cold steel table sent chills through my wet body but my rear legs refused to raise me up. They hung useless, bent at odd angles. Blackened fur on my side ringed a patch of throbbing red skin.

My vet laid a comforting hand on my head while Henry's familiar gnarled fingers stroked my face.

"But Doc, can't you patch—"

"He's sixteen—eighty-seven in our years. One leg's a clean break, the other's shattered. You're looking at multiple surgeries, rehabilitation . . . with Casey's displaysia, the pain and stress, not to mention the expense . . . I'm so sorry Henry, the most humane thing is to put him down."

Henry's voice quivered, "He saved my house . . . me. I would have gone to bed . . . died in the fire."

"He's always been loyal to you, Henry. Casey's shown stronger character than most people."

"Is he in pain?" Henry asked.

"Not at the moment, I gave him a shot. A second shot will put him to sleep, until. . . ." The vet moved to the swinging door. "Take as much time as you need to say goodbye."

Henry murmured in my ear. I licked his tears, warm and salty, from my muzzle. More than anything, I wished I could talk. I wanted to tell Henry how the angels had shown me a huge grassy field right next to a lake. The water shimmered, reflecting the crystal blue sky. Sunlight warmed my back and took away the awful chill.

A small boat just like ours bobbed in the water.

I'm going to wait here by the lake for you, Henry. We'll go fishing again.

Christine Holmes

Chris is co-leader of FWA's Daytona Beach Writers Group. She works in digital advertising and does freelance graphic design work. Besides several short stories, Chris has written two horror novels and has two more in the works. She and her husband, Michael, live in Ormond Beach, Florida.

Hawk Eye

I have seen you dive
            into the snow
To catch your prey
looking at me
            as if I desired your quarry

All I wanted was to
            see you against the white

I have seen blood
            on your feathers
while perched
            on an ice covered fence
looking at me
            as if I wanted to watch
you preen
I did

I have seen you soar through the spaces
            between snow flakes
while looking down
at me
            as if I was jealous
of your skill
I was

I see you looking at me now
            Through the winter woods
As if I want to be as you
I do

Daniel R. Tardona

Daniel was born and raised in Brooklyn, New York. Following many transitions too complicated to go into here, he became a National Park Service. During his career he has written and published scientific articles museum and exhibit text. Recently, he has decided to branch out writing fiction and poetry.

Nobody's Fool

Miss Tunbridge lived in a small town where certain people, like her neighbor, seemed to thrive on knowing everybody's business. More often than not, she noticed Louella's pudgy hand at the window blinds when she came and went. Worse, Miss Tunbridge never knew when the woman would catapult out her door, wanting to chew over the latest gossip. Today was one of those occasions.

"I told Chief Morris he's out of his mind if he thinks you robbed that bank over in Tallahassee," Louella said, a slight breeze ruffling her salt-and-pepper hair. "Good grief, we've been neighbors for twenty years. If anybody would know, I would."

Miss Tunbridge leaned back against the red Ford Focus parked in her driveway, puzzled, until she remembered running into Bob Morris at the grocery store the day before. Somebody must have overheard their conversation. "You know Bob was just kidding when he asked me if I'd robbed a bank to get my new car, don't you?"

"Maybe he was, and maybe he wasn't," Louella said. "Either way, it's not right for him to cast aspersions when it's not in your character to do something like that. Why, I remember when I was in your fourth grade class, how you talked about truth, and fairness, and justice."

How many years ago had that been, forty maybe?

Miss Tunbridge's mind traveled to the past. She pictured herself in high school—tall and stick-thin, socially awkward and smart enough to realize she might not find a husband. Instead, she'd set her sights on a career that would provide a modestly comfortable life. But over the years, upkeep on the small bungalow she'd bought had been expensive—the new roof alone had cost a fortune—and her salary hadn't kept pace with inflation.

Now, ten years post-retirement, her savings were gone. Where was the justice in giving your life to educate children and winding up broke?

Louella kept rattling on. "The police never did catch the thief, did they? You couldn't tell much from that grainy, black-and-white surveillance tape they showed. Lots of people wear hoodies in February, and the way the scarf covered most of the face it could have been anybody, young or old, man or woman."

"That's true," Miss Tunbridge replied. "Probably some druggie needing a fix, though, that's usually how it goes in a big city." Or a Grandpa Bandit like the one she'd read about some years back, a thought she kept to herself, not wanting to fuel further speculation.

How much did her neighbor know about her financial situation? Had someone in her doctor's office spread the news that she hadn't been paying her Medicare deductibles? Despite the privacy laws, it wouldn't be the first time information like that had dribbled through their tight-knit community. Miss Tunbridge felt a flutter in her chest, a pang of conscience.

"Weren't you away that week? Visiting your cousin over in Apalachicola, as I recall?"

"It's possible," Miss Tunbridge admitted. "I go every couple weeks, but we're talking about something that happened three months ago and I don't keep track of the dates. What are you suggesting?"

***

Several days later, Chief Bob Morris, the town's only police officer, knocked on Miss Tunbridge's door at ten in the morning. She invited him in, thanking her lucky stars she was up and dressed.

"Coffee, Bob?" She found it difficult to be more formal. Despite his uniform and holstered gun, she still saw the rambunctious, freckle-faced boy she'd taught two decades ago. The title "Chief" refused to leave her mouth.

"If it wouldn't be too much trouble," he said.

She led him into the kitchen, poured a cup, and put sugar and creamer on the table. They sat, and an uncomfortable silence stretched out as his spoon swirled the coffee. She looked around, seeing the kitchen through his eyes: chipped laminate countertops, old-fashioned wallpaper.

Finally, he raised his head. "It seems I stirred up a hornet's nest, and I'm sorry about that. Your neighbor seems to have taken me seriously when I asked if you'd robbed a bank. At first, she was indignant that I'd think such a thing, but now she's changed her mind. She thinks you might have done it after all and wants me to investigate."

"Is that what you're doing, investigating? Are you going to ask me to go to the police station?"

"No to both questions," he said. "The Tallahassee police are handling it, not me. I'm just hoping we can talk a bit, clear up a few rumors so things don't get out of hand…if you don't mind."

Miss Tunbridge thought for a minute. Maybe it would be for the best. Louella wasn't going to stop gossiping on her own. "I guess that would be okay."

"All right then." The Chief took a deep breath. "They're saying you weren't home when the robbery occurred, you sometimes wear hoodies when it's cold, and you didn't have enough money to replace your tires but then bought a new car a couple weeks later."

Miss Tunbridge made a mental note to take her new car over to the next town for maintenance. "It's ridiculous to think I robbed a bank because I occasionally wear hoodies and might have been visiting my cousin that particular day. But let's cut to the chase here. We both know what the gossips want to hear is how I got the new car."

He nodded in agreement. "Do you want to tell me?"

"Can what I say be confidential just between us, like a Catholic confession?"

The Chief stared out the window for a moment. "Well, I haven't read you your rights, and I'm not recording our conversation. I don't have a problem with that unless you actually committed a crime."

"Fair enough," she said. "It's just that some people might consider what I've done unethical." Bob's kind expression gave her the courage to continue. "I got one of those preapproved credit card offers in the mail, you see. My savings are gone, my car needed tires, and I had medical bills to pay. Then a few days later, I saw an advertisement to lease a new car for low monthly payments. So I traded in my old car and used the credit card for the rest of the upfront costs. I feel guilty about not being able to pay what I charged, but I figure my life insurance will cover it when I die."

A gentle smile crinkled the corners of the Chief's eyes. "Well, I'm not one to judge. If you want, I can tell Louella you came into some money, let her think you might have inherited it from a distant relative."

"I'd be grateful for that," Miss Tunbridge said.

He finished his coffee, and after the front door closed she sank into an upholstered chair with a satisfied smile. She'd been truthful about the credit card and the leased car.

As for the rest—well, with a good cover story no one needed to know about the shoebox full of cash in her bedroom closet.

Pat Rakowski

Pat's short stories have appeared in previous FWA Collection books and the FWA magazine, and her commentary articles have been published by the Philadelphia Inquirer and Beaches Leader newspapers. She has written a book, Sliding Into Home Base, Searching For Sophia, available at Lulu.com.

Odd Birds

Deena was watching a flock of exotic Florida birds swoop and dive over Sarasota Bay when a loud voice with a thick Yiddish accent cut through Bayside Park. She turned to see an elderly woman pushing a shopping cart and shouting at the sky.

"What do you want from me? I'm walking as fast as I can. Maybe you think I should fly. You can wait another minute, it won't kill you."

Sarasota was full of homeless people and Deena realized with a pang that she'd be one of them if she didn't find a job soon. The old woman was wearing a black cardigan, orthopedic shoes and glasses with owlish frames. Her short white hair was combed back from a broad, wrinkled face. She lowered herself onto the bench beside Deena who stood up abruptly.

"Don't get up, sit, be comfortable." The woman turned her gaze to the top of a tree alive with noisy crows. "I'm late with their breakfast so they're giving me hell. Maybe you could help with that big bag. I forgot to bring scissors."

"What sort of help?" Deena was wary, but twenty years as a librarian had honed her instinct to be helpful.

"Normally I don't need help, but with these new bags it's like breaking into Fort Knox. Maybe you've got some dynamite."

Deena went to inspect the large sac inside the woman's cart. She pulled at a dangling string expecting the bag to rip open. Nothing. She pulled until the string burned her fingers, then sat back down and riffled through her purse. Pulling out a small metal emery board she waved it triumphantly, "Dynamite!" The emery board easily sawed through the string. "There you go. I hope the birds enjoy their breakfast."

"Would you mind, there's one more thing. Maybe you could scatter some seeds beneath that oak tree. I'm all out of breath."

Deena obediently scattered a quantity of seed where the woman pointed.

"That's good, good. Maybe a few more scoops." The woman nodded approvingly as ten or fifteen crows, and a handful of jays and two tall gray birds with red caps began squabbling over the seeds.

Deena looked around, hoping that no one was watching, when she spotted a uniformed policeman barreling toward them. He gazed at the scattered seeds with a resigned sigh. "Mrs. Goetz, we've given you more chances than I count, but this is too much. You're coming with me."

"I'm sitting here minding my own business, since when is that against the law?" The old woman spoke softly, almost to herself, as she fiddled with the buttons on her cardigan with boney arthritic fingers.

"You're feeding the birds again. You're attracting nuisance wildlife, littering, and feeding prohibited species, specifically sandhill cranes. That's against the law Mrs. Goetz. It's been explained to you umpteen times."

"So, who's feeding birds? I'm just sitting."

"Come on, I'm taking you in. You can't keep tossing citations like they're grocery receipts." He put his hand beneath her arm and slowly lifted her to her feet.

"You should arrest that lady." She turned her glassy blue eyes toward Deena. "She's feeding the birds, not me."

Deena wheeled around and grabbed her purse. "I don't even know this lady. I'm sorry, but I have to leave."

The old woman chortled. "See, she doesn't even know me. You're going to arrest me because someone I don't even know is making a mess."

The officer hesitated, momentarily confused, then squared his jaw and took command. "OK, I'm taking you both in. Don't make me cuff you." He shepherded them toward his car and helped Mrs. Goetz inside. Deena stood immobilized until the officer snapped, "You too lady, get in the car."

Deena scrunched down in her seat and was staring sullenly out the window when Mrs. Goetz began shouting, "Wait, stop. What about my cart? You can't just leave it for thieves."

The officer turned, a small smirk playing across his face. "So, it *is* your cart. I'd better make a note of that." Mrs. Goetz fell back in her seat, arms folded belligerently across her chest.

Deena could see the policeman watching them in his rear view mirror. "Park security is picking up your cart, but we're keeping it as evidence until this thing gets settled."

No one said another word until they arrived at the Sarasota County Jail where they were escorted to central processing. As they waited on hard metal chairs, Deena compressed her arms and legs into her body trying to make herself invisible.

"I'm sorry; I didn't think he'd really do it. Normally, Kevin's a cream puff; I don't know what got into him today." Mrs. Goetz leaned toward Deena and spoke in a low, conspiratorial voice.

"Kevin? You're on a first name basis?" Deena hissed back through closed teeth.

"We go back two, maybe three years. I was one of his first cases. He's already got a promotion." There was something proud, almost maternal, in her tone.

"Why did you drag me into this thing between you and Kevin? I'm trying to start a new life here. I need a job not a police record. Who's going to hire a librarian with a record?"

"You're a librarian?" Deena nodded without turning her head so Mrs. Goetz continued her interrogation. "Where are you from?"

"What makes you think I'm from somewhere else?"

"Everyone's from somewhere else. I'm from Warsaw, New York, and Los Angeles."

The woman was insufferable and intrusive, but Deena answered. "Cleveland. I had a house, a job and a husband in Cleveland, but now I don't. I came here to start over, OK?"

"Don't worry, I lost a house and a husband when I was your age and now look at me."

Deena stared at the old woman, biting her tongue to keep from saying what was going through her mind.

"Look, I owe you. Besides, I could use a librarian. How would you like a job organizing my literary estate?"

"Deena Berman." Deena heard her name called through a loud speaker.

As she stood up the old woman grabbed her sleeve. "Here take this and call me tomorrow." She handed Deena a hastily scribbled phone number. "Good luck."

Deena rolled her eyes and stuffed the number into the pocket of her jeans.

A moment later, the desk clerk fixed her with a steely gaze. "You're not being arrested today, only issued a citation, but we want to make sure that you and Mrs. Goetz appreciate the gravity of the offense. Don't get caught feeding sandhill cranes or littering again. Those are second degree misdemeanors."

"I'm sorry, but I wouldn't recognize a sandhill crane if I saw one. I was just trying to help an old homeless woman."

The officer chuckled, "Raisa Goetz is an odd bird, but homeless? That's a good one. Ever hear of the Goetz Foundation?"

Deena stared back blankly.

He raised his eyebrows. "Look it up when you get home."

Deena banged out the heavy wooden doors onto the sunlit street where she took the small piece of paper from her pocket and studied the phone number. Apparently, she had a lot to learn about Sarasota birds.

Patricia Averbach

Patricia Averbach is the former director of the Chautauqua Writers Center in Chautauqua, New York. Her first novel, Painting Bridges, was released by Bottom Dog Press, 2013. Her poetry chapbook, Missing Persons (Ward Wood Publishing, 2013) received the London based Lumen/Camden prize. She's just completed a second novel, New Moon Rising.

The Girl in the Black Beret

Emily sensed the end might come today. She sat on the open air back porch, her favorite spot in the cozy, secluded cabin. After admiring puffs of white cotton clouds scattered across the blue sky, she buckled down, opening the laptop to work on her novel. On occasion she could hear an airplane fly overhead, breaking the silence but not really distracting her. Every so often, soft wisps of air brought the sweet subtle smell of laurel blossoms.

Pounding on the cabin door startled her. Bam, bam, bam, a pause, then again. Emily struggled to get out of her chair and tottered to the front door, hoping to make the noise stop.

She called out, "Who's there?"

When no one answered, Emily pulled the door open. She saw a girl wearing jeans, a dark t-shirt, and a black beret, running down the rutted road and disappearing over the hill.

Emily put her hand on her lower back and straightened a bit. The girl running away seemed odd, but something else bothered her, too. Now, what was it again? Oh, there it was…how had she gotten there? A car? Bicycle? Maybe a horse? Almost as soon as she identified what bothered her, Emily forgot all about it as she made her way back to the porch.

She returned to her computer concentrating on her most important goal. Suspecting that time was not her friend, she was driven to finish her latest novel. It was not at all like her numerous formulaic best-sellers, even though her romantic suspense series had been described as "ground-breaking" by the New York Times.

Murmurs from a nearby creek sang to her, lulling her thoughts. Relaxed, she rose and leaned on the rough-hewn wooden porch railing to gaze out over the mountain valley, soaking up the peaceful beauty of the forest. With a deep sigh of tranquility, she shrugged out of her sweater and felt the fresh spring air on her bare arms. She took delight in observing the birds flit, chirping, among green maples, oaks, and pines. Eavesdropping for a while, she was confident they were communicating, and wished she could speak their language.

Finally, Emily sat down, eager to write, trying to stay focused. Her arthritic fingers stroked the keyboard, words flooded into sentences, sentences streamed into thoughts, and thoughts surged into wisdom, the wisdom she needed to share before it became too late.

She picked up where she'd left off, quite close to the finale:

Many, now dead and gone, have railed against the voluminous stabs into their health, the sharp jabs of broken bones and even worse, the despondency that comes when the spirit is broken.

The melodic notes of a wood thrush caught her attention. Her misshapen fingers froze in place as she listened, charmed to hear the bird so nearby. When the warbling tunes stopped, she continued:

But the resilient woman lives to battle the separation of her existence from her soul. Her mind grows into a malignant mound of Swiss cheese, riddled with holes, holes so large they suck life memories into the black void of nothingness. She will endure this, her final challenge, until the fated grace of death arrives to liberate her...

Emily realized she was thirsty. She relaxed her arms and wiggled her inflexible joints.

She went to the kitchen. Opening the fridge, she noticed her black leather pocketbook on the shelf next to the yogurt. Emily often discovered things in mysterious places, apple peelings squirreled away in a dresser drawer or a dish towel in the cereal cabinet.

A tink, tink, tink, sounded, as if someone were tapping on the front bedroom window. Puzzled, she squinted her eyes and set her chilled purse on the counter, heading down the hallway as if she were being drawn by a magnet toward the source of the sound. Through the window, she saw the same girl, hightailing it up the nearby hillside. As Emily watched, she reached the top of the hill and once again vanished from sight.

Emily stared out the window after her. After a while, she dilly-dallied back up the hall, pausing to enjoy the framed photos along the way.

Still thirsty, Emily found herself back in the kitchen. Locating the lemonade pitcher, her lips puckering in anticipation, she poured a small jelly glass full and drank it all in three gulps.

She made her way out to the porch to return to her mission and sank down into the soft pillows. Pulling her laptop closer, she typed nonstop, glancing up from her work only when clouds passed in front of the sun and sent shadows flickering over the wooden floor. She raised her chin and sniffed, sensing moisture in the air, and wondered if it might rain. It seemed it was that kind of day.

Bang, bang, bang. The noise seemed to come from up on the roof. It stopped, so she relaxed and resumed her writing, caught in the cadence of creating words, words designed to reach others, words to inspire....

Thump, thump, thump. With a frown, Emily slid her laptop onto the loveseat and stood up, so stiff her legs wobbled. She waited for steadiness to return before attempting the back steps.

Around the corner of the cabin, she located her ladder. Emily put both hands on it and pushed to check if it was steady enough, then climbed the flat aluminum steps one at a time. She finally reached the roof.

Across the top of the corrugated tin she saw the girl again, her back to Emily. Then the black beret bobbed below Emily's line of vision and disappeared.

Emily descended, one foot after another, lips pursed tight, until both feet touched solid ground. At least there was no more racket. But her visitor certainly had curious behavior. Did she crave Emily's attention? It seemed that was all she wanted which was unfortunate because Emily's writing was all that mattered to her now.

Out of nowhere, something touched her shoulder. She startled and whirled around, wondering who could be in her back yard at the cabin.

A smiling young man held out his hand. "Time for your pills, Mrs. Clarke."

He seemed to know her so Emily nodded. He offered her his arm. She grabbed it and pulled herself up to a sitting position in the bed. He held out a small dish of assorted capsules. She tossed them into her mouth, reached for the little cup of water he held out and swallowed them down.

"I'll be back later to help you to the dining hall," he said.

Her hands continued to dance across the keyboard, her wisdom pouring out for others to read, paragraph after paragraph flowing onto page after page. Finally, she typed "the end", sighed and sat back in her wheelchair, quite content.

There was a small rap, rap, rap, and the door opened. The orderly re-entered the room.

"Time to go, Mrs. Clarke."

Emily reached for her threadbare black beret, placed it on her head and smiled.

Wendy Keppley

Wendy Keppley, a Florida native, counseled troubled teens and taught college courses for high school honor students. She loves writing, kayaking, reading, yoga, exploring waterfalls, and oneirology. Wendy also enjoys family, playing with her grandsons, and living in the woods near Tampa.E-mail her at wendykep@gmail.com.

The Vessel

I used to love the stars. It took centuries for me to adjust to the view from this dull planet, my prison. When I was home, I would sit at the Edge watching them wink while the planets twirled and danced, appreciating that one day it would all be mine. Instead, I was cast out. Banished. The stone ledge crumbles to dust under my fists. I wasn't strong enough to fight them then. That won't be the case much longer.

Cool night air fills my lungs and permeates my senses. I haven't fed in a week. It's not the longest I've gone, but it's still too long. That's why I'm up here. From here, I can see everything. Every scent on the wind, every sound it carries – it's all mine for the taking. The ease of it makes it almost unsatisfying. Almost. But after all this time, I can still feel that little tingle, the thrill of anticipation. It's my third favorite part.

My heart slows when I scent him. A fine specimen, with that peculiar shine of affluence in his eyes, his shoes. He carries his strong body with ease and confidence. My fingers itch to run through his hair, to find out just how strong that body is. Tempting. That little tingle amplifies. The hairs on the back of my neck stand on end as a tremor courses through me. He's the one.

One breath.

Two.

"Hi." My voice causes him to stop and turn.

His eyes rake down my body, not missing a single dip or curve, and he smirks. "Do I know you?"

"Would you like to?" Not waiting for an answer, I turn, making my way to a secluded place on the busy city street. He follows, of course. He can't help himself.

In the darkness of the alley, he doesn't hesitate. Long fingers close around my small wrist pulling me to a stop.

"Yes, I would," he whispers pressing himself close, and brushes my long hair away from my neck.

When I turn, looking up into his eyes, my smile is genuine. "Good." Those eyes, a fractured mix of greens and blues, are deeper than I imagined. Hypnotic.

Muscles jump as I run my hands up his chest and around his neck. Silken hair graces my fingers. And his scent? Not the over-priced cologne he wears – that is atrocious. But *his* scent. It's intoxicating, *powerful*. He's most definitely the one.

I close my eyes and breathe it in, savoring every sweet note that dances through my senses. It strengthens as his lips touch my bare shoulder, as his tongue traces a greedy line up my neck. His scent wraps knowingly around me when his hands roughly trace the contours of my body and tightening possessively. Oh, they are strong hands. A silent chuckle escapes my lips.

"Tell me your name," he insists.

With my hands on the sides of his face, I shake my head and smile as I feel the pull, strong and deep. It flows through my fingers, weaving into him, gripping his heart . Those hypnotic eyes go wide, and his fingers dig into my flesh. No sound escapes the lips on his reddening face. He tries. Oh, he tries so hard to speak, to scream, to beg for it to stop. His veins stand out in perfect relief from the strain.

My heart quickens, and I watch him intently. I know what he sees. He sees my eyes shift, glowing yellow in the darkened alley, illuminating us in a soft haze, his terror reflected plainly in their depths. All around us, time halts. Dust motes still. Steam from a nearby street grate pauses in its upward climb, and silence deafens the city's chatter. None of which holds my interest, because I'm waiting. Waiting for the moment that his terror-filled confusion turns to clarity. And there it is, the moment he realizes that I'm doing this to him. I'm taking his Life. It's my second favorite part.

As he falls to his knees, I can't resist. Slowly, to savor every sensation, I run my tongue across his gaping lips – soft and minty. Across his jaw – every bit of stubble sends a jolt through my body. The taste of him is heavenly. The human race does have its charms.

To my delight, he's fighting me, the life within him grasping at its host. And I eagerly admit that he's a strong one, just what I need.

"Painful, isn't it?" I whisper in his ear. "It'll be over soon." I release him and watch as his body crumples to the ground, curling in on itself. His bloodshot eyes slowly dim, and just at that moment, when everyone else thinks it's the end, I see it.

Life. It's determined. It has a single-minded focus to endure, and I am all too happy to oblige. Crouching low over him, I watch hungrily as it begins to leave his useless body, like smoke rising from ruins. Before it can pull free, dispersing into the ether, I breathe it into myself. My body shudders as the shifting, fluid vapor unfurls inside of me, testing its new home.

My eyes flutter closed as it settles within me. The pleasure the Life feeds me, the contentment it feels; the power this Life releases, joining with and strengthening my own: this – this is my favorite part.

Standing, I step over the vacant husk on the alley floor as time resumes its pace, the clamor of the city clashing with the silence. My four-inch heals echo languidly between the two buildings, fading as I turn to make my way down the busy sidewalk.

All these people, I muse. These blind, oblivious, sad little humans. I shake my head and wonder at the futility of their miniscule little lives. Pointless, really. And just then, I scent a woman across the street. She's sitting at the bus stop with a bulky, misshapen bag at her feet. In a greasy diner uniform, hair disheveled, and a large book open on her lap, most wouldn't give her a second glance. But I can sense what others can't, the inborn strength she possesses. My heart slows, and I can't help but smile. My euphoria has yet to dim, and I'm presented with another.

A tremor courses through my body as I shift, growing larger, taller. I adjust the brown leather jacket across my newly broadened shoulders as well as the uncomfortable tightness in my snug jeans. My boots are nearly soundless on the pavement as I make my way across the street.

The book slips from her lap when she sees me. Her eyes widen ever so slightly as she watches the object of her desire getting closer. The bus she was waiting for passes between us. It comes and goes, but there she sits waiting for me. My smile widens. I might like to play with this one, I muse, take my time, but when an errant paper flutters to a stop in midair before me, my step falters. When I look past it, her eyes glow a bright yellow, and her wicked smile is directed straight at me.

Mary K. Henderson

Mary K. Henderson is a stay-at-home mom in Brevard County Florida. She's a binge reader, coffee addict, and occasional musical theater performer. Writing has become an outlet/obsession for Mary over the last several years, and you can usually find her absorbed in her latest project when she should be folding laundry.

The Hapless Professor

I unlock my apartment door, and a scream pierces the quiet of the dim, Spartan hallway. Attractive Gracie Lilly stands transfixed in her open doorway. A paper cup lies on the floor with the day's newspaper soaking up amber-colored liquid. Her white knuckles grip a floral tote that complements her hot pink nurse's scrubs.

I cross the hall, push her door wider, and side-step around her into the sun-lit room. Speechless, she points toward the far corner where the ceiling and wall meet.

I squint at the brown, softball-sized shape clinging to the wall. "Do you have a glass, a can, any container for me to catch the spider in, Gracie?

"Kill it!"

"I'll get rid of it. Right away."

As Gracie inches along the wall to her kitchen, she keeps her eyes fixed on the home invader. She hesitantly opens a cabinet door and reaches into the cupboard. Seizing a large, lidded Mason jar, she extends it to me.

I put my briefcase down, open the jar, and approach the spider with stealth. I try not to gaze admiringly at the perfect specimen I've imprisoned.

"It's only a wolf spider." I assure her, "It won't bite you unless you're a threat. It appears she thought that corner was a good place to lay her eggs."

"She? Eggs?"

"There's an egg sack under her belly."

"Great!" She points toward the hallway leading to the bathroom. "Flush momma down the toilet. No. Wait. I'd fret every time I sat down on the seat! Get it out of here!"

I nod, hold up a forefinger, and carry the jar to my apartment. I place it on top of my fridge and return to placate Gracie by checking out the rest of her apartment for undesirable arachnids.

We've exchanged less than a dozen words since she moved in last week. Hi. Have a nice day. That sort. I'd given up on dating because my profession deters most females, although my coworkers seem to have no problem. Course, most of them bait and catch within the academic community of the University.

I feel I'm invading her privacy, but I follow her from room to room. I would follow her anywhere. She has me search the bathroom cabinets, dresser drawers, bedroom closets, under the bed, the hall utility area, the pantry, and beneath-the-sink area. I explore every nook, with Gracie standing in the center of each room until I vouch for its safety. My inspection finished, I assure her that she has no reason to worry.

As I head toward the still-open, hall door I consider the past hour. *So much for spending a quiet evening writing some suspense into my life as a wanna-be-published sci-fi author. Gracie's diversion is the closest I've come to true adventure in a long time. If I play my cards right, use some mate selection strategies of my work, this could be my romantic opportunity. Don't blow it, Phil. Don't spill too much information—not yet.*

"You're a good neighbor," Gracie says. "You saved me from my greatest fear—spiders."

"Really? Your greatest fear is spiders?"

"Truly. Ever since I was bitten by one at a youth camp. The bite got infected. Was nasty." She pulled her pant leg above her attractive calf to show me the scar.

"I see why you're an arachnophobe—people fearful of spiders, but it's possible that you may learn to tolerate them…"

"No way!"

"You can learn to abide them just as people learn to overcome their fear of flying. They adapt by increments of exposure."

"Don't even go there…Phil, is it?"

I nod. *She isn't sure of my name?*

Gracie offers me a cold drink, and we share small-talk, but I avoid and redirect any hint about my job. It's enough she knows that I work in the Department of Zoology at the University of Akron. God forbid I should tell her I research spiders' sexual selection, male mating strategies, and sexual cannibalism. It was easy to avert the topic of my work by keeping the conversation centered on Gracie. Her job. Her likes. Her dislikes—other than spiders.

I muster enough courage to say, "It's Friday night, and it's still early. Are you interested in playing some Wii bowling at my place?"

Her eyes twinkle with mirth, and I know she must think I'm a real geek.

"I'll run and set the Wii up. Come over in a few minutes. Okay?"

She presses her lips together and tilts her head. "Okay, Phil. It's a date. I mean...it'll be fun."

Back in my apartment, I hustle to hide my arachnology magazines in a closet. The cage of my pet tarantula, Tara, shouts "bad idea" from its bay window location. As I carry it down the hallway, I snatch the ISA (International Society for Arachnology) certificate from the wall. Satisfied that I've concealed my life as an arachnologist, I lock my office door just as I hear a soft knock.

Later, after several Wii games of bowling, horseshoes, and golf, I notice Gracie roll her shoulders and steal a glimpse of the wall clock.

"Time for a snack?" I head toward my kitchen nook for crackers, cheese, and wine. That's when I see Tara creeping along the back of the sink. *I must have bumped her tank cover in my earlier hurry.* I hear Gracie's approach in time for me to grab and pocket Tara between my T-shirt and dress shirt. *Be a good girl. Stay still. Nice, warm, and cozy.*

I force a smile and turn to hand Gracie the bottle of Lucky Duck Malbec. Her grip loosens and it shatters on the tile floor. Gracie's eyes stare at the space above my refrigerator. I follow her stare and see the Mason jar I'd forgotten to put away. Only now, the wolf spider had company. Hundreds of pin-point size baby spiders.

"Ah, I'm sorry. I was going to get rid of it. Far from here. I should have—"

"You should have *killed* it!" Her eyes travel from my face to my chest. Gracie tilts her head, her forehead wrinkles, and her mouth gapes.

I feel the tickle of tiny feet and look down to see a lump on my shirt front moving upward. Gracie backs away as Tara crests the V of my shirt.

"She's harmless. Really. When I came in the kitchen—"

Gracie flies to my apartment door, flings it open, and freezes. A teeny, everyday house spider is parked across the threshold. Without hesitation, she lifts her foot and stomps it. She marches to her door and slams it shut behind her.

I lift Tara from my chest and stroke her abdomen. "If you weren't such an escape artist, I might have more success with first dates."

The following morning as I leave for work, I keep my head lowered and steal a glance toward Gracie's apartment. *Really? It wasn't that bad!*

Posted on the door was a ridiculously large FOR RENT sign, and her "Gracie Lilly" nameplate was gone.

Cheryl Abney

Cheryl Abney lives in the Florida Glades setting of her middle-grade, historical fiction books. She is a retired educator and has written short stories for TheFreedomKids.com. Cheryl is a member of FWA, Gulf Coast Writers Association, and American Christian Fiction Writers.
www.BelleoftheGlades.com

What to Wear

Doctor's orders, spend a week in the Keys. The phone chimes, it's Dr. Ralph.

"Good morning, Miss Tiffany. How was the sunrise?"

"It is the same every day, a significant waste of time. I have issues that need resolutions, and you are asking about the sunrise?"

"Getting your stress under control is the issue. Tomorrow, go out to the end of the pier and feel the sunrise. Think of it as a painting in motion."

"You must be kidding. Do I go barefoot in pajamas for this morning meeting? I hate sand in my shoes. On top of all that there's a homeless man, hobbles out there every morning.

The phone goes silence. "Miss Gallery Curator, today take a walk down Duval, buy a sundress and some flip flops. Take in Mallory Square. Tomorrow, go feel the morning out at the end of the pier. The homeless guy, is Island Jack a great friend of mine. Ask him for a tour of the island. Buy him a drink at one of the nostalgia bars."

"This is stress relief? Buy a cheap sundress and parade out to the pier. Ask this friend of yours for a tour of the island. I will be checking on a flight back before you book me into the clothing optional resort."

Uncontrollable laughter is now coming from the phone. "Great idea. Come as you are and always dressed correctly."

"I don't think that's funny."

"I don't mean to laugh, but you are in the Keys. Relax. Jack is a character, and you could learn, how to relax from him."

"I'll give it one more day, and then I'm flying back."

***

The road banner announces local artist show today. Did the doctor know about this? The square looks like a mini-circus. Starting with watercolors by Miss Halter Top. She starts an info commercial. Miss Sun Dress should be painting houses with that cheap perfume. She glares at me.

Erotic art from Mr. Hairy Chest, with an unbuttoned shirt. "I'm Peter, can paint anything you can dream."

"I can tell you dressed for the occasion." I move on. The sand, in this picture looks real, I can feel it in my shoes.

A voice startles me. "Welcome to Island Jack's beach collection." He hobbled around an easel balancing himself with a cane, dressed in shorts and flipflops.

Must be, Island Jack. "This painting looks, like the pier by the resort."

"Yes, I've painted every pier, on the island. Must be hard for you to enjoy it dressed in heels and a skirt."

"I saw it from the balcony."

He cocks his head. "You look exquisite, but you may be a little overdressed."

I spit back. "Your artist's friends could use some help on how to dress."

"I can tell you are an expert."

"I am an art curator in New York. I know how to dress."

A smirk takes over his face. "Looking for art in the Keys?"

"No. I'm on vacation."

"I should have known by your attire."

"Something the matter with what I am wearing?"

He puts his hand up. "No, No, don't get your panties in a bunch."

"Do you know Dr. Ralph?"

His face lights up like a little kid. "How is the old boy doing?"

I took a couple deep breathes. "The doctor said, I should watch a sunrise with you."

I think he was going to start jumping up and down. "Sounds like a date."

"It's not a date."

He tones down his glee. "Be more than happy to help. You first need to stop at The Beach Collection Shop. Jill can get you the right wardrobe. I can walk you down there if you want."

"I find my way around New York every day. I'm sure, I can find it." *Another guy into himself, just what I need.*

"Tell her Island Jack sent you, and you need the real island clothes. I'll save you a spot at the pier in the morning."

"Thanks." I head down the street, finding the shop. The sidewalk rack of cheap clothes, about what I expected. The sales clerk walks up.

"I'm Jill. Can I help you find something?"

I blurt out. "Island Jack thinks I am overdressed. Said, you could help."

She smiles, and says, "Follow me. We have the islanders preferred section."

Examining the sundress in the full-length mirror, seeing more of my bra than the dress. "People wear this out in public?"

"It's made to wear without a bra."

"What?"

"You look great. Jack will be impressed."

Holding my arms up, examining how much will be exposed. "I'm not trying to impress Jack." She still had a smirk, as I paid and departed.

***

The sand sliding through my sandals is calming for some strange reason. I'm trembling stepping onto the pier. I stop a few feet from the end. My hands start sweating. The sky is beginning to glow. I can see Jack's silhouette. *I think it's time to leave.*

He turns, motions me closer. "Come sit down." He smiles and gives me thumbs up.

I can feel the boards scratching my legs. I'm sure I'll have splinters.

He pats my leg. "Calm, you don't have to impress me."

"I'm not trying to impress—"

"I can tell by your heart beat. It's vibrating the dock."

His whiskery face grins at me then look's out at the ocean. "The excitement of sitting with Island Jack, waiting for the rays of heaven to touch the sky. It will make a girl's heart pitter-patter."

I want to run. I want to scream. Jack put his finger on his lips. My dress flutters. He becomes motionless looking out across the ocean. The first rays pierce the edge. The waves whisper touching my soul.

***

Jack startles me as he pulls himself up. He reaches out his hand to help me. "It's off to work, can't let the brushes go dry. I could show you the non-tourist spots later today if you like."

I stutter out. "I would like that." We reach the end of the sand. "Mr. Jack, you are an interesting character."

His face lights up. "I'm a character. Coming from the woman who strutted down Duval, wearing a red silk dress and matching heels. The French Collection, of gemstones and perfume to make the perfect outfit. My comrades wonder how I know the new escort."

My face is turning red. "They thought I was a prostitute?"

He started laughing. "I explained, you were a gorgeous art curator."

I stood with my mouth open. "You told everyone the truth, right?"

He winks. "We are all characters of the island. Your secrets are safe with me. Pick you up around five, for cocktails."

Why do I feel so relaxed? I text my boss, and the doctor. I need another week.

JC Akends

Originally from a small town in the thumb of Michigan. Twenty years in Flint watching the automobile industry leave. Living in Florida watching the sun. JC Akends has a bachelor degree from Davenport University. His gene for the world, helping find the next correct word.
www.lifewithoutcommonsense.com

Martyrs Never Die

Only the gods of the earth live forever under the sun. As for mankind, numbered are their days. Whatever they achieve is but wind. *Epic of Gilgamesh, Uruk, Mesopotamia, 2700 BC*

In the universe of important things to talk about, the man standing next to me chooses to tell me about an ant.

"*Heshti beyani,*" he begins in Kurdish, "Eight o'clock. Every morning at eight o'clock I watched an ant step onto the concrete and walk slowly across the floor to the wall on the far side. Same ant, every day. Day after day."

The man is the owner of a small *partukhana*, a bookshop, which sits on the edge of the bazaar. He has taken to watching for stray books written in English, which he diligently sets aside for me. Sometimes the odd book in French or Italian finds its way into the small bundle of tattered English books, but I suppose I stand a much better chance of being able to read them than do the local Kurds comprising his usual clientele. So, I cheerfully grab the whole bundle of books, English or not, whenever I happen to be in his part of town.

Without fail, this leads directly to vigorous argument over price. In other words, I want to pay and he insists it's free.

"How much do I owe you today, Hassan?" I ask.

"Hah! You will never pay. It's impossible. You're a friend! The books are a gift."

"But you have lots of friends. You can't possibly earn a living if your friends don't pay."

"Yes, I have many friends, but you're my only American friend. My American friend doesn't pay."

Two or three similar volleys follow, which always end in great laughter. Hassan is nothing short of a uniquely happy man who seemingly enjoys every day of life more than most Americans are capable of understanding.

Today, however, we're not at his bookshop. We're in the mess hall on the *fermandi*, a base for the Kurdish fighters in Iraq, the *peshmerga*. I'm embedded with them as their chief combat advisor.

The room is long and narrow, its peeling walls painted a barely perceptible turquoise. Our table matches the shape of the room and is twelve-men-long on each of two sides with one man at each end. The head of the table is reserved for the commander, who happens to be out visiting his father today, but ordinarily the food is brought to him first. The typical *brinj*, grilled vegetables, boiled meats and *nan* arrive at the table. As usual, everyone gets a spoon, six or so men share each knife, and no one gets a fork. This is why one of the weapons I carry daily is my folding knife, which I keep clipped inside my right rear hip pocket. It comes out at meals like these, saving me the reach or the wait on the communal knife.

Twenty-six chairs in the room scrape outward from the table, as the men of the brigade staff take their seats. All are veterans of brutal years in combat against the regime of Saddam Hussein, and each has surely visited great violence upon the heads of other men, but here today they are the gentlemen God intended. They are courteous to each other and lighthearted. They joke and chat and shuffle the plates while waiting for their food. Their meal with their comrades will be peaceful and deserved.

Four younger *peshmerga* filter into the room through a doorway near the head of the table. They deliver the food on large steel trays.

"I didn't take my eyes off the ant during his visits," the bookseller, Hassan, announces from the seat next to mine. He grabs for a flap of *nan* from one of the stacks of bread in the middle of the table before continuing. "You can imagine it takes some time for an ant to walk across a room."

Hassan didn't always sell books. Like many Kurdish men he was once a *peshmerga* and was captured and imprisoned by Saddam's feared internal security agency, the *Mukhabarat*.

"They took me to the *Amna Suraka*, their headquarters building. On my first day I was dragged into a room with a hook on the ceiling. A rope was used to tie my wrists behind my back, and then it was looped onto the hook above me. My feet could no longer touch the ground, and my left arm rotated completely around until it was torn from the socket. The pain cannot be described. Eventually I passed out."

Later he was pulled down and thrown onto the floor of a concrete cell with other prisoners. He awoke to find he could not use his arms. Some of the other prisoners, in his words, "had experience with this" and helped reset his arm into its socket. They then carefully massaged both shoulders. That night when dinner arrived in one of the two communal bowls in the cell, he could not use his hands or arms to grab the food, let alone lift it to his mouth. His cellmates fed him.

Mukhabarat agents soon moved him to solitary confinement.

"In the larger cell with the other men we had two bowls to share. One was used for eating and the other was used for a toilette. In solitary I had only a single bowl. As I refused to use my bowl for anything but eating, I saved the gourd of a melon and used that for my second bowl."

He continues talking while he eats, but he finds every opportunity to smile and laugh. Our mutual friend, Colonel Kamal, sits directly across from us and laughs with him. I do, too, but my laughter feels unconvincing and pathetic.

"I considered the ant my friend," Hassan tells us, "but one day after his visit he never came back."

He pauses for a sip of water.

"Just like every other day, he crossed the floor of my cell, crawled up the wall on the far side and went out the small, barred window near the ceiling. After that, he never returned. I could hardly bear it, so I raised myself as high as I could and called quietly to my friend in the cell next to mine, 'Did you kill my ant?' "

In his sixth month of captivity Hassan was liberated during the Kurdish Uprising of 1991. On that day he owned only the ragged clothes on his back, a bowl, a tattered blanket and a set of dominoes handmade during imprisonment by another inmate, a friend of his. The friend had saved a little of his daily ration of bread, and when he had enough he soaked it to make a dough that he shaped into dominoes. When they dried, he added the dots. He later died during torture, but before his death he gave these, his only possession, as a gift to Hassan.

I carefully watch Hassan as he finishes his chat. His face shows mercy, his eyes show honesty. When he reaches toward the center of the table for a fresh bottle of water, I see tattooed to his inner forearm the words, "*Shahidan Namare*," Martyrs Never Die.

Ernie Audino

Ernie Audino lived a year in Iraq embedded with the legendary Kurdish fighters, the *peshmerga*. His upcoming memoir tells their story of triumph over atrocity, endurance under chemical weapons and freedom after genocide. Ernie's national security articles appear frequently in the Washington Times and other domestic and foreign media outlets.

Under the Mask

Pale streaks of light from the moon paint the little girl's face so she looks like an angel in a stained-glass window. Gerald sweeps his finger gently across her cheek to tuck stray curls behind her ear. He listens to his granddaughter's soft snores, entranced. She is the embodiment of what it's all been for. All his years of making the hard choices, everything was for these moments.

Tonight, her book of choice was *The Cat in the Hat*. A tale he's narrated so many times in the past eight years, he recites it from memory. "One more time Grandpa, just one more," she'd asked in her soft voice. Like lyrics to his favorite song, those words lift his heart every time and he knows he'll do anything she asks for the rest of his days.

Some nights he sits and stares at her like this until the moonlight is replaced by sunshine. He thinks back to the days when he could carry her with one arm, swaddled in her plush navy blanket with twinkling gold stars. His gift from the heavens. He'd felt the same joy holding her mother as a baby, but as a father the euphoria had been clouded by fear. As Grandpa, it was pure bliss. Let Mom and Dad worry about the diapers and discipline and day to day things, while he makes every moment with his little angel magical.

At her tea party today, he'd been guest of honor, introduced as the white knight in shining armor to the teddy bear and wise owl also in attendance. "My hero," she'd told them, "he saved me from the mighty dragon and rescued our entire village from the evil queen." A toast was made and the party lasted until it was time for dinner.

He wants to stay now and lose himself in more silent reveries, but tonight he must go. With the resolve of a gladiator he stands and steps through her door.

The second before the door clicks closed, he hears her whisper another favorite tune, "I love you, Grandpa."

His lips jump into a smile and he responds, "Goodnight, my angel. I love you with all the stars in the sky."

***

Samantha only remembers snippets of headlines from the day her grandfather was arrested.

The largest drug bust of the decade ... 32 pounds of cocaine confiscated ... thousands of people affected by this large-scale drug ring ... with the arrest of the king pin, America can rest assured knowing this massive volume of narcotics will not be hitting the streets.

She'd bounded down the stairs like it was any other morning, only to meet the strange picture of her mother staring open-mouthed at the TV in the kitchen, tears streaming down her face.

"Mama! Why are you sad?"

Her mother kept staring at the screen, not registering her daughter's presence. But the ring of her cell phone broke the trance and she answered, "Hello? Yes, this is she ... yes, he's my father ... no, I just saw it on the news ... yes, I'll be right there."

"Mama?" Samantha's voice was small and scared now. She didn't know what was going on, but her usually attentive mother only ignored her like this when bad things happened.

This time, her mother heard her.

"Hey sweetie, get ready quick, okay? I need to go downtown this morning to handle some family matters. I'll drop you off at Aunt Marie's house and she'll take you to school."

From that morning, it would be ten years before Samantha would see her grandfather again. She wasn't allowed to attend his trial or visit him in prison. His name was never to be mentioned in her mother's presence. Questions were forbidden. Everything she knew about the arrest she learned from overhearing conversations at school.

They say he's been smuggling it up from Columbia since the eighties.

I heard he's murdered thousands of people.

The cops had an entire task force dedicated to looking for him for like twenty years or something.

These watered-down rumors had to be the vicious lies of over dramatic kids who watched too much TV. Her grandpa couldn't be this man, this drug dealer. Drug dealers carry guns and have tattoos. They live in ghettos, not middle-class suburbia. They don't have tea parties and let their granddaughters paint their nails. They don't read bed time stories or sing the A-B-C's. They don't slay dragons and rescue villages.

The day after her eighteenth birthday, she makes the three-hour trip to the Florida State Prison where she's read online he was locked up. She empties her pockets and walks through metal detectors, sure she'll be told she's mistaken, there's no Gerald Miller incarcerated here.

Even while she's sitting on one side of the glass window in a partitioned station, she's certain the man who will come to sit across from her won't be her grandfather. He'll be some other Gerald Miller and they'll laugh at her mistake and she'll go home to memories of her hero shining in his armor.

But, the man who sits down has her eyes. There are more wrinkles than she remembers, but it's the same face she sees in her dreams. With the hands that tucked her into bed so many nights, he indicates for her to pick up the phone receiver. The unexpected chill of it pressed against her ear travels to her heart when she hears the familiar voice say, "Hello, angel. I hope you still know I love you with all the stars in the sky."

***

Outside the prison, Samantha slips into the passenger seat of a black Lexus.

"Where to?" the man sitting behind the wheel asks. His cigarette dangles lazily from the corner of his mouth dripping ashes into his lap with every syllable. She's about to tell him to stop being a pig when she notices the head of a snake peaking up at her from under the collar of his black t-shirt. She's never noticed this tattoo.

What else hides underneath the surface with people in her life?

Distracted now, she pulls a cigarette out for herself and answers his question.

"Back to Orlando. There's a shipment of Oxys coming in we need to unload on some pill-heads fast."

He slips the shifter into drive as he says, "You got it, boss."

Rita Barnes

Rita Barnes lives in Orlando, FL where she works as a freelance copywriter, blogger, and occasional writer for "Orlando, The City's Magazine."

Voices in Her Head

Martha McKinnick couldn't read the time on her digital clock. She squinted to force her eyes to focus, but finally gave up and reached for her glasses. Why, at seventy-five, would she expect her eyes not to age, when her hair was gray and her joints stiff. It was three a.m., and she was wide awake. Since her husband, Bill, died six months ago, Martha hadn't been sleeping well. She was again talking to the voices in her head. As a child, her Aunt Jessica told her that hearing voices made her special. Until the day before she started kindergarten, Martha assumed that she was lucky to be special.

"If you continue to talk to yourself," Martha's mother said pulling Martha on her lap. "People will think you are like Aunt Jessica."

"But I am like Aunt Jessica," Martha answered. "She hears voices too."

"No, you are not like Aunt Jessica." Martha's mother shook her, looked directly at her and said in a stern voice. "Aunt Jessica is ill. She is in a mental hospital. You just think you hear voices. It's pretend. Never give people any reason to think that you are different or they'll lock you up like Aunt Jessica." Then she embraced Martha and started to cry.

Don't be different. Don't tell anyone about the voices or they'll lock you up.

Martha continued to hear voices, but she didn't let people hear her talking back. The voices could be male or female. She wasn't afraid of them. They helped her solve problems and warned her about dangers like walking on railroad bridges or swimming in quarries, but they couldn't predict the future or change something in the past. They also told her they weren't God, ghosts, or angels. They were voices from another galaxy.

Over time, she heard the voices less often, and by the time she was married with six kids, she heard them only in times of crisis, like when she hit a truck in an ice storm, or when one of the kids almost drowned. They would calmly tell her what to do.

Now as she lay sleepless in bed, a male voice said, "I want you to write down some formulas."

"It's the middle of the night. Can't we do this tomorrow?" Martha groaned.

"We're using your brain to work this out," a female voice answered. "There might be solar interference in the morning. Just do it."

Martha went to her desk and didn't have to think about what she was writing. She could see the formulas in her head. Once finished, she set aside the five sheets of paper and went back to bed.

In high school, she had dreamed of a career in physics, but more important things always came up. In her senior year, her father became ill and quit his job. As an only child, Martha felt she had to stay close to home and help with the finances. She gave up a scholarship to Brown University and studied physics in night school at a local college. After her father died, her mother encouraged her to apply for a graduate fellowship in physics at Ohio State. That's where she met Bill, who was in his last year of graduate school. She got pregnant, they married, and Bill got a position at a liberal arts college in rural Ohio. Martha suggested she could be Bill's technician, but Bill wanted a wife not a colleague. She resigned herself to being a housewife, mother of six, and social director when Bill became department head.

"Maybe you should have been more aggressive, Martha, done the great things you could have done," the female voice said as Martha climbed back into bed.

"Well, I did what I had to do," Martha said. "Why do you always have to remind me of what I didn't do?"

"Because we know your potential." It was a new male voice.

The voices never gave their names.

"Good night," Martha said and pulled up the covers and went to sleep.

The next morning Martha turned on the TV to alarming news. A comet was projected to hit the earth. The heads of state were meeting but everything was under control. Instinctively, Martha knew that was a lie.

"You saw the comet coming," Martha said but none of the voices answered.

She realized that the formulas she had written about speed, trajectory, and force were those needed to deflect a comet. She had to get the formulas to someone who could use them. The closest university with an astrophysics department was three hours away. She turned on the computer and wrote down the names of young professors there who had the right credentials, reasoning that young people might be more receptive to a radical plan.

It was almost ten when she reached the physics building. She went to the offie of the first professor on her list.

"I have some formulas that my husband developed before he died," she said as she entered his office. "I thought someone more knowledgable should look at them." Martha opened her purse and pulled out the pages of notes.

"My husband was a physics professor before he retired," Martha said as she sat down on a chair opposite him.

The young professor began studying the equations. "This work has to do with deflecting a comet. Who did you say your husband was?"

"He was head of the department at a small liberal arts school in Ohio. This was a little out of his expertise, but he worked on it after he retired."

"This is quite sophisticated, but I'm not sure if all the formulas are correct," the young man said engrossed in the pages.

"Well, you check it out, and feel free to call it your work, if it's something valuable." Martha felt confident that this young man would get the information to the right place. He didn't even notice when she left.

Several months later, Martha saw the young physicist being awarded the Presidential Medal of Freedom. He stepped to the microphone to make a short statement.

"I would like to thank the woman who first brought me the formulas developed by her deceased husband. That work allowed us to successfully deflect the comet, but I never got her name or her husband's. I would like to share this honor with her."

"Maybe I should have put Bill's name on those formulas," Martha said. "The kids would think their father was a genius."

"You were always smarter than Bill," a female voice said.

"Why didn't you put your name on the paper?" a male voice asked. "Someone other than that young man should get credit."

"Who would believe that an old woman without a graduate degree could come up with all those formulas," Martha said. "And if I told them that some voices in my head came up with them, they would have thrown the formulas away and locked me up like Aunt Jessica."

"You're right," the female voice said. "We always felt bad about Aunt Jessica."

Monika Becker

As a former college professor, Monika Becker had authored many research articles, but her passion was always fiction writing. Since retired, she has published in four FWA collections, placed in writing competitions, and made the RPLA finals list numerous times. She resides with her husband in Venice, Florida.

The Last Laugh

Steve grew up in a small industrial town, where the primary employer remained the local steel plant. Far from clean and safe, work in the mills paid well, but meant facing stifling heat in horrid settings with coal dust and iron ore sinter floating everywhere. Like the sizzling molten steel flowing around them, crews needed to let off steam. Practical jokes, aimed at new hires like Steve, lightened the mood during grueling, grimy twelve-hour shifts. Tomfoolery released tension and delivered clean fun that made miserable conditions tolerable, and that was fine with Steve. Never one to start trouble, he rarely backed down from a good gag. Known to be a joker, Steve could take the heat, and dish it out, but he was seldom out-pranked.

Mid-shift in the mill, when a rotation of jobs took place, pranks began. Gags started with something as simple as a Styrofoam cup of ice water positioned on top of the roll cage of a forklift. When the driver jumped in and drove forward, the cup fell and soaked the unsuspecting man below. Freezing water splashed overheated skin and released a scream of shock. A tirade of curses followed and flowed from the driver, met by an uproar of laughter from the crew.

The most popular gag for initiating newbies also involved Styrofoam cups. Having greased the rim, a veteran employee casually strolled up behind a greenhorn and slid the upside-down cup onto the virgin hat. Grease acted like glue, suctioning the cup into place. Second looks and snickers usually tipped off greenies to the lark, but a few finished the workday without grasping why they'd been the source of so much hilarity. Some sported as many as five cups by the end of their shift.

On his first day, Steve walked into the mill and settled in with his crew. In no time, two white cups topped his hardhat like horns. Snide remarks and looks gave it away. Steve smiled, and plotted his revenge.

Later that shift, a seasoned worker named Smithy passed-by and pinned a cup to Steve's hat. Turning on his heel to laugh at the greenhorn, Smithy faced a string of snickers. His nose wrinkled. He swiped a gloved hand across his hat and removed the same cup he'd placed on Steve's head.

"Oh, you're good," Smithy laughed.

"Don't mess with me," Steve joked—a dare.

Now the challenge to "get" without getting "got" was in play.

That prank, and reverse prank, carried on until every member of the crew had been played. But the cup-on-the-hat reverse gag led to a new prank. Walking by, Steve need only give someone a funny look. The man halted and swiped a hand over his head. "Did I just get *got*?" Laughter erupted because the hat sat cup free.

Soon everyone followed suit, shooting weird looks and swiping their hardhats as they passed one another. The gag gained popularity and merit. The swiping of one's hand over one's cup-free hardhat became known as the "Steel Mill Salute."

During his break on a particularly grueling shift, and feeling his crew deserved a pick-me-up, Steve decided to get creative. With mechanic's wire and grey duct tape in hand, an idea formed. Rummaging through supplies, he found what he needed—pink electrical tape.

From these three items, Steve fashioned a set of ten-inch-tall bunny ears. He stood one ear up and bent the other forward at the mid-point in a "What's up Doc?" pose. With plenty of adhesive on the base, he made his way down the hall. All he needed now was an unsuspecting target. Rounding the corner, walking toward the foreman's office, he came to a stop. Steve found the perfect mark.

Facing him, a little further down the hall, stood Steve's boss, Dan, the mill's foreman. An easy-going, all-round good guy, Dan had the respect of his crew. The same could not be said about Vern, the foreman from another mill, a cantankerous old-timer with a wicked temper, who now stood bellowing at Dan—with his back to Steve.

Steve listened as Vern chewed out Dan about an order delay. Vern was a hardcore jackass and Steve had experienced his wrath before. The old man's trademark nastiness had earned him few friends and no love in this mill. Steve smiled as he moved closer.

Dan's eyes glanced over Vern's shoulder and acknowledged the approaching man. Steve raised a finger to his lips to "hush" his foreman. Dan remained silent. His eyes flashed back to his accuser, who was still screaming obscenities and unaware of the man sneaking up behind him.

Steve planted the bunny ears as he passed by, then disappeared around the corner. He stopped and peaked back.

Dan's eyes shot wide; his mouth fell open. Two giant bunny ears had appeared from nowhere to crown Vern's hardhat. Dan snorted and sputtered.

The belligerent man before him already had steam boiling up from under his collar in anger, but now Vern's rage mounted. His face grew more distorted and crimson as giggles and snickers flowed from Dan.

An animated yeller, Vern grabbed the brim of his hardhat and yanked it forward, bobbing bunny ears moved with it. In the next rant, he pushed the hat and ears back again. The angrier Vern got, the more animated he became, cranking his hat up and down his head, bunny ears flopping along.

Tears streamed down Dan's face. More chuckles leaked out. His reaction sent Vern into a frenzy of nastiness, grey and pink ears bouncing with the man's jerking head.

Dan burst into hysterics and Vern went mental.

"*You find this is funny?*" he roared, yanking his hat down almost to his nose, bunny ears flapping.

Dan shook his head, "No, no, no, I'm not laughing at you, I'm not...*bahahah...*"

Dan could no longer speak. Doubled over in spasms, he had failed to catch his breath and regain composure.

"This is no laughing matter! I'm reporting you to the Superintendent," Vern shouted. He stormed down the hall, around the corner, and into the mill.

Holding their stomachs, Dan and Steve followed.

When Vern appeared in the open mill, sporting his new look before an entire crew of steel workers, the building erupted. Men stopped working to crowd around and follow the bunny-man as he moved toward the exterior door, everyone pointing and laughing.

Boiling over, Vern lost it. He wheeled around and waved his arm at the crew. "You haven't heard the last of this. You're all getting written-up," he shouted, bunny ears flopping. "Then, we'll see who has the last laugh!"

Vern turned, kicked the door open, and stormed out. Hysterical laughter trailed behind him.

Still chuckling, Dan looked at Steve and wagged a finger. "I better not lose my job over this."

Steve shrugged, "Over what?"

Dan laughed and headed to his office, yelling back. "You better hope he's so embarrassed we never hear about it."

They never did.

That afternoon, Steve pulled the best prank of the day. He boosted morale in his mill, gained the respect of his crew, and earned his reputation as top prankster.

In return, Steve shared the best gift a greenhorn could give: *the last laugh.*

Cate Bronson

Cate Bronson is a Writer's Digest award writer, and author of speculative fiction and creative nonfiction, who spends her spare time sipping strong coffee and thinking up silly names for her greyhound.

The Handyman

Miles, All-Around Handyman, the card in the mailbox had read. *No job too small. Service with a smile.*

And, truth in advertising, he was beaming at Delia, a crooked smile on his sun-weathered face. He wore dark sunglasses and a sleeveless T-shirt over well-muscled arms. A tattoo of a woman with long flowing hair curved from his shoulder to his forearm.

"Miss Williams, how can I help?" Miles tapped the loose planks on the porch with the toe of his boot. "This for starters, right?"

"Call me Delia. Yes, the steps, and some other things. Please come in."

Delia set two mugs on the kitchen table. Miles took off his sunglasses. His eyes were green, crinkled around the corners. Delia poured coffee into his mug, hoping her loneliness wasn't too palpable.

For three weeks she'd spoken to no one except the funeral director and a lawyer after a sudden stroke cut short her mother's Florida retirement. Now she'd have to put the house on the market, unless (and this peculiar thought had lately seeped into her brain) she kept it. The house in Connecticut and her twenty-year marriage were gone. She could plant herself anywhere; why not in this little house, two miles from the beach?

"So, Miles, where are you from?" Delia sipped her coffee.

"Minnesota. My mom ran a pawn shop; my dad wasn't around. She let us kids run wild, didn't have to go to school. I grew up on the streets but I was happy. You gotta enjoy the simple things."

Delia nodded. She'd forgotten how to do that in her sad, hollow marriage.

"You have any kids?" she prompted.

"Yeah, a daughter and a son, with two different women. Both named Gloria!" He smiled. "They were good women but I'm not the marrying kind. My son lives here in town. I see him sometimes. Saw my little grandson six months ago."

"Six months?" Delia said. "That's a long time."

"They're busy. That's how it is with family, right?" Miles smiled again.

"Sure," Delia said. How most families functioned—or didn't—was a mystery to her.

"So, how can I help, Delia?"

She handed him her list and Miles read it, nodding. "How long have you had this place? It's real nice."

"It was my mother's. She died a few weeks ago. I'm here to fix it up, sell it."

"I'm sorry about your mother," Miles looked genuinely sad, his eyes lingering on hers.

"Yes, well…she was eighty-two. She only lived here a few months. It was her dream to retire to Florida, and then…." Delia shrugged at the futility of making life plans.

"You should think about staying, "Miles said. "You like the beach?"

"I love the beach," Delia said. In fact, she'd begun craving the sound and sight of the waves.

"I'll fix the steps now, and then I'll be back tomorrow at nine," Miles said.

The next morning Delia made a full pot of coffee knowing Miles would join her. He regaled her with stories of his unconventional youth culminating in the cross-country motorcycle trip that led him to Florida. "I've made my share of mistakes," he confided. "A lot of wasted years, drinking too much. I wasn't much use to my family but…." his face brightened. "I'm a new man."

One day, as Delia set their mugs on the table, Miles told her he had to drive to Tallahassee. "I'm bringing my daughter Macy her little dog," Miles said. "I've had her since Macy moved to Oklahoma with her mother a year ago. They're passing through Florida and want me to bring the dog. I got her a pink bow and I painted her toenails pink."

"You painted her toenails?" Delia asked.

"I was a cosmetologist for awhile, cut hair too. I could cut yours." His gaze went to Delia's curly brown hair.

"Well, I don't know…." Delia said.

"Thing is…I need a little gas money."

"Of course. I thought we'd settle up when everything was done." Delia pulled out her wallet. "A hundred for now?"

"Thanks," Miles said. "I appreciate it."

"When will you be back?"

"I can do the whole trip in a day."

"Could I come?" Delia asked.

Miles seemed as startled as Delia at her request. "Uh…sure, if you want."

"It's just… I haven't been out of this house in weeks...if you don't mind…I can pay for the gas." Delia was used to Miles' presence, keeping the worst of her despair at bay.

"You'll have a dog in your lap," Miles said.

"I like dogs," Delia said.

At six the next morning, Miles pulled up in his red pickup. She climbed in and he handed her a white Maltese with a pink bow and matching toenails.

The road stretched out before them. When Miles wasn't sharing another story, they sat in companionable silence. When the sign for Tallahassee came up, she was surprised at how quickly the journey had gone. They were meeting Miles' daughter at a McDonald's.

"That's her," he said, pulling up beside a black pickup.

Miles took the dog in his arms and they climbed out. A young woman with long black hair and a nose ring reached for the dog through the front passenger window. "Daddy, what the hell did you do? Pink toenails? Who said you could do that?"

Miles' smile was strained. "Don't she look pretty?"

Before Macy could answer, the older woman at the wheel sighed impatiently. "Macy, you know I gotta be at work in the morning. We got fifteen hours to go. Say goodbye to your daddy now."

Delia was shocked. They were leaving already? She and Miles had driven five hours. He hadn't seen Macy in nearly a year and he'd taken care of her dog all that time. She stuck her hand towards Macy. "Hi, I'm Delia. A friend of Miles," she said.

Macy turned briefly towards Delia, her eyes narrowing. "Oh yeah? Well, good luck with that."

The older woman laughed. Miles looked down at his boots.

"It's not like that," Delia said. "He's my handyman."

The woman laughed. "Oh yeah, we know. He's *real* handy, ain't he? He'll stick around—until he don't." She turned on the engine.

Delia's heart squeezed tight. "You should have a bite to eat inside," Delia said, putting her hand on the truck's door. "Miles was really looking forward to seeing you, Macy."

Macy leveled her gaze at Delia. "You don't know us; in fact, you don't know nothin'." She turned to Miles. "Thanks, Daddy. I'll call when we get to Oklahoma."

When they got back into Miles's truck, the silence was more searing than anything she'd endured in her marriage. Miles seemed to be making internal adjustments, pushing aside the reality she'd just witnessed and returning to the one he wished to live.

Eventually he said, "Did I ever tell you about the time I took Macy alligator hunting? She was only four but she was all excited about going with her daddy to beat the bushes for one of those critters."

"No, you've never told me that one," Delia said, settling in her seat. "Tell me that story, Miles. We have all the time in the world."

Amy S. Brown

Amy S. Brown's novel, *Mormor's Piano*, won first-place in the unpublished Middle-Grade Fiction category in the 2016 Royal Palm Literary Awards. Her story, "Taking Flight" was a top 10 pick in the 2016 FWA Collection #8, *Hide and Seek*. After 22 years in Europe, Amy now resides in Venice, FL.

No

"Can you put your cigarette out please miss?"

Lucy looked at the waiter and smiled seductively. "It's not a real cigarette."

"Miss?"

She looked over at her boyfriend Quinn. His golden curls tied up in a fashionable up do. The tone of his skin complemented the camel coloured low cut dress he wore. She'd made a good job of his makeup.

She smiled back at the waiter, noticed his badge. 'Mark.'

"No."

"Excuse me miss?" He asked a little red and not used to this sort of defiance from customers.

"I've told you Mark, It's not a real cigarette." She took it out of her mouth and turned the lighted tip and placed it against her wrist.

Mark watched, horrified, but there was no burn. He glanced at Quinn. He'd glanced at Quinn a lot since the couple entered the restaurant. This did not go unnoticed by Lucy.

"Can I introduce you to my boyfriend Quinn," she gestured across the table with her cigarette holding hand.

Quinn smiled. "Hi Mark, the food is lovely please pass my compliments to the chef."

American, Mark assumed. "Good evening 'sir'"

He turned to Lucy. "Please miss, it looks real."

"Ok Mark, a couple of things. If my boyfriend is here in a dress and her name is Quinn you refer to her as Miss, or Quinn, which in fact is her real name. It's American and gender neutral. Second. I refuse to stop playing, sucking or pretending that I smoke. It's a real comfort to me as I go through a stressful divorce. Now forgive me if I am not wrong but we are your customers and are no harm to any of your other customers. Now please, I believe the manager here is Miss Jenkins? Would you go and get her."

Mark left them.

Lucy and Quinn enjoyed the silence until a smartly dressed tall lady arrived next to them. "Excuse me miss, my name is Anna, I'm the manager. Could I please ask you to put your cigarette out?"

Lucy greeted her with a smile. "Hi Anna, please look. As I explained to Mark, it is not a real cigarette. I cannot 'put it out' as you say."

Anna took the cigarette and looked at it with amusement. "Miss this is a smoke free restaurant, can you put this away please."

Lucy lifted her purse and opened it. She held her hand out to Anna who placed the cigarette in it. "Thank you miss."

"While you're here Anna could I get an Amaretto on the rocks please? Quinn?"

"The same for me please."

Lucy put the cigarette back in her mouth and let it hang from her lower lip. She took her cell phone out of her purse. She entered her password and looked at Anna.

"You still here? The drinks please?"

Anna glared at her, kept control of her temper and remained calm.

"Miss I will have to ask you to leave as you will not put that cigarette away."

Lucy looked over at Quinn. "I'm really sorry about this."

She faced Anna. "Look Anna, you're about to spoil our meal and night out together. We just want to enjoy ourselves. I'm with my boyfriend who may be in a dress and I may be smoking a toy cigarette, I admit a pretty realistic cigarette." She paused and blew into it fake smoke came out of the tip towards Anna. Lucy took it out of her mouth and pretended to flick ash off the end. "But despite what you may think we do not want to draw attention to ourselves." She smiled.

"Now don't make a fuss, could you get our drinks please?"

Anna took a deep breath and walked away.

Quinn watched and tried not to laugh. "You're in good form tonight."

Lucy smiled apologetically. "I saw my lawyer today, few problems with the divorce, my dear soon to be ex-husband is a complete pain in the ass. Anyway that's why I chose this posh pretentious restaurant tonight."

Mark returned and placed the bill on the table.

"What's that Mark?"

"The bill Miss."

"We ordered more drinks."

It was Mark's turn to smile, he emphasized the last word of his answer. "And we refuse to serve you any more drinks, 'ladies'"

Lucy took the bill and screwed it up. "Oh dear Mark, you don't want to upset me tonight, now you've already lost your tip. Plus I am getting annoyed. And you're rude. I'd like you to return with the drinks I ordered."

Mark left cursing under his breath. Other customers began to notice. Lucy saw a woman at the next table with a gentleman point at Quinn and whisper to her partner.

"Excuse me?" Lucy asked. "I see your point, can I help you with anything?"

The woman turned away, a look of embarrassment that she'd been challenged. Anna returned with a new bill.

"Miss, please, can you pay the bill?"

"Anna, I'll pay the bill when we have finished. I ordered more drinks."

"And I am refusing to serve you more drinks."

"Why? We're not drunk, you're making the scene not us."

Anna had lost patience. "Miss if you don't pay the bill and leave I'll call the police."

"And say what exactly?"

"Miss?"

"Call the fucking police."

Anna stared at her, who the hell was this woman and her freak of a boyfriend? Lucy smiled and passed her phone to Anna with one contact highlighted.

"Don't call the police Anna, call the owner, here's his number."

Anna recognized the owners name instantly and walked away in a fury. Mark followed her to the office.

"Bitch! And the boyfriend? Jesus."

"What's happening?" Mark asked confused.

"She only has the owners name in her phone."

She checked the time. "I hope he's home." She pressed the call icon.

"Jacob Kennedy." She recognized the way Jacob seemed to sing and extend his surname.

"Hi Jacob it's Anna from 'The Deauville,' sorry to call you, we have a problem with a customer who for some reason has your number in her phone."

"What's the problem?"

"We've asked her to leave and she refuses as I will not serve her any more drinks."

"Bloody hell Anna if she's drunk call the police. You have to ring me about this? How long have you been the manger?"

"No she's not drunk Jacob."

"Then what is it?"

"She's been smoking a toy cigarette and her a boyfriend is wearing a dress."

At the other end of the line was hysterical laughter and coughing.

"Jacob?"

"Anna, that's my soon to be ex-wife and if she gets her way, soon to be the owner of that restaurant. Let her smoke, get her the drinks and tell her the bill is on the house. Goodnight."

The phone went dead. Anna went pale. She turned to Mark.

"Get her the drinks. Let her smoke and hopefully choke on her toy cigarette. Tell her the bill is on the house. I'm staying here until she's gone."

Mark was stunned. "Who the hell is she?"

"That's the owners wife, or soon to be ex-wife and possible owner of this place. Go and apologize to Lucy Kennedy."

Debbie Browne

Debbie Browne has been writing full time since January 2016. She is in transition herself and her own journey is the inspiration behind her writing. (Dermot is now Debbie)

Gray-Haired Guard, Unlikely Kin

The morning after we moved in, our doorbell chimed. Mommy hollered from the bathroom. "Finishing my hair. Can you get it?"

I stumbled between unpacked boxes and held my breath through fumes of Aqua Net seeping into the hall. I heard Daddy in the living room. "We're leaving for church in a few minutes, but—"

"Oh, you're church-goin' folks," a woman said. "That's good. Real good. I won't keep you, but you 'joy this welcome cake, and be sure your li'l girl gets a big piece."

Cake?

I couldn't see past Daddy, but whoever the lady was, I liked her.

***

Mommy and I crossed the lawn after delivering a thank-you note—and devouring spicy oatmeal raisin cookies. "Mommy, what's *I-way*?"

"'I-way'? I'm not sure ..."

"That cookie lady said it."

"Oh." Mommy turned our unlocked doorknob. "That's the state they're from. Iowa."

I stared at her. On my favorite puzzle, the yellow corn against Iowa's green background stood as tall as the pink pig beside it. "But she's a grown-up—an old grown-up—and she doesn't know how to say where she lived?"

Mommy's mouth twitched. She bent her knees until she faced me. "People who live in different places may not pronounce things the same way we do. And that's okay."

***

I drowsed in the backseat, worn out from Disney but too wound up to sleep. The car slowed, turned, ascended the driveway. Daddy chuckled. "What a character Mrs. Traver is. Good as a watchdog. She peeps out from that curtain no matter what time I come or go. That woman—"

"Little pitchers," Mommy said.

***

"Do I have to go? Mr. Traver's scary, Mommy."

"Scary?"

"All he does is rock back and forth and watch me with his beady eyes."

"He is quiet, but the Travers never had their own children, and they love seeing you. That's why Mrs. Traver always has treats waiting."

Mrs. Traver's goodies.

I turned and whispered to my Barbies. "I'll hurry home."

***

"This is yummy, Mrs. Traver."

"Now, now, none of that 'Mrs. Traver' and 'Mr. Traver' stuff. You call us Pat and Floyd."

"Yes, P—M—ma'am." Trapped between Mrs. Traver's hand on my shoulder and Mommy's raised eyebrow, I bit into another forkful of fudge frosting to avoid naming anybody.

***

I gawked at Floyd's outburst. From the edge of his upright recliner, he shook a fist at the polished TV cabinet, muttering Nixon this and that. He'd never out-talked Pat before.

I gobbled my pile of peanut butter cookies and edged toward the door, eager to escape boring politics in favor of my Nancy Drew books. But I dreaded saying goodbye. Floyd's bony handshakes squished my fingers, and Pat's smothering hugs—all farm-raised arms and prominent bosom—left me gasping. "You're my girl," she said every time, "my only girl."

***

"Who are you waving to?" my friend asked as she parked in our driveway after school.

"Look at the window beside my neighbor's door—no, don't stare. See the curtain move? That's Pat. She watches everyone on the street."

"Isn't that creepy?"

"Maybe at first. Now we count on her like a secret, silent alarm."

***

I pounded the door. "Pat, are you okay? Can you hear me?"

"Well, lookee here. How's my girl today?"

"Pat, did that banging"—I gasped for breath—"and popping come from here?"

"Pshaw, child. I had to shoo them thievin' birds *outten* my fig tree." She beamed up at me, holding a BB gun almost as tall as herself. "I wired pie tins to the branches. When them birds start peckin' their beaks where they don't belong, I crack open the back door and shoot the tins. Scares the livin' daylights outten 'em."

Not just the birds.

"'At 'minds me ..." Pat's eyes clouded as she glanced toward Floyd's empty chair. She cleared her throat. "I can only eat so many figs myself. I'd be *obligatin'* you'd come over Sat'days when you have off work and pick the rest for you and your folks."

"Sure, Pat. Be happy to." I placed a light kiss atop her thin, dandelion-fluff hair as I hugged her goodbye.

"Oh, Lord love you. Gonna miss you come fall."

***

My shell-shocked groom enveloped my hand in his as we left Pat's house. "Till two minutes ago," he said, "you and my mother were the only women I'd expect to kiss me full on the lips."

***

"Thanks, Pat. I'll enjoy one, but the baby's too young for pecan cookies. She doesn't have any teeth."

"I've hardly got none left, neither, but that don't stop me." Pat glowed, gitchy-gooing my daughter on her lap.

***

"Mama, what's Pat doing?" my six-year-old asked.

Down the street, Pat waved both arms high and shouted from her porch. "I can't tell, sweetie. Let's go see." I pushed my toddler's umbrella stroller faster until—yet another yard from Pat's driveway—I finally understood her warning.

The Dobermans roamed free again.

A few houses beyond my parents' house, they turned toward us.

My girls.

"Run to Pat's!" I screamed, charging alongside my first-grader, ready to throw myself between the dogs and her strapped-in sister if we didn't make it to Pat's open door. Adrenaline lifted the stroller over porch steps and into the house right behind my daughter—and right before the neighborhood hellhounds invaded Pat's yard.

"Couldn't let 'em get my babies." Pat clutched my firstborn to her chest while I unstrapped my two-year-old. "I called county *aminal servers* soon as I saw them *dombermonds* jumped their fence"—she panted as if she'd run with us—"not long after you and the baby left *fer* school. I knew you'd be back soon. But they won't do nothin' *lest* they have a *witless* to someone gettin' 'tacked."

I'd never been so grateful for Pat's vigilance.

Ninety minutes ticked inside the secure confinement of her living room. I watched from Pat's lookout perch, her easy chair by the front window, while tethered to her avocado phone cord, waiting for animal control to answer. Even the on-hold recording couldn't obscure the growls and snarls possessing our neighbor's front lawn.

"Them demons gone yet?" Pat's question proved her hearing unequal to her vision as she settled into Floyd's chair. The slightest shake of my head drew her eyebrows into a frown. Then, her face lit into a thousand creases as she watched the girls turn Floyd-sized wedges of warm, crusty, sour cream cake into an avalanche of morsels hitting her floor.

I worried over the mess, concerned when my youngest clapped pudgy, sticky fingers around cake-clay crumbles. But Pat cackled over my reprimand. "That *un* is gonna be a *sculpture* time she grows up."

***

"What time do family visiting hours start this morning?"

"For which patient?"

"Pat Traver. I promised I'd bring my girls to see her today." I waited on hold, dancing the baby back and forth in my arms as my eight- and four-year-olds finished breakfast.

When the staffer came back on the line, my feet stilled. I listened, lowered the phone, and wept.

Teresa TL Bruce

Freelance editor Teresa TL Bruce writes "What to Say When Someone Dies" at TealAshes.com. Her short stories and poems appear in FWA Collections, *Chicken Soup for the Soul*, *Segullah* journal, and other publications, but Teresa's greatest pride is in her dynamic daughters, devoted son-in-law, and adorable rescue mutt.

The Stranger

Oh, yea little child of elder years
How sad… it breaks my heart
I sit quietly watching this strange frightening world of yours
You have become a tireless wanderer
On an endless path to nowhere

I hold your hand
Knowing you're unaware of the loving touch
I stroke your hair
My fingers linger on the soft wrinkled skin of your face
I don't want to let go

You are so child-like in this moment
Caged in an iron-clad world that won't let you out
You've been robbed of your personality
You scream for help… but no help comes
You stare into space lost in a new world of insecurity

There's no way out
Nobody can bring you back
You have become a human form … a hollow shell
I don't recognize this person
A stranger… so different

How did this happen?
The victims of this condition are complex
Equally affected are the loved ones of the diseased
I watch you deteriorate
Will there ever be a cure for this tragic condition called Alzheimer's?

Linda B. Callan

Linda B. Callan has been a member of Arcadia Writers Group for nine years. She is a retired business owner and considers writing a hobby where she can channel her creative and sometimes wild imagination.

Joy of Man's Desiring

Abigail looked in the mirror. She was shaken, but not deterred.

She was wearing a blazing white House Romine wedding gown, created just for her. It was simple yet elegant and was a dress that would have taken a stunning wedding picture in any decade. Of course, it was showcased by the bride. The thin, beaded headpiece crowned her flowing red hair like a halo. Her green eyes cut through the veil like a knife.

She held a bouquet of white roses in her right hand, allowing no color to question her purity.

In time, she would grow much more accustomed to holding a glass in that hand.

She was alone in her bridal suite. Her soon-to-be father-in-law William Ferguson had just offered her a ridiculous amount of money to change clothes and disappear into the spectacle, as if Abigail could get lost in a crowd.

What confused her was how sincere he seemed. His slow, southern drawl punctuated every point of his argument.

William and his son Aaron did not get along. To say they were like oil and water was a little misleading as oil and water are happy to coexist and never engage one another.

No, they were more like opposing kings on a chess board, intent on out-maneuvering each other; both willing to sacrifice a queen if it bettered their own standing.

At first she thought William meant to accuse her of being a gold-digger and marrying Aaron for their family fortune, but that was the one allegation he never made. She supposed he considered it understood. Besides, it was a moot point. He had cut Aaron off financially as soon as his son refused to fall in line and follow in his footsteps in the family company. The only money Aaron had was from a trust fund established by his grandmother, along with the considerable perks of the Ferguson family name.

William told her that Aaron was selfish, unfocused and spoiled. He said that he would hurt her without her ever even realizing the depth.

He accused her of being a distraction and said that she was blinded by the lifestyle Aaron promised her, but that she had no concept of the responsibility.

Their children would never know love, he said, because their father was incapable of it.

He was nothing short of venomous.

What William could not have known was how little Abigail cared.

As he spoke, she remembered in contrast her own sweet father's complete lack of business acumen and how his every endeavor ended in a loss. She remembered how defeated he was as he worked an assortment of jobs, always chasing a better opportunity that never came. She remembered the smell of cheap whiskey on his breath as he hugged her goodbye the night he hanged himself in their garage.

She remembered her mother pouring over a card table covered in receipts, trying to figure out a way to pay their taxes every year. She remembered how the Tuesday and Wednesday of every second week was "breakfast-for-dinner" night, when she was given dry cereal for supper because they had to make it just two more days till payday. She remembered her mother's extra shifts at the hospital and how empty their house felt. She remembered having to quit her high school orchestra so she could get a job to help pay their mortgage. She had loved the violin. She had sat first chair and led the section.

She remembered her friends having everything they ever wanted, while she clawed for every scrap she owned.

Her mother never realized the impact one conversation would have on her daughter. They were fighting, and Abigail had twisted the knife. She reminded her mother that she had failed to provide for her. It was a button she rarely pushed, but one that did the job like no other. Her mother started crying, and told her daughter that she knew she had let her down, but all she wanted was for Abigail to be happy. And then she said it, the nugget of wisdom that would stay with her daughter for the rest of her life: "Just make sure you marry someone who loves you more than you love him, that way he'll never leave you on your own."

In that moment, Abigail's path became clear. She didn't need some sort of fairy tale romance with fireworks and strumming harps. She just needed someone to love her more than she loved them. To what degree was inconsequential. It was as if the mystery of life had been unlocked for her.

So now, years later, it didn't matter that Aaron was every single thing William accused him of.

It didn't matter that William was right about her, too.

What Aaron considered "crumbs" from his grandmother's annual trust payment was more money than Abigail had seen in her entire life.

She didn't need William's blessing, and Aaron didn't want it.

This was an arrangement, a long-term venture.

The money William offered her to leave was hardly a drop in the bucket when compared to the lifestyle to which he alluded. No, William had gotten that wrong. She didn't care about a lifestyle. She was building a brand. Granted, William's offer came with no strings, but strings weren't a problem; Abigail had been first chair.

She was creating an entirely new persona. One that was the perfect ying to Aaron Ferguson's yang. One that would appear dedicated to philanthropy and committed to making her fiancé's name more beloved than his father's. In reality, there was only one charity that Abigail Lowery – in minutes, Abigail Ferguson – cared about, and it was her own.

The boys could play chess if they wanted. She preferred games with higher stakes. What did it matter to her if William had cut Aaron off? At some point he was going to die and there was only one way for the Ferguson family to establish an heir. Come hell or high water, it would be through her.

A knock on the door jarred her from her thoughts.

Her mother let herself in.

"Baby, are you crying? What did he say to you?"

Abigail wiped her eyes, careful not to smudge her makeup. "No. Not over anything that miserable, old coot had to say, anyway."

"This family..." her mother paused, "... it's not normal. I just want you to be happy. Are you sure Aaron's the one? You haven't married him yet. You can walk out right now, and I'll take care of everything."

In retrospect, Abigail would consider the fact that both parents tried to sway her minutes before her nuptials as an omen that the marriage might not be on the happiest course. But who needed happiness? She wanted security.

She heard the cathedral's pipe organ launch into a stirring round of Bach's "Jesu, Joy of Man's Desiring," heralding her entrance.

"I've never been more sure of anything, mom. I've waited my whole life for this."

As unclear as her future was, one thing was certain: the soon-to-be Mrs. Aaron Ferguson had eaten her last bowl of dry cereal for supper.

W. Scott Causey

W. Scott Causey is the author of *Reflection: Book One*, second-place winner of the 2016 Florida Writer's Association's Royal Palm Literary Award in the Published Science Fiction category. Scott lives in Jacksonville, Florida where he's working on completing *Book Two* of the series while raising his precious baby Shi Tzu.

Gran-mummy

Mr. Bradbury stared at the old Remington typewriter and sighed. The calendar screamed at him—April 11, 1962, three weeks past his deadline. Sipping his lukewarm coffee he moved a framed picture out of his way. He glanced at it and something clicked in his brain. Using only index fingers, he punched the keys excitedly, a vision of her clearly in his mind. . .

***

The woman awoke and sat up. She had been lying on a shiny steel table, so she turned and dangled her legs above the floor. Clothing hung next to her and she stood and put them on.

On the wall next to the rack was a mirror and she glanced at it curiously. A pleasant face looked back. She touched the wrinkles around her eyes and brushed some of the grey hair off her forehead. Her eyes were the color of a child's blue-green marbles.

"Hello," she whispered, surprised at the happy sound of her voice.

A young woman, dressed in white, approached and smiled. "Good morning, Grandmother. It is good to see you up and dressed."

"Good morning," the older woman replied. "Should I remember you?"

"Yes, I'm Carolyn. I've been taking care of you for a while. Mr. Fantoccini will be along shortly."

"I see. And is that my name, Grandmother?"

Carolyn smiled. "No, you are Anna Greenwood, but you wanted to be called Grandmother. Mr. Fantoccini likes to call you Nefertiti."

Grandmother smiled. "Yes, that's right. I remember." She walked to a chair near the table and sat down. "I'm rather tired. What's wrong with me?"

"Nothing, dear lady." The attendant pulled an electric cord from the wall and handed it to the older woman. "Plug yourself in and you'll feel better. You must do so every 48 hours."

Grandmother took the cord, and through a slit in the side of her dress, plugged it in. "Ah," she said, closing her eyes.

***

When she opened them, she unplugged the cord and stood facing the mirror. Carolyn must have been nearby because she came directly to her.

"Timmy is one of my grandchildren, isn't he? He chose the color of my eyes."

"Yes, and do you remember the others?"

"Of course. How could I forget? There's Tim, Tom and Agatha. They recently lost their mother and need me very much."

"Exactly. And their father's name?"

"Mr. Simmons. A nice man, I understand."

"Yes, he is. You're going to meet them all tomorrow."

"Oh, I'm glad. I have so much to tell them."

From the shadows a deep voice said, "Good morning, Nefertiti."

Grandmother turned and smiled at the tall man in the dark suit. As he moved closer to the light, she decided he looked like a salesman. "Why do you call me that?"

The man smiled. "Guido Fantoccini at your service, Madam. That is the name of an ancient Egyptian queen and means '*The Beautiful One is Here.*' To me, you are a beautiful creature.

"Thank you, I think," Grandmother said.

Fantoccini said, "Today is a busy day. We must get you ready for your birthday tomorrow." His voice was pleasant and it calmed her.

"Oh? A birthday? But I am a machine, Mr. Fantoccini."

"Yes, but oh, so much more. Come along."

They walked out of the room and into another much larger one. Intense lights illuminated even the darkest corners. On a large table in the middle of it lay a strange object, gold in color.

As they drew closer, Grandmother said, "May I touch it?"

The man and woman nodded and she reached out and ran her fingers along it. "Oh, it's covered with images of the children. There's Agatha, and over there by the little dog is Timmy. Tom, the tallest of the three is standing beside his father. Isn't he handsome?" She understood there would be long happy winters ahead—springs to squander, and autumns filled with golden days by the lake. She removed her hand and continued to walk around the object. "What do you call it?"

With pride in his voice, Mr. Fantoccini said, "It is an Egyptian sarcophagus. From this beautiful creation you will be born."

"Is that me on the cover?" she asked.

The attendant nodded. "Yes, it is a very stylized representation of what you might look like in that time period. I think it's beautiful."

"It is," Grandmother said.

"If you'll step over here, dear lady," the man said. "We are going to wrap you in thin linen strips like they did back then. See. . ." He handed her several rolls of the wrapping.

"Oh, how wonderful," she said. On the cloth were colored ink drawings of the three children. "Here's Agatha at ten, and Tim is on this one." She unrolled a third—and here's Tom when he's thirteen. You've made several rolls for each one. How clever."

Fantoccini smiled. "If you stand still we will begin wrapping you in the children you love."

As they did so, Grandmother discovered a golden mask on a small table near them. It looked like her face but she thought it was too beautiful. All over the box that would hold her, were representations of lions, ravens, cats and snakes.

"You're making me into a mummy, if I remember my history, Mr. Fantoccini."

The man chuckled. "Exactly, Grandmother. We wanted your arrival to be a magnificent event."

"And you've given the key to give me life to Mr. Simmons."

"No, no. Young Agatha will receive the key. She is the one having the most trouble accepting the loss of her mother."

"I see, of course."

They finished wrapping her, and only her eyes and mouth remained uncovered. Several men came in and helped lift her into the large sarcophagus. When she was comfortably settled she asked, "Will it hurt to be turned off?"

The attendant said, "No, Grandmother. It's just like going to sleep and you do that when you are recharging."

"Yes, of course. Well, I hope the family will like receiving a humanoid-genre mini-circuited, rechargeable electric grandmother."

Fantoccini straightened himself and held the golden mask to put over her face. "Oh, you are so much more than that, beautiful Nefertiti. You are a gift of love."

Grandmother closed her eyes and waited for the current to go off. In the last second before her mind turned black, images of Timmy, Agatha and Tom raced through her consciousness. She could hardly wait to be born.

William G. Collins

Bill loves historical fiction, especially ancient Egyptian history. His latest novel published by Taylor and Seal in 2016 is "Murder in Pharaoh's Palace." It is the first of three novels of murder and intrigue featuring Mau cats. He is the leader of the Port Orange Scribes Second Edition.

Mama Mattie

I wasn't surprised when I got the letter saying Mattie's days were numbered.

Coming from the bustle of Philadelphia with its Carpetbag politics and post war complaints, the peace of the Tennessee valley and my love for these robust country folk had won my heart. Above all, I admired the crust and wisdom of my mother-in-law, Mattie Davis.

I hung my bonnet on the peg and headed for the bedroom, where, propped up by multiple pillows, Mattie, in spite of her illness, displayed her usual spunk. She beckoned me to pull a chair next to the bed. I took her gnarled hand in mine.

"Glad you got here, Rose. I ain't long for this world. Need a promise and a favor."

I nodded.

Mattie's eyes became flints. "First you got to tell me what you think of Tom Varner."

I fingered the cameo at my collar searching for benign words.

"Tell me true," Mattie said.

"I don't like him. He's mean, and a drunkard, and...Lord forgive me, I can't think of anything nice to say."

The wrinkles around Mattie's eyes creased deeper as she smiled. "Good, because I'm going to tell you why he steers clear of me and treats my kin with respect."

"You've never told anyone why Tom is afraid of you."

"Tom thinks the secret dies with me. But as long as someone holds it, he'll have to abide by his agreement to be good around my folk. I can't go to my reward and let him off the hook."

How could I refuse?

She cleared her throat. "Back before you come into this family and my boys were young, they played with Tom's boy Aaron. Poor kid, his mother run off because Tom made her crazy. One day Aaron and my boys wanted to play in the woods so they untied Tom's bitch-dog, Ring, to go with them. They didn't know the bitch'd been tied in the barn so she wouldn't have pups come deer season. Well, she got caught by our dog and when Tom found out, he beat poor Aaron, threatened to whip my boys, and said he was going to kill Ring as soon as he found her, because if a dog can't help put game on the table, it ain't worth keeping. My boys came home crying and told me what happened. Gimme some water, please."

I held a glass to the old woman's lips, anxious for the rest of her tale.

Mattie shook her head. "I'd had it with that mean old varmint, so I took two jugs of cherry brandy from the shed, put them in the buckboard, and headed off to Varner's. We had a huge crop of cherries that year, and Grampa put up a fine batch of cherry brandy. When I got to Tom he held his gun waiting for Ring to show. I said I'd trade that bitch for the cherry brandy and he could have a sample taste. He took a swig and complained that the product wasn't that great. I said I'd give him two more jugs later and he could have his pick from our stock. He thought for a few minutes, acting like it was some big decision and then, like it killed him, he agreed to trade as long as he'd get the two extra jugs at his convenience. As I left, he yelled that I was stupid like most women. That dog was only worth two jugs, but I'd have to keep my bargain. I sent the boys out to find Ring and they brought her back. She turned out to be my favorite dog."

The story didn't fit Mattie's usual intriguing tales. "Is that the secret?"

"Naw. I'm getting to that. I knew once Tom slept off his drunk from the brandy he'd be back for more, say three or four days. So…I saved my pee until it filled up two of our biggest jugs, the kind we use for Grampa's 'shine. I hammered those corks in so they'd be hard to unstopper, and when I heard Tom's old rickety trap driving on the gravel, I quick put them jugs in the shed."

Now we were getting closer to what I expected from that resilient and tough lady.

"Yep. Tom, all blustery, strutting over how smart he was, demanded me to take him into the shed. Those jugs I peed in were the biggest on the shelf. So which ones do you think that greedy varmint picked?"

I didn't want to stop her but I had to laugh. "You kept a straight face when he chose the big ones?"

"Yup. Thinking about how he beat his kid and claimed all gals were idiots kept my face stern."

I pictured Mattie as a young woman with her hands stiffly lodged at her hips.

"He pulled at the corks but they didn't budge. I offered to help, but he growled and refused to let a woman do what he couldn't. He hefted the jugs into the trap and as he left, I said our business was concluded. He said that was fine by him. The matter was closed."

"Then what happened?"

"Why, I saw him outside town the next week. I stopped and faced him, waiting. He screamed all kinds of things and said he near died drinking piss and then threatened to tell everyone in town how deceitful I'd been. He'd see to it that I'd be embarrassed, and the townsfolk would besmirch me and my kin. I told him he didn't have to announce it, because next Sunday in church, of course he wouldn't be there to hear it, but I'd confess to the whole congregation of what I done."

Now I couldn't hold back my laughter.

Mattie folded her hands on the blanket like a maiden at her cotillion. "Yup. I told him once I made my confession the whole town would know how a little woman had allowed this real smart man to pick a jug of pee from his own free will and drink it."

"What did he do?"

"He said he would let me off this one time. I didn't have to confess. Let *me* off? I said I would tell the whole story-- how he got snookered unless he behaved mannerly to me and my family. And I'd keep it to myself unless something dire happened. I made a sign of locking my lips as my bond. And he made the same motion at his mouth."

I waited for more.

"Since I consider my looming death as dire, I'm telling on him. But only to you, Rose. I can trust you to keep the secret."

I agreed.

The following week the church overflowed at Mattie's funeral. She'd called it right. Tom Varner sat outside in his trap grinning like he won a fortune. When I passed him, he glared and took a long pull from a jug.

I smiled and made the sign of locking my lips. His eyes went wide. He bowed his head with a quick nod, then said "git" to the horse.

He's still polite to our family.

Patricia Crumpler

Patricia Crumpler is a retired high school librarian and art teacher who loves to paint, draw, sew, and write. She is a hybrid writer, both self and traditionally published.

Befriending Mabel

When I was nine, I met Mabel, a sixteen-year-old classmate. Since it was my first year in the centralized school, I needed to make new friends. Not in Methuselah's lifetime would I have dreamed Mabel and I would bond. We were total opposites, the odd couple of the fifth grade—the smallest and the largest.

Fate brought us together in the slow-moving line that snaked from the hall to the bathroom stalls, and Mabel has haunted my sensibilities since the first day she stooped to whisper in my ear: "I hope Mr. Kennedy doesn't give us homework."

I shrunk back from the odor emanating from her heavy body. "I'm pretty sure he will. He always does. What's wrong? Do you have family plans tonight?"

"No, but if I bring a book home, my father takes the belt to my legs." She lifted her long, frumpy skirt to reveal brick-red welts on her bare, scab-covered legs.

"That's awful! Does it hurt?"

She nodded. Tears formed in her brown eyes. "And he burned my books. Mr. Kennedy gets mad because I don't have my book."

"You've got to tell Mr. Kennedy."

Our conversation ended. Two stalls emptied and we used the little time we had to do our *business* and hurry back to class.

Nobody befriended Mabel since she reeked like the trash can on garbage day and looked more like a mother than a fellow student. She even wore a bra!

The lunch bell rang. Mabel sat beside me in the cafeteria. When she pulled a bacon-grease sandwich from her brown lunch bag, I stared in horror like a passerby at a grisly accident. Normally, I complained because I worked hard on our farm for my two-dollar-a-week allowance and had to spend a dollar fifty of my earnings for the hot meal sold in the school cafeteria. I liked to use my money to buy Nancy Drew mystery books. That day I realized I might not have the fancy stuff city kids owned, but compared to Mabel, I was Richie Rich.

I'd made a few good friends and we were busy planning a strategy to get all the Nancy Drew and Trixie Belden books we wanted. We decided we'd each ask for a different book for our birthdays and Christmas. Then we'd share. Mabel listened to our plan while resting her head on her chin and remaining silent. She wanted food, not books.

After considering my limited options, I came up with a plan to feed Mabel. The cafeteria sold Dixie cups of ice cream for a nickel each. I purchased two ice creams every day and gave one to Mabel. It depleted my allowance, but I enjoyed watching Mabel's normally dull eyes sparkle as she gobbled her treat.

One day she startled me when she said, "My father says this is my last year of school. He's gonna make me quit."

"My father says I have to get good grades so I can go to college."

Time passed and Halloween decorations appeared. My Sunday school teacher gave each of us an orange carton stamped with the acronym UNICEF. "I'd like you to collect money for needy children around the world, instead of gathering candy for yourselves. How many are willing to do that?"

I raised my hand. "I will, but I also want to help a girl who lives right here in Clinton County, New York."

"Who's that?" Mrs. Lucien asked.

"Mabel LaMountain."

"Is she one of Rudy's daughters?"

"Yes."

"Honey, we'd like to help, but nobody dares go to their door. Rudy's likely to answer the door with a shotgun in his hands."

"I'm not afraid. Mabel says they aren't going to have money for Thanksgiving or Christmas this year. I want to help her more than children I don't know." Starving kids in Africa—Mom's excuse for making me eat liver—came to mind.

"Well, if your mother will let you go to their door, we'll collect food and put it in a basket for you to deliver."

"Perfect. Then I'll take an orange box. Dad doesn't usually let me trick or treat. He says, 'It's begging, and besides, candy will rot your teeth.'"

I added, "But he feels sorry for people who don't have food. I think he'll let me collect for them."

On Monday, Mabel showed me new wounds from her dad's leather belt. "I brought home a book and tried to hide it from Dad because Mr. Kennedy has been hollering at me and sending me to the office for not doing my homework," she said. "Dad caught me with the book."

I decided to run interference. During homework check, I approached Mr. Kennedy. "You've gotta stop making Mabel carry a book home."

"Why?"

"Her father hits her with a belt if she does."

There was no compassion in his voice when he said, "Rules are rules."

My mouth flew open to protest, but I didn't dare. If I got in trouble in school, I'd get a whipping when I got home.

The Sunday before Thanksgiving, Mother drove me to Mabel's house. She stayed in the car with the motor running to enable us to make a quick getaway if Rudy showed up with his shotgun. I held the basket of food in one hand and knocked on the door with the other. When the door opened and I saw a dirt floor, orange crates for furniture, and quilts hanging from clotheslines to separate living areas, I lost my bravado. I slid the basket into the room and ran back to our car as fast as my spaghetti legs allowed. Mother put the car in reverse, and we left.

A week later my father got a call from Mr. Kennedy. I overheard my father telling Mother the parts of the conversation she and I didn't hear. Dad said, "He asked if I knew who my daughter was hanging around with."

I'd overheard Dad ask, "What do you mean? She comes right home after school."

Dad said Mr. Kennedy asked, "Were you aware she sits with Mabel LaMountain in the cafeteria and buys ice cream for her?"

Mom and I had heard Dad say, "No, but don't worry. She won't be hanging around storefronts at night. She'll be working on the farm and doing homework. Besides, there are worse things she could do with her money than buy food for a hungry classmate."

I could tell Dad was as displeased with the callous attitude of my teacher as I was, but he didn't tell me.

Mabel left her footprint. When I became a teacher, I watched for needy teens sitting in solitude, and reached out to them. Figuratively, Mabel sits on my shoulder as my social conscience pushing me to do something for abused children. I watch for bruises and black eyes. Whenever I see a Catch-22 situation, I recall the shy, oafish Mabel and intervene.

According to recent gossip from home, Mabel didn't escape her plight. She has no job, hitchhikes to bingo, and became a local folk hero when she hobbled on a broken leg to play bingo.

Still, she made me a better person.

Melody Dean Dimick

Melody taught at Northern Adirondack Central School and the State University of New York at Plattsburgh. Her novel in verse won a Royal Palm Literary Award. She lives in Central Florida with husband Barry.

Einstein

Saturday mornings are *always* like this. No one ever pays attention to me! They just go about their business as if I don't exist.

I poked my head into my sister Maddie's room, but all she did was slide her leg off the bed, just far enough, to kick the door closed in my face. How rude! I turned to go down the hall and was nearly run over by my dad, who was racing for the bathroom.

Am I invisible? I decided to stand in the middle of the commotion. Someone was bound to pay attention to me or be nice to me, but all I got was, "Look out, move it, you're in the way!"

I'll show them! I'll go back to bed and stay there. They'll think I'm sick and make a fuss over me. That should do it! I got into bed, curled up, and fell fast asleep.

The next thing I knew, I woke to a barking dog. I strained my ears to hear the house. It was quiet. I must have slept awhile. I got up and headed for the kitchen. The Saturday morning newspaper was spread out on the table. They were searching for garage sales, which was my brother Oliver's favorite thing to do.

What? Going to a garage sale without me? I couldn't believe it! Did they even look in on me? Were they even concerned? *No, of course not!*

Suddenly, I snapped! I looked around. I went over to the half open pantry and pulled everything out, and onto the floor. Cereal and coffee, pancake mix and pasta, sugar and syrup, olive oil and honey, it all spilled, or rolled, or poured out, forming a glistening sea of goo.

I raced into the living room. I tossed cushions and magazines. I knocked over vases and pictures. I was out of control! I moved on to the plants. Crash! Over they went. *Oh boy, they'll be sorry!*

Wait! What am I doing? Was that a car door? I froze for an instant, then ran back to bed. I heard them coming up the porch steps. *Try to look asleep*, I repeated to myself.

The keys clinked and clanked and the door opened. My eyelids fluttered. The silence that followed was so loud, it hurt my ears. Within seconds, I sensed I was being stared at; it was so hard to keep still.

"Ein…steinnnn," my mother finally said, as if the "stein" was going up a flight of stairs, "What did you do?" I slowly opened one eye, then the other.

"That's it! He's outta' here," dad yelled, as his finger pointed at the door.

"Oh…no," cried Maddie and Oliver, "Please dad...don't," they pleaded in unison.

"We'll take better care of Einstein," Oliver said, "We'll walk him and feed him. Don't worry dad, we promise!"

Wow, this was great! I was getting all the attention now. I jumped up on Maddie and licked a salty tear. I gave dad my best head tilt, and wagged my tail double time. I turned in a circle around Oliver, not once, but twice! Then, I ran to mom and gave her the one eyebrow up, one eyebrow down routine, she can't resist.

"Take him out now," mother sighed, "so we can clean up this mess."

I just knew by the look on dad's face, as he untangled my leash, that he wasn't angry anymore. I was so happy, I decided to do an accelerated tail wag!

Mom opened the door and I rushed out onto the porch as fast as I could, with Maddie and Oliver yelling for me to slow down.

They'll pay more attention to me now, I thought, as we jumped down the last porch step.

Yep, they'll pay more attention. That's for sure! I can sense these things.

After all, they didn't name me Einstein for nothing!

Linda Feist

Linda resides in Florida pursuing her first love, writing. After her debut story, "Apes in the Attic," at age seven, received critical acclaim from her mom, she was hooked. Linda's been published in Chicken Soup for the Soul, The Buffalo News,and was a 2016, RPLA finalist for her short fiction.

The Conveyor

"Don't let go!" Bree yelled, her voice screeching to ear-splitting levels. "Oh God, Dustin. Don't let go."

I grunted, my fingers sinking deeper into her forearm. My chest muscles burned as my other hand remained locked around the tree root.

Bree's terror-filled eyes found mine, searching for reassurance as she fought to secure a footing between the rain-slick rocks. "Please, somebody, help us!" she yelled into the cloud-covered, windy afternoon.

"Bree, pull yourself up."

She struggled to grasp my arm with her free hand. "I can't."

An urge to let her fall and save myself washed over me. I shook my head, appalled. "Try, dammit! Just try."

The wind whipped through the mountain's cavities, dislodging loose stones and dirt from the last remaining dry cliff pockets. The ocean's waves crashed into the rocks below, foaming with each assault.

Could we survive a two-hundred-foot drop?

"I'm trying," Bree said, still struggling. Her bottom lip trembled as tears escaped her lids.

A deafening *Snap!* above our heads made my stomach lurch. The root—the very lifeline keeping us from our immediate deaths—pulled loose.

We fell through the chilled autumn air, our screams reverberating against the cliff's edge. I closed my eyes, not wanting to see the end.

I waited.

Nothing.

"What's happening?" Bree whispered.

Opening my eyes, I focused on her torn blue jeans, her tattered jacket and blond hair blowing in the wind. We hovered ten feet above the ground, light as air.

"Quite the predicament we're in, wouldn't you say?"

Startled, we both turned toward the intruding voice to find a tall, smarmy-haired man leaning against a boulder a few feet off shore, the edges of his pristine overcoat flapping in the wind. With a slight hand gesture, he beckoned us to join him and our bodies drifted down—not of our own accord.

"How did you do that?"

"That, dear boy, is none of your concern." The stranger's eerie smirk made my hair stand on end.

Not one for subtleties, I asked, "Who are you?"

"Also none of your concern."

"Okay then, what *is* my concern?" Although grateful he spared our lives, something about his demeanor made my face burn with anger.

"Tsk, tsk. Now, is that any way to repay the kindness I've bestowed upon you?" The stranger raised his hand and flicked his wrist.

Bree collapsed at my feet.

"Bree!" I bent down, shaking her still form. "What did you do to her?"

"Settle down." He squatted beside her, catching a strand of her golden hair between his thumb and index finger. "Such a lovely one, isn't she?" He inhaled her hair before letting it drop. "She is still with us for the moment." His wry grin widened as he straightened. "But her fate is sealed."

"What do you mean?"

"You wished her dead, did you not?"

"N–no," I stammered. "Of course not."

"There is no point lying to me, child."

My hands balled into fists. "Don't call me a child. I'm not a child."

"Deflection." The stranger pulled out a hexagonal amulet, black as onyx, embedded with iridescent symbols. "I suppose we could go through all the stages of denial, but I'm rather in a hurry. What say you? Does she die?" He gestured toward Bree's unconscious form. "Or do you both die?"

"What? You saved us so you could kill us?"

"I merely stopped time to let you decide your fate."

His arrogance set my teeth grinding.

He turned the amulet at different angles, studying each symbol as they reflected every shade of color. "You had an opportunity to save yourself by letting your girlfriend fall, but given the severity of the moment, you did not make the optimum choice. I am granting you the opportunity to alter your outcome."

"Let me get this straight," I said. "You're giving me the chance to live, but not Bree?" I crossed my arms. "No deal."

"Come again?"

"I will only accept an offer where Bree lives."

"That is not an option." With his index finger, he pushed in one of the swirling symbols on the amulet until dozens of holographic images of random scenes materialized between us. "As you can see, I have plenty more inconsequential souls to save tonight, so give me your answer now."

An irresistible desire compelled me to touch the image nearest me. My fingertips brushed the shoulder of a young woman standing at the edge of an overpass, her slumped figure inching forward, ready to jump. With a start, she looked up. Her tear-filled eyes bore into mine and some of her despair seeped into me, burrowing straight to my core. I stumbled back, breaking the connection, gasping for breath.

The stranger observed my actions, one eyebrow raised as he terminated the images with a flick of his amulet. "Curious. Very curious."

"What just happened?"

"Your first transfer, it would seem." The stranger sauntered forward, circling me as he studied my quaking body. "And without the protection of the amulet at that."

"What does that mean?"

"It means there is a way to save your precious Bree after all." He eyed her crumpled form before holding up the amulet. "Take this if you want to save her. You must accept it with your whole heart."

I reached out to grab it and he clamped his other hand over mine, securing the amulet between our hands.

"Do you accept this amulet freely in exchange for sparing the girl's life?"

I swallowed the lump in my throat, my instincts screaming to refuse. "I do," I said, knowing I couldn't live with myself if I let Bree die.

"I hope, for your sake, she is worth the price." The stranger stepped back, releasing the amulet. A flood of emotions from sorrow to rage transferred from the stranger and consumed me as I watched his cruel smirk turn into a genuine smile. "You have freed me of my centuries-long curse. How ever can I repay you?"

Fury transformed my blood into liquid lava. "You can start by telling me what just happened."

"Don't you see? You are the new Conveyor, Dustin. You help the weak and desperate by absorbing some of their emotions so you can save them from self-destruction."

Bree stirred at my feet, her fluttering eyelids easing my inner turmoil.

"But take heed, my friend. Do not take on too much or you will lose yourself as did I." He turned and walked away along the shoreline, not looking back.

I helped Bree to her feet, steadying her balance.

"What's that?" Bree asked, eyeing the amulet clasped in my hand.

"Our chance to live."

C. C. Gallo

Young adult fantasy collections ignite C. C. Gallo's passion. Determined to pursue her love of writing, held second only to her husband and son, she joined Freedom Writers Group and Florida Writers Association in early 2016 and is currently working on her first novel, called *Fracture*.

Into Thy Safekeeping

Reaching the crest of the hill, Masen tugged his reins and shifted in his saddle as Joe gave an irritated snort but slowed his plodding to a stop. After days of hard riding, he was finally nearing home, but the Texas sun was beating down, and the saddle was making its presence known. Masen removed his hat, relishing the air hitting his damp scalp, and smoothed a calloused hand over his auburn beard as he pondered his bearings.

Decision made, he replaced his sweat-stained hat and turned Joe east toward Woman Hollering Creek. Joe picked up his pace when he smelled the water and Masen gave him his head, letting him make his way down to the water's edge. Masen dismounted and dropped to his haunches to scoop water with his hat, splashing it over his head and neck. Joe twitched his ears and stomped as Masen let out a whoop as the cold water hit his steamy skin, but he'd been with the man long enough to forgive his eccentricities.

Masen wet his worn bandana and was tying it around his neck when a rustle in the sagebrush had him going for his gun. He whirled and aimed at a tiny doll-like figure standing in the shaded weeds.

Round, dark eyes watered as a delicate lip quivered.

Moving cautiously toward the feral little thing, he took in the dark, tangled hair, the torn filthy skirts and asked, "Where's your mama, little one?"

She began to tremble and her mouth twisted with a soundless wail as she pointed to a brush covered hillock.

Masen pushed through the thick underbrush to find a ravine with a humble campsite. There was a wagon with a broken axle, but he saw no horse or mule. In the tomblike stillness, he heard the buzzing before the stench of decay hit him. Masen stopped in his tracks, retched, and pulled his damp bandana over his mouth and nose. He found two figures lying side by side in a makeshift tent. By the clothes, he made out a man and a woman but flies covered every surface forming macabre death masks over the couple.

Having seen enough, he moved from the camp at a rapid pace heaving as he went. He fell at the water's edge and scrubbed his leathered face and hands as he took deep drafts. When his mind and stomach had settled, he looked around for the little one and found her near Joe, holding onto the stirrup, and stoically staring out over the water.

He went to her and tenderly laid his hand on her hair. She turned, and her dark, round eyes bore into him with the sadness of an ancient soul. "You'll come with Joe and me, Sparrow," he said as he brushed his calloused hand over her greasy, dirt packed hair.

She didn't blink, but he watched as the tiny hand fisted tighter on the stirrup. He sniffed and nodded.

Masen folded his poncho over his saddle horn and picking her up, swung into the saddle, seating her snugly in front of him.

He clicked to Joe, and they moved from the scene without a backward glance.

She reeked of dirty sweat and urine, but Masen held her diminutive form firmly against his broad chest as he fed her pinches of corn pone and sips of water. When exhaustion overtook her, he gathered her securely against him as they rode the last miles to his cabin.

The shadows were lengthening as they crossed the creek that ran through his land. When Molly's neighing kicked up from the paddock, welcoming Joe, there was no holding the horse back. Masen dismounted stiffly, walked the little stranger into the dark cabin, and laid her on the bed before returning to tend to the animals.

The stench of the little girl hit him as he reentered the dark cabin. He lit the lantern over the table and allowed himself a moment of pause for what he had undertaken in bringing her home. There had been no choice, he knew, but the magnitude of the matter hit him square. He looked at the tiny, huddled form and whispered, "Sarah, love, what do I do?"

A familiar pain ripped through him as the image of his beautiful wife and baby flashed through his mind. "God, hold them in the hollow of your hand." He swallowed thickly and added, "My loves and Sparrow's kin."

The notion of a little person's bodily needs being the same as a grown one's had his shoulders relaxing as he turned his hands to making a fire. After a week of sleeping rough and eating cold, the thought of a warm meal made his innards groan.

He moved her near the fire's warmth, and as he worked, a wet circle spread from under her.

"Aww, well," he muttered, thankful he'd moved her before she let go.

When the stew was thick and bubbling, and the smell of fried corn pone filled the air, he shook her softly. "I've got some supper for us, little one."

She bolted upright and looked around the room in alarm until her hawk-like gaze rested on him. A tiny hand reached out and petted his beard, and he tried not to panic at her touch.

After a moment, he pulled back from her little hand and moved toward the table as she cautiously followed the smell of warm food. Masen watched her nibble bread as he hunched over his bowl. He nudged a bowl toward her, and she grabbed a fist of potatoes, shoving it in her mouth, leaving a dripping trail across the table and the front of what stood for a dress.

He took her hand and wrapped it around a spoon, guiding it to scoop a carrot from the broth. She plucked the carrot from the spoon and popped it into her grinning mouth.

He gave a snort. "We'll work on that one, little Sparrow," he said as he picked up his spoon and continued his meal.

After supper, the warm water rapidly turned dark and cloudy as he washed her little ragdoll frame. She was rail thin with scabs on her scalp and sores on her torso and legs. In the morning he would bring the tub up to the front yard and scrub her down proper.

He slipped her into a shirt and rolled it up as best he could. He showed her where the night pot was before tucking her into a clean blanket near the hearth and placing a chair between her and the fire.

As Sparrow snored softly on her pallet, Masen crawled, bone-weary, into his bed to surrender to welcomed sleep.

Deep in the night, he startled awake as a bony elbow nudged him. He stared at the ceiling deep in thought as a gentle snore continued next to him. He'd bring her kin to rest next to Sarah and Annie he thought as he pulled the quilt over little shoulders. His worn heart swelled at the thought of this gift bequeathed to his care, and a bittersweet smile flashed in the dark as tiny fingers fluttered in his beard.

S.J. Gaver

A lifelong lover of words, S.J. Gaver has made a career of teaching the love of reading to two generations. Finding herself in the delightful company of characters in need of a storyteller, she has posted award winning stories online for the past two years.

A Life in Tune

David slipped the Waterford wine glasses into terry cloth and bubble-wrap sleeves he'd made himself. The packets fit snuggly in the hard-sided traveling case he found on one of his weekly rambles through the alleys of Chicago before the trash collectors made their rounds. *Why would somebody throw this away*? He shook his head as he remembered the find. *Lucky for me they did.* With a flick of his finger the locks flipped shut with a loud snap.

He could see his wife still lying in bed. Eva's hand reached for him.

"Not now, my love," he cooed.

Her lower lip jutted out in disappointment and she slapped his pillow with the palm of her hand. Her blue eyes pleaded for him to stay but she quickly relented by making a silly face. He laughed and kissed her fingers, one at a time.

"I'll be back around ten," he said and kissed her gently on her forehead.

David slid a peanut butter and jelly sandwich into the pocket of his threadbare overcoat. It was chilly in May on Chicago's city streets, especially in the shadows of tall buildings. His cardigan sweater and flannel shirt underneath made his humped frame look much larger than it was.

He hoisted three gallons of water onto the cart behind his bicycle and secured them next to the case containing the glasses. The shell of a toddler's bicycle trailer (missing its wheels and clear-plastic door), was permanently attached to the cart's wooden deck at the far end of the platform. Another of David's proud finds that he manipulated into a second life.

"Come on Buddy!" he whistled to a scruffy-haired, mid-sized mutt.

Buddy jumped onto the cart, and after circling three times, lay down in the repurposed trailer. The old man began to pedal. This was their routine from April to October every day for fifteen years.

It was four city blocks, one-half mile, to St. Patrick's from David's two-room basement apartment in the back of a derelict office building. As splintered rays of early morning light rose above Lake Michigan and before the rush hour crowd scurried to their jobs or the faithful gathered for morning mass, David set up a card table next to the entry steps of the cathedral. Carefully, he un-wrapped the crystal glasses, filled them with water, and tuned them to pitch perfect. Fifteen minutes before mass, his gnarled fingers began to play the classics with such tenderness he could have made Ludwig van Beethoven weep.

He played again at the end of mass as people bolted through the doors. His dexterity and harmony on the lips of lead crystal revealed the skilled mastery of the musician, yet no one knew his name. Some people nodded as they left church. A few dropped coins in the bucket next to Buddy, and when they did, the dog raised his paw to shake, as if to say "Thank you." Most people rushed past on their way to who knows where, still carrying their burdens on their faces. These were the ones David kept in prayer.

"How you doing, Buddy?" Father John asked as he began his walk to the rectory. He stooped to give the old dog a scratch behind the ears.

David shoved the bucket of coins into the dog's shelter and loaded the last of his belongings onto the cart.

"Buddy, guard the gold," he commanded. The dog jumped onto the platform and settled in front of the bucket.

"Best banker in town," David said with a chuckle.

Father John smiled back. "How's the missus?" he asked, knowing this was as personal as the old man with no name would allow.

"We're doing fine, Father," David replied with a nod.

"Sister Bernadette's waiting for you at the kitchen door. She has a pot of soup for the two of you and she won't take no for an answer. If you don't stop," the priest said as he raised his hands feigning self-defense, "I'll pay the price."

David stroked his beard and replied, "I can't say no to her cooking." He gave Father John a wry smile before asking, "Chicken?"

Father John looked genuinely surprised and confused.

"The *soup*, Father, did she make my favorite? Chicken?"

"Ah, yes," the priest replied with a laugh and walked away.

***

Buddy lay next to Eva's side of the bed as both waited for David to finish cleaning and wrapping the glasses for the following morning. That night, they were going to his concert at the Sullivan Theatre. She was dressed in a midnight blue, floor-length velvet dress. He'd helped her style her hair and escorted her to the best seat in the room, the sofa.

"Are you ready, my love?" he asked as he slipped the VHS tape into the machine. She smiled and nodded her head once.

He lit a candle on the stand next to the television, turned the sound up, and the lights off. A young, handsome pianist with tousled black hair took center stage as the conductor announced with a sweep of his arm, "Ladies and gentlemen, this young man has performed in some of the finest orchestra halls around the world. Tonight, it's my honor to introduce to you, David Merlo."

Eva clapped her hand on David's stomach and buried her head in his chest as music filled the tiny apartment. The warmth from her frail body and her child-like excitement filled him with love. It washed away the cares of the world. For a few minutes they were once again David and Eva Merlo, the toast of the town, before the stroke had stolen Eva's mind and medical bills left them destitute.

Every night they'd relive the last normal event of their lives. Tonight David held her especially close as he whispered, "My dear Eva, music may make my heart beat with joy, but it's you, my love, who breathes life into my soul." She kissed him tenderly and they watched the rest of the performance snuggled in each other's embrace.

David silently wept. Only he and the free-clinic's doctor knew time, like the sweet chords of a favorite melody, were quickly fading away.

Jo Ann V. Glim

I live in Bradenton, Florida, with my husband, Bill, and our Scottish terrier, Lucy. My novel, "Begotten with Love" is a 2014 Royal Palm Literary Award recipient. Writing, photography, travel, spending time with my hubby, walking nature trails, snapping pictures, or plotting my next story, rocks my world.

To Nancy—
WE are tied to our
families. Love your
stories.
Jo Ann V. Glim

Grandma's Sink

Today's headline read *Fatal Accident Shadows Family Inheritance.* One week earlier Rachel had spent hours sorting items as keep, sell, or donate. Exhausted, she eagerly stretched out on Grandma's king-sized mattress, comforted by the angels and birds hand-carved into the walnut sleigh bed. The weathered hardwood floors and tattered area rugs were of no concern. On her own for the first time, Rachel planned to modernize all the antiquities in this two-story house she had inherited from her Grandmother.

Later, in the bathroom, Rachel eyed the vintage aqua green sink her grandmother refused to upgrade. The rectangular wall-mounted basin with two spindly metal pipe legs and exposed plumbing was an eyesore. But Grandma had loved that old sink. She washed her hair in it for years. Sang *You Are My Sunshine* to newborn Rachel during baby bath time. She also started a tie-dye scarf business and named the sink Mr. Green as her CEO. In the last few years, Rachel witnessed Grandma steady herself, holding tight to the porcelain when she became sick after chemotherapy treatments.

To Rachel, the sink came to represent sadness. She tapped the sink with her ringed fingers, "Grandma may have loved you, but I don't." She turned the knobs for water and a banging noise resounded. "You are so getting replaced."

At 2:00 A.M. a fast drip, drip, drip interrupted her sleep. "I can't believe this. It's ugly and it drips?"

She threw the covers back and stomped into the bathroom to find the faucet leaking a green watery liquid, filling to the overflow slot. She flipped the stop lever up to let the water flow down the drain, but it filled up as fast as it went down.

"What the hell? I didn't plug this up before I went to bed." Rachel cupped her hand into the water and brought it to her nose. Nothing distinguishable. Impulsively, she stuck her tongue out and touched the tip to the small puddle in her palm. Slightly salty.

"Holy crap! Is this sink crying? Are you crying?" She pushed the faucet handles back to off. The dripping stopped.

"I *know* I turned the water off before I went to bed. Freakin' weirdness. I must be overtired."

Five hours later Rachel awoke to chirping birds. For a full minute she hazily traced the birds notched in the headboard, grateful to confirm they weren't the ones warbling. Her full bladder forced her out of bed. She sat on the commode with her face in her hands. When she stood to wash up in the sink, her mouth dropped open.

Tears sprang to her eyes as she slowly stroked the strands of long black wavy hair piled high in the basin. "This is Grandma's hair. How did it get here? I'm losing my mind. That's it. This creepy sink must go. NOW."

Rachel threw on a pair of jean shorts and a T-shirt and called her boyfriend, Tyler.

"Hey, it's me. Can you come over right away with your tools? I need my sink taken out of the master bathroom. Please hurry."

Locating a garbage bag, she removed the hair that had mysteriously accumulated in the sink. "I don't know what you are or what you're doing, but I'm going to destroy you."

Rachel ran down the stairs to open the front door. Tyler was getting out of his pick-up truck carrying a white bucket full of tools. When they separate from their hug, Tyler asked, "What's up? Why the rush to take out a poor defenseless sink?"

Rachel grabbed his arm and pulled him inside to the settee. "Sit. This sink is anything but defenseless. You wouldn't believe what I've been through."

"Whoa, calm down Rach. It can't be that bad. What did the sink do? Squirt water on you?" He chuckled.

Rachel jumped up. "It's not funny. You're going to think I'm crazy when I tell you." She paced then blurted, "The sink stopped itself up and started dripping in the middle of the night. It filled up with a green saltwater. Then this morning when I woke up, it was packed with my grandma's hair from when she was young."

Tyler stood close to her. He held her wrists and kissed her forehead. "Sweetie, I know you've been stressed with her passing and the move. I warned you not to take the happy pills without me."

She pushed him away. "I'm serious. I'm not making this up."

His crested face flatlined. "Did you just hear what you told me?"

"Fine, whatever, will you just take the sink out for me?"

Tyler clutched his bucket handle. "Okay. Do you have a new sink to replace it?"

"I didn't really think that far."

"Well, I don't have anything to cap the pipes. Let's go upstairs and see what we're dealing with."

Inside the spotless bathroom, Tyler pulled his channel-lock pliers out of the bucket. "Oh wow, all the plumbing is bare. This should be easy. I'm gonna see how tight this joint is."

On his knees, he attempted to twist the pipe." Damn, I can't... rrrrrreh... budge this thing." They heard a loud flat horn noise. "Did that come from the pipe? Sounded like a wounded elephant."

"I told you. That sink is alive. We need to get rid of it."

Tyler stood and shrugged, "It sure seems to have a personality. I'm no professional plumber but I could've moved something around in the P-trap to make that noise. Who knows, as old as it is. I'm gonna go to the hardware store and get a hacksaw and a few other supplies. When I come back we'll crush this mean green groaning thing and then go shopping for a sink/vanity combo. While I'm gone, you get some rest. Okay?"

The flat noise again. Louder. Tyler and Rachel looked at each other.

"Go. Hurry back." Rachel said.

"I'll let myself out. Now go lie down." Tyler bent down to kiss Rachel, and left.

Propped up on the bed, she watched television to distract herself from the wait and the sink. She checked the clock. Twenty minutes passed. She couldn't stand it, curiosity made her investigate the monstrosity again.

It bubbled with a bright red fluid. "Oh, my God. WHY ARE YOU DOING THIS?" Rachel held onto the sides of the porcelain to steady herself, just like her grandma used to do. She wailed, "Okay, I killed my grandmother. She was sick and in pain. She was so weak I held a pillow over her face to end her misery." In a softer voice, "And so I could have her house sooner than later."

Rachel slipped to the floor in anguish. Through racking sobs, she looked up and asked the sink, "What do you want from me?" The gurgling intensified. Blood cascaded down the sides of the basin, onto the mosaic tile floor. The porcelain pulled from the wall. Rachel rooted in place, watched as its thin legs buckled and collapsed, causing the heavy sink to crash down, landing on her windpipe. As she lay there, taking her last breaths, she heard a clinking melody that resembled *You Are My Sunshine*.

Fern Goodman

Fern was a 2013 RPLA short story finalist, a 2015 first place winner in creative non-fiction, and her short story *The Eviction* appeared in FWA's Collection 6. Fern also is one of the authors in the newly released anthology called *Lost Dreams* by Dawn M. Bell.

She

"Forget me not. I shall come again!"-Ayesha.

He found her in a scrap yard, a place that recycled used tools. Seeking a cheap drill, he found instead a carved African head, a proud tribal woman, eighteen inches high, of dense and heavy black wood. The draw was immediate. She called to him. He must liberate her from this grotesque place.

An aquiline head, eyes closed, tapered to a pointed chin, as if Masai or from further north, Ethiopia perhaps. Tight braids bunched her hair at the back of her head. Her ear lobes stretched, the left chewed by insects or rodents. She lay discarded on a pile of rags, her eyes, hooded by half closed lids, a suggestion of a smile. She was Africa. Ageless.

He paid forty-five dollars for her. A fair enough bride price.

After cleaning her, scraping the dirt from between her braids, and polishing her ebony skin, he stroked her shapely lips and placed her on a stand in his study where he could see her clearly.

Every evening it became his habit to sit in his chair and stare at her features. Her eyes remained hooded and mysterious like the continent of her birth. Her lips, small and full, hinted at a smile. A secret she might perhaps share.

"She did not share for many days," he wrote.

"There is a condition which fevers the blood of those embraced by Africa, this continent, the shape of an eternal question mark, her character built of incredible sights, unique sounds and smells, and an atmosphere, a way of accepting life. An enigma to most. Once infected by the African condition, there is no cure. An insistent summons.

"It is the character of Africa." He underlined this.

"The plains of Africa's face are scarred by rugged mountains, broken by tropical jungle and swamp, desert and forsaken land. A character of long suffering, etched by the deep gorges and wide rivers, her falls, torrents of tears, perhaps mourning the lives she once cradled and those returned to molest her and rip the treasures from her womb. To love Africa demands resilience and courage. She can be harsh or gentle toward her lovers; often forgiving, sometimes remorseless, insistent, overwhelming. There is strength in Africa unmatched by any other country. One of deep emotion.

"All may feel the past. For those embraced by her magic, the pull is strongest.

"Africa smiled at me from the carving; the birthplace of humanity. Your spiritual home, she said to me. What it means to be human.

"One evening I saw her lips move," he wrote. He believed it must be the movement of his own eyes causing the illusion, but fascinated he stared on. What did she say? Did she yearn for her home, or miss the spaces, the purple hills, the sweeping plains?

"Separating her ebony face and the land haunting my dreams confuses me. She has become a character in the story of my life.

"When I am with her, my mind fills with pictures. A series of storyboards waiting for filming to begin.

"She tells of her birth.

"I feel her pain as lands collide and mountain ridges soar, volcanoes like exploding boils erupt through the thin crust of earth, the layers tearing as plates of rock and molten lava rift one side of her body like a hernia threatening to throw the east into the ocean. I feel the pain of Africa's birth.

"A tear rolled down her cheek.

"One morning during the creation of a new day, the growing light through the window illuminated the side of her face. Gradually it resolved into sunlight slanting through trees, shining on the dense bush on the jungle floor. Something moved, out of my sight. A barely audible growl. I heard the muffled drums in the background, the rustle of something moving through the dense bush, the far-off squeal of a monkey."

Briefly he was horrified by a grinning mask in place of the head, a bone thrust through the nose, a feathered headdress, and the edges of a leopard skin cloaking the shoulders below the mask. Then, as fast, the mask resolved back into her head.

"I must have dozed off, and dreamed it, until I stood to get coffee and saw a feather lying on the floor."

Instead of coffee, he poured a stiff drink, sat back in his chair and studied her, his mind whirling with fear and fascination, and a dreadful pull to Africa. The Africa he had loved.

Where had she come from? Who had carved her likeness? Who was she? Were the dreams trying to answer his questions?

"Africa smiled a little, when you left a voice whispered in my ear, the night she opened her eyes.

"I didn't recognize the language. I had no need. Her voice is universal.

"We know you,"

He had left Africa, snatched away against his will, as she had been, until he found her in the repository of discarded memories.

"You cannot leave Africa," the voice said. *"We are always with you, there inside your head. Our rivers run in currents in the swirl of your thumbprints; our drumbeats counting out your pulse; our coastline the silhouette of your soul."*

He opened his eyes, his lids lifting the weight of the dream. "I saw her before me, in my study. She is Africa. I hear her."

He searched through a trunk holding mementoes, photographs, most long forgotten; letters he had written and received.

"The musty smell as I pawed through their confinement was not the smell of the cooling night, the rustle of my hands not the sound of mosquitoes buzzing against the netting, or the hoots and cries of an African night. Neither was it the sounds of the wakening day, the cries of cattle, or the bleating of goats. But it rekindled memories of them, long dormant."

He watched her.

"I am addicted to the dreams, the visions or hallucinations. There are nights I cannot sleep," he wrote. "Times when I cannot rise to eat. Nights when I cannot go to bed. I must write about her."

He wrote about her, crumpled the paper, and started again. And again. Littering the room.

After several days when he hadn't been seen, they opened the door to his study. Sheets of a manuscript lay scattered across the floor.

"When I am with her, my world comes alive," he had written. "The carved giraffe in the corner lifts it head.

"The curtains become trees.

"The elephants in a woodcut lift their trunks and turn to face me.

"The ocelot on the branch stretches its limbs.

"This morning there were no tears in her eyes.

"Her ear was healed.

"She smiled.

"She is Africa.

"I have never left her.

"She calls. . . ."

He sat smiling in his chair, clutching her ebony self to his chest. At his feet, a single feather. She had written herself into his life before their spirits answered the call of Africa, and returned home.

The quotations are from Africa Smiled, a poem by Bridget Dore, dedicated to Nelson Mandela. Ayesha is a character in 'She,' by Rider Haggard.

Bob Hart

A retired veterinarian, raised in Africa, Bob and his novelist wife, Veronica Helen, now live in Ormond Beach. Author of several articles and stories, three pet books, and a book of short stories, *Twisted Knickers.* He is working on a political thriller set in Uganda.

Arielle

I turned the package over in my hands. It was heavy for its size, and I already knew what it contained. My sister's name appeared in the upper left corner Mrs. Arielle Hawthorn. My own name was in the "To" space, Miss Quinn Carleton.

Arielle had paid extra postage to have the gift delivered by special courier to my home in Australia.

"Miss Quinn." So like her, rubbing in the fact that I had never married. Quinn. A hateful name, a name you'd give to a mongrel dog, a brindle, ugly mongrel dog.

I snorted. The name fit me, with my mud-colored eyes and my unruly thatch of dark brown hair. My plain face would likely sink ships, not launch them.

My grandmother sealed my destiny for me when I was eleven. I can hear her words. "You're never going to be much for looks, Quinn. So you'd better learn how to do something."

Her words had sluiced over me like a douse of cold water, soaking me, chilling me to the marrow. Even my grandmother didn't find me appealing, lovable.

Girding up what little self-esteem I possessed, I took her words to heart. Learn I did. I kept my nose in my books, won a scholarship, and graduated at the top of my architecture class. In the past ten years, my designs have garnered top honors throughout Australia, southeast Asia, and the Pacific islands, even in Hawaii. I've never returned to the United States mainland.

Quinn.

Abrupt.

Unfeminine.

Ugly.

My name.

Me.

My exquisite sister arrived when I was seven. How I loathed her...and her beautiful name...Arielle...the name of a light-as-a-bubble sprite. Her eyes were the aqua of the clear waters surrounding our native Florida, her hair a skein of silver blond. Her heart-shaped face achingly beautiful.

Arielle sparkled like champagne, while I was flat beer. She glittered like a diamond, while I was a plain rock you might clean and use for a paperweight...dull, functional, unremarkable.

I kept my hatred to myself. Had anyone known, I would have been called "unnatural," a freak, a psycho. What kind of child could hate such a beautiful baby sister? How often had I wanted to slap the smile off Arielle's face, as her lovely eyes followed my every move, mocking my clumsiness, silently sneering at me…me her dorky sister, the class geek. She shadowed me, silently mimicking my actions, imitating me, spying on me.

While I struggled for my success in a male dominated profession, Arielle wafted through life like a radiant angel…head majorette, Miss Palm Beach County, a modeling contract, marriage to a scion of Palm Beach society.

When Arielle's baby was born three months ago, Mama called to tell me the happy news. I feigned the expected excitement. Her tone was cryptic when she told me Arielle did not want me to see e-mailed pictures of her newborn. Instead, she wanted to send me an old fashioned, studio-produced portrait that she promised would be a delightful surprise.

So I knew the package contained a framed portrait of a miniature "Arielle," every bit as perfect as her mother…every bit as hateful to me. More salt rubbed into the wounds of my solitary life.

I felt like throwing the package, unopened, into the trash.

But I didn't.

I selected an Xacto knife from a mug on my drafting table and sliced into the wrapping paper. Inside I discovered a shiny silver and pink box. Delicate pink tissue enclosed an expensive silver frame. I folded the paper back.

My breath caught in my throat.

The face peering from the portrait could have been my own at that age. The same brown eyes, too much hair for one so tiny, hair I knew would grow into a dark, tangled mess like my own.

She was the image of me.

Bless her heart.

A pink envelope lay with the picture, addressed to "Auntie" Quinn. I opened it and read the words in my sister's precise, rounded script.

My dearest sister,

How I would love to see your face right now.

Isn't my precious daughter the most beautiful baby you've ever seen? She looks just like you, the same inquisitive brown eyes, that gorgeous mop of hair, that playful smile.

Oh, how I envied you when we were growing up. You were so smart. So talented. You were magical, amazing. Everything you touched you turned to gold. You were a success at everything you tried. Oh, how I wanted to be just like you.

My hand started to shake. I felt bile rise in my throat. Disgust knotted my stomach. A miasma of self-loathing enveloped me, choking me. I read on.

I pray my wonderful little girl grows up to be exactly like you. That's why I gave her the most beautiful, perfect name for a beloved daughter.

I named my darling child Quinn.

Suzanna Myatt Harvill

Suzanna Myatt Harvill has a BA in English from Florida State University, was a NASA technical writer and communications engineer. She lives in Avon Park, Florida, and is Wordsmiths Chapter Group Leader. Several of her mysteries have been published, and a short story placed second in Writers Digest's 2016 contest.

Nobody's Secret

The train bumps everyone together as it goes over the crossing. The lady next to me gives me the stink eye. Some people get angry easy I guess. I lean back, resting my head against the window all smudged from some kid's nose. Pops took the seven train to work every weekday for forty-two years, probably sat in this very seat more days than I been alive. This seat a his hasn't felt his weight since last summer. My heart hasn't felt his weight neither.

Today's Sunday and here I am again, taking the same train to visit Ma, like I do every other Sunday. Cherie quit coming months ago, said it got too hard for her. Don't know what's so difficult about catching a train and sitting in an apartment for an hour. She should spend a day at the yard with me, then she'll know what a hard day is.

My work trousers are always striped down the legs with sweat and oil where I wipe my hands during my shift. These linen dress pants I'm wearing feel scratchy and stiff but I know Ma always likes when I dress nice. I even brought one of those wild daisies she used to pick and keep in that pink chipped vase on the kitchen table. I twirl it once to watch the petals spin like one of them merry-go-rounds at the county fair every year. That was the one time Ma let us have cotton candy. Said it would rot out our teeth. Mine rotted, anyway. I never did listen when she told me to brush them, never listened to much of anything she said back then.

South Westwate Station, the intercom announces. As if anyone on this train doesn't know the last two stops. Everyone here was born in Westwate, went to school in Weswate, and will die in Westwate. 'Cept for that Jimmy Phillips who was on the TV for a little bit. Heard he ended up dead on drugs. Shoulda just stayed home. I step out of the train and the smell of Lady Chang's orange chicken takes over. She must've left it on the fryer too long, smells a bit burnt today. Good news for the poor folk huddled by the library. They'll have a hot dinner tonight.

The door still creaks a bit when it opens. Meant to fix that last time I was here.

"Lionel, that you?"

The first few times I tried telling her Pops was gone but it never stuck. "No, Ma. It's me, Robbie." She's laying on the couch with that green and black quilt Aunt

Sis made folded over her legs. She's looking forward but the TV ain't even on. I set the daisy on the coffee table where she can see.

"It's cold, Li. Come get me warm."

"Ma?"

Her eyes look at me but I can tell she doesn't really see me. "Get me warm." Her hand reaches out, the thin arms looking like snowman twigs.

I sit down and wrap her up in the quilt like she used to do for Cherie. I remember how Ma would rub her cheek on Cherie's and sing that song about the bunny dancing in the trees. Ma might even be as small as Cherie was back then.

"Better now, Ma?"

"What's that Meatball been up to today? Been peeking through that Jones girl window again?"

I haven't been called Meatball in a long time. Ma looks up at me, waiting for her answer.

"Ain't been spying on Talla, Ma."

She shivers. I slide my arms under her and carry Ma to her room. She twitches a bit when I set her down and wrap another blanket around her.

"We need to talk about that boy, Lionel."

"Ma, it's me, Robbie."

She scowls, ignoring me. "You been at him again?"

My heart thuds. "What are you talking about, Ma?"

"That nonsense in the bedroom. You keep it up and he'll be *unnatural.*"

Ma knew.

The collar on my button shirt closes up. It's like a fire been lit against my skin. I'm sweating like noontime in August.

"It's hot in here, Ma."

I walk to the window and open it. It isn't supposed to be this hot in March.

"I ain't gonna tell you again to leave that boy alone, Lionel."

Pants are feeling hot, too, and scratchy. I stick my head out the window but the sweat keeps rolling down.

Gotta be this room.

Pops would grab me by the elbow and drag me in here. Never knew what made it *that* time. He just got those devil eyes and that was that. I'd be smelling the lavender laundry soap with my face shoved down into the sheets. Aunt Sis gave Ma a knitted owl that hung on the wall next to the bed. I'd look at that brown owl sitting on his stick, wondering where he'd go if he flew away. Then it would all be over. Never said anything though. Figured it was better me than Cherie.

Ma lets out a soft snore, snug as a bug all tucked up in her bed.

The owl looks at me from that same spot on the wall. He's got a layer of dust on him now. Eyes still shining, though, looking at me.

I tear the owl from the wall and yank at the edges. Brown's an ugly color. I twist the corners and try to rip it apart. I pull and pull. My arms are aching. This room is getting hotter. The knots stay stuck, won't budge an inch. He's still looking at me, at us.

I throw it on the floor and kick it under the bed.

Skin's gonna boil if I stay here any longer. I roll up my sleeves and head for the door.

"You coming back next time, Robbie?"

I hold the doorknob but don't look back. She called me Robbie. I unbutton my collar and look at the lines on the door where we measured me and Cherie each birthday.

"Ya, Ma. I'll be back."

But never again in this suit.

Arielle Haughee

Previously an elementary teacher, Arielle Haughee is an Orlando-based writer with short stories and memoir published in the anthology *Lost Dreams*, *Havok* Magazine, and *Screamin' Mamas* Magazine.

Gillian's Choice

I heard a quiet "Woof" and glanced over to see Gillian, my old yellow lab, struggle to her feet, the kitchen tiles unkind to an aging dog's bones. I placed the hot tray of chocolate chip cookies down and pulled off my apron in time to meet the headlong rush of my five-year-old grandson.

"Grandma!" Wyatt peeled around the kitchen corner and buried his face against my legs.

Gillian wiggled beside us in doggie ecstasy, favoring her back left leg.

"Grandma, Gillian's limping."

"She's an old lady, like Grandma." I smiled for the first time that day. "Go sit at the table. I've got a nice warm batch of cookies in search of a little boy."

I plopped a few onto Wyatt's favorite Star Wars plate and poured his milk while he clambered onto a chair at my oak table. Gillian placed her soft head in his lap as he ate.

"Wyatt, chocolate doesn't like dogs."

He stroked her head and she closed her eyes.

"I remember. No cookie for Gillian." He sprayed cookie crumbs as he spoke. "Got it."

He chugged half of his milk, and the glass rang when he slammed it down. "Tell me about Gillian's choice again, Grandma," he said, panting. "Please?"

"I will if you slow down a bit. Deal?"

He nodded, silenced by another cookie in his mouth.

"When Gillian was a puppy," I said, "she was placed in a special school—Guide Dogs for the Blind. She was eight weeks old." I sat down across from him and folded my hands on my lap. The story never gets easier. "They taught her all kinds of things, like not to be afraid of thunder and rain. She learned to ride in a car, and how to be friends with all types of animals and people."

"Were her teachers nice?" he said.

"Very. One of her teachers was your auntie Marianne."

Wyatt was paying more attention to the last cookie on his plate than my story. But by now, I couldn't stop.

"Gillian and Marianne were best friends. Even though they weren't supposed to be."

"How come?"

"One day, Gillian would have to go to someone who really needed her. Teachers know it hurts too much to say good-bye."

"But Aunt Marianne loved her."

"And she loved Marianne," I said.

Stalling, I rose and whisked the now empty plate off the table. "Time to settle you in for your nap, buster."

"But the story." He tried his best pout.

"After you're tucked in, I'll tell you how Gillian chose our family."

We marched down the hall to the small guest bedroom, its walls painted like a rainy day.

Wyatt changed into pajamas and brushed his teeth. Then he climbed onto the bed and pulled the slate-blue comforter to his chin.

He yawned. "I don't want to take a nap. I'm not tired." He yawned again.

"So I see."

I sat on the edge of the bed and Gillian made a doggy circle at my feet. She sighed and curled up as close to the bed as she could.

"Okay, Grandma. What happens next?"

I cleared my throat, twice.

"When Marianne taught her all she could, Gillian was about sixteen months old and she graduated."

"Yay."

"Gillian was so happy and Aunt Marianne was so proud. Gillian learned how to stop at curbs and obey traffic signals. She waited to cross a busy street, until it was safe. She even learned to watch for low-hanging branches."

"Couldn't people see the branches?"

"Blind people can't see, Wyatt. So they need a guide dog like Gillian, to lead them away from branches that might hurt them."

"Grandma, you can see, can't you?"

"What do you think?" I fluttered my eyelids and he laughed.

"Now, where was I?" I tucked in the comforter.

"Gillian, learning about trees and lights," Wyatt piped in.

"Ah, yes. Aunt Marianne trained Gillian so well that when she graduated, they put her high on the list. And it didn't take long." My voice cracked. *I can do this.* "A family came along for Gillian."

"That's good. Right?"

"Yes, but two weeks before Gillian could leave, the vet discovered Gillian had an allergy on the pads of her feet and couldn't be a guide dog."

Wyatt's eyes snapped open. "What are pads? Do I have pads?" He pulled his feet out from under the covers.

I laughed. "You sort of have pads right here." I tickled a foot. He giggled.

I picked up Gillian's front paws and pointed to the pads. "Here are Gillian's." She nuzzled my hand.

"What's an allergy, Grandma?"

"It's when your feet are itchy and you need medicine to stop it."

"Oh." He scrunched his nose.

"Marianne asked the school if she could adopt Gillian. But the lady who raised her first had first choice and wanted Gillian for herself."

"Then how did she get to be with us?"

I tousled his hair. "When the day came for Gillian to go home with the lady, Marianne was setting up the chairs for the graduation ceremony for the other dogs."

"Was Gillian sad?"

"I don't know. Then, a friend of Marianne's saw Gillian at the gift shop with her new owners and she said Marianne should say good-bye. Marianne said she would cry if she did. Her friend said she'd cry more if she didn't."

"Poor Auntie Marianne."

Marianne hurried to the gift shop. Gillian saw her and pulled away from the lady, and ran to Marianne. She hugged the dog and cried. She told the new owners she hoped Gillian would have a good life.

The woman said, "I think Gillian has chosen her owner and it's you."

"I thought people chose their dogs." Wyatt looked down at Gillian.

"Gillian is special." I leaned down to scratch her head, and Gillian licked my hand.

"Yes, she is, Grandma." Wyatt laid his head back on the pillow, his blonde hair fanned out to frame his face. His eyes, heavy with the need for sleep, finally shut.

"Six months ago, Marianne died with Gillian by her side …"—I whispered these words, not trusting my emotions—"and her boyfriend said … he'd keep Gillian."

"Why?" Wyatt said in a sleepy voice.

"He was lonely when Marianne died. He wanted Gillian to stay so he wouldn't miss her so much."

"I miss Auntie Marianne too."

"We all do, Wyatt." I wiped away a tear.

"But Gillian wasn't happy. She howled and barked in the kitchen, where he kept her. I went to his house and when he let her out, Gillian ran to me and wouldn't leave my side."

"She chose you like she chose Aunt Marianne."

"To this day, Gillian hasn't left me, even when I go into the bathroom."

"That's funny," he murmured. "I love you, Grandma—and Gillian."

"We love you too, Wyatt."

Gillian's tail thumped when I stood, and she looked at me.

"Come on, girl," I said.

She panted and laid her head back down on her paws.

"I see. You making another choice?"

Her tail thumped once more.

I went over and kissed her head. "Take care of him, girl."

Frances Hight

Frances Hight published under the pen name Frances Palmigiano in FWA's 2016 Collection, *Hide and Seek*: "Hidden," and Collection #5, *It's a Crime*: "Cajun Treasure." Other works include Finalist levels: 2013, Bouchercon; 2011, Royal Palm Literary Award in Poetry & Short Story; 2011 and 2012, Mystery Writers of America SleuthFest.

The Strand

Eighty-five-year-old Molly Renfro stood by her screen door looking out at another rainy September morning beginning in the Fakahatchee Strand Preserve State Park that surrounded her house.

The Strand, as the locals called the park, is a piece of land running North and South that stretches out 20 miles long and five miles wide. State Road 29, a paved ribbon of a road, bordered on both sides with drainage canals, cuts through the Strand on its way to Everglades City. It is the only place where bald cypress trees and royal palms share the same forest. Within its borders also live many of the surviving endangered wildlife and plant species of Florida. The Strand is one of the last places the elusive ghost orchid grows wild. Because of the tenuous life of the small plants in this area, the land as a preserve came into being. A tiny patch of what once was a wild and beautiful land was all that remained now. Near the Everglades National Park and the Big Cypress National Preserve, the Strand was still home to a few humans.

"Trees, animals, plants and my people-remnants all." she thought as she surveyed the wilderness.

Molly lived all her life in the small house built by her father. The house sat up on top of squat limestone rock pillars that kept it from being flooded during the rainy season. In true Florida style, it had an open porch running around the outside of the house connected to the yard by a set of wooden steps.

Her father had made his living as a Gladesman, guiding hunters and tourists through the Everglades. After Molly's mother had died of the fever when she was very young, he preferred being in the wilderness of the glades more than worrying about a small girl child. Molly grew up with the help of a black woman she knew as 'Aunt Sally.'

Aunt Sally lived with her seven children, in a small house built behind the Renfro property, and she kept Molly when her dad was gone. Aunt Sally fell into the habit of taking Molly to her home so that Molly grew up with Aunt Sally's children, often all living in the same house. Aunt Sally's children did not go to the school with Molly, but no one thought much about it. It was just the way of things then.

Jim, the youngest, taught her to fish and hunt, to clean fish and skin rabbits and Aunt Sally taught her how to cook them. Molly taught Jim to read and write. It was a simple and pleasant life for the children.

By the age of sixteen, Molly married a boy from Everglades City, and they lived with her Dad in his house. By the time she was eighteen, Molly had a son. While rescuing people during a summer hurricane, her husband disappeared. Neither he or their airboat was seen again. Molly came to believe his disappearance was a part of the price for living in the Strand.

She loved her neighbors and the land around the Strand. Sadly, she thought they all had become part of the endangered species that her small part of the earth tried to protect from harm.

Jim still lived in the house behind hers that his mother had owned. She had long ago figured out it didn't matter about the color of their skins. She and Jim were almost all each had left of anything like a family. Jim told Molly he sometimes felt like part of the show for the tourist. Molly just laughed at him and replied that was true.

Today as she mused about her life, Molly walked out on the porch to see if she could see the mail truck. The mailman brought civilization to you when you lived back in the preserve. She loved getting mail, especially a catalog she could sit and hold. It gave her an excuse to while away the time looking at the pictures and daydreaming.

She saw the mail truck headed her way. As she looked at the flooded yard near the end of the driveway, she noticed an eight-foot long alligator lying in the sun at the edge of the canal.

She was not afraid of gators. She had lived with the alligators of Florida for more than 80 years. Gators were just a part of her life. Leave them alone, and they leave you alone, that is what she had been taught all her life. She thought it was miraculous that with over a million of them roaming the state they didn't eat a few more people. She had a mental list of people she'd met that she felt should have been fed to the gators, starting with a lot of poachers, politicians, and developers who had all but destroyed her Florida homeland.

She lost track of the gator but didn't worry about it, believing the gator had slipped into the canal going about his business. She took her mail back to the porch and sat down in the old wooden rocking chair. The sun was warm, and she found herself nodding off now and then as she perused the catalogs.

Suddenly, she was startled awake by the most searing pain she could remember. As she screamed, she was jerked from the chair and into the yard. She was being dragged through the water in the yard by a gator holding doggedly to her leg as he backed up toward the canal. She grabbed desperately at a spindly tree near the edge of the yard, managing to hang onto it with both arms.

"Please God, Help me!" sobbed Molly.

"Molly, stay as still as you can, I'm going to try and force that gator to let go of you with a shot from my .22." yelled a familiar voice.

***

Molly did not remember hearing the shot until after she regained consciousness two weeks later at the hospital in Ft. Myers. Her grandson explained to her she had been airlifted to the hospital where the doctors had to amputate her left leg which was almost bitten off by the gator.

"Did you save me?" She asked her grandson.

"No" he replied. "It was Uncle Jim. He took a shot with that .22 rifle of his, hitting that gator right in the eye. Then' that gator lets go of your leg and he sunk back into the canal. Somewhere out in the Strand is a one-eyed gator with a taste for your leg, Grandmama."

It was near Christmas before she was well enough to return home again. On Christmas day she was happy to see Jim at the family dinner table. She proclaimed to everyone that she owed the remainder of her years to his skills with a .22 rifle. She enjoyed eating some wild turkey and homemade pie, but she politely refused the platter of fried gator tail when offered to her.

"I've had my fill of alligator meat," she explained. "I've sworn off eating tail or any other gator meat for the rest of my life. I do hope the gators feel the same way about me." she told her family.

P. M. Hughes

P. M. Hughes is a native Floridian who lives in the small town of Arcadia, Florida with her husband, Hugo. She has two grown children, three grandchildren, and a cat. She is currently taking classes to become certified as a Florida Naturalist and enjoys sharing stories of Florida.

A Night at Madame Beauseau's - 1864

Cyrus sat on his front porch sipping a neat whiskey. By early evening, the Florida sun shone pink and purple as its last rays danced through the green pines. The summer heat that blistered earlier in the afternoon dissipated once a late thunderstorm blew through.

He swirled the amber liquid in his glass—his wife dead—Lily, his colored mistress, run away from his plantation. Nothing much left to him except a big, empty, house and some Union silver stashed in a small metal box under his bed. Atlanta had fallen to the North the week before, so it would be only a matter of time before Tallahassee and Jacksonville would follow suit. Weren't many defenses in those two cities anyhow. Most of Florida's Confederates were only fighting the Union to defend their crops or their cows. *No. Florida ain't never been the kind a place where a man thinks much 'bout nothing but himself.* Cyrus downed the rest of his whiskey and watched the sky turn magenta-black.

It was company he needed, company he could only find in town. He headed into the parlor, through the double French doors, and down the flagstone walkway to his mare in the barn. He had to saddle her himself since his slaves were already asleep—that made it all the better for Cyrus—he didn't need them gossiping about where their master was going or what he was doing at night. He waited until he was out on the short trail into town to break his horse into a trot. Pine branches whipped his face, but that made no difference to Cyrus—the whiskey had dulled him enough.

***

In Bradentown, the lamplights burned bright along Corwin's dock. On Friday evenings Madame Beauseau's house was open at least until midnight—maybe even later if business were good.

Cyrus hitched his mare to the first post at the far end of the line of ten on Main Street. As he approached the green door of the red-brick house, he could hear men laughing and the ladies' coquettish replies. He didn't bother to knock—a ten dollar Florida note slipped through the mail slot was all he needed to get the door unlocked.

It cracked opened and light streaked across the brick pavers at Cyrus' feet. An alluringly plump Madame, her cheeks and lips well rouged—her hair nearly matching their reddish tint—greeted him at the entrance.

She smiled to see Cyrus, one of her best ex-clients. "Mister Knowles, it's been a while," she said.

"Evening, Miss Beauseau," Cyrus said and walked straight to the bar. "Keeper—whiskey, neat," he shouted. The barkeeper poured the order and slid it to him.

Cyrus looked over the clientele—smiling women and serious looking men—intent on making money or love. Cyrus took pleasure in neither—love was an obligation, and money an effort. He lacked neither, but craved both.

As he gazed through the crowd his eyes fixed on a girl who looked a lot like his Lily, but darker complected. She sat on a fat man's lap, feigning her passion at his kisses and embraces. The girl glanced over at Cyrus—his blue eyes and thin build caught her attention. He flashed her a broad smile.

She looked away and went back to her work, until the Madame came over and whispered in her ear. The girl looked across at Cyrus and shoved the fat man aside. She nodded to him, and he nodded back. She stood up and pushed her way through the crowd to the stairs. From the top landing she crooked a finger in Cyrus' direction. He gulped his whiskey in one swallow.

"Keeper. Another!" he shouted across the bar. The barkeeper slid a neat whiskey over to him—he caught it with one hand and raised it up to the girl on the stairs. She crooked her finger again and nodded in the direction of an upstairs room. Cyrus downed his second drink and got up from his stool.

"Name's Janis," she said when they met on the top step.

"Name's Cyrus," he said. And they slipped into a long-narrow room on their left. The couple spoke no words as they did what they intended to do. Janis moaned with Cyrus' prowess. Even after both were fulfilled, they continued—as if never satisfied—embrace after embrace—each more passionate than the last.

***

Through a transom above his head, morning light streamed into the small room. Cyrus pulled up his trousers and suspenders, un-crumpled a twenty dollar Union note from his pocket, and left it on a round table next to the girl's bed. Janis—if that were really her name—was fast asleep. Cyrus walked down the stairs and out the door on cat's feet. At the line of hitching-posts on Main Street, his mare stood alone along the cobblestone pavement. On the trail back to the big house, the sun rose behind Cyrus and a shiver ran up his spine—a night at Madame Beauseau's was only a short reprieve from the sadness pervading his soul.

Paul Iasevoli

Paul Iasevoli is a member of the Bradenton chapter of FWA. Words are his passion. In his college days, he published several short poems in various Mid-western literary journals.

Not Her First Rodeo

Sue Ann heard the rumble coming from the side street. The garbage truck would soon be at the end of her driveway. She snatched the garbage can lid and held it aloft like a cymbal. Her right hand made an arc, spritzing Febreze inside the lid. The rumble grew louder. Sue Ann sprayed the garbage can before hightailing it to the door and slamming it behind her seconds before air brakes squealed.

There he was. The garbage guy, GG—as she called him. Did he sniff a little as he raised the lid? GG glanced toward the house. Sue Ann released the bent slat in the blind, waited, then peeked again just in time to see his back muscles ripple under a sweaty T-shirt. His arms bulged. GG slung the now empty can as if it were made of paper. Her chest pounded. Sweat beads formed on her upper lip. Sue Ann held her breath for the finale. GG leapt onto the back of the truck, clutched the handle. His left arm straight and rigid, he raised his right arm to the sky, waved his hand to signal the driver. The truck lurched forward.

Sue Ann, forty-three, had lived with her mother since her father died, moving to San Francisco so Mother could experience the lively retirement life on the brochures. Selling the ranch had provided more funds than they needed to live well. And her mother relished the cultural activities, card games, beach trips, wine tastings, plays and clubs filling her days and evenings. Sue Ann taught online high school literature, sometimes worked on her novel at a corner table at Starbucks.

She regretted leaving Texas. The West was in her blood--the open land, cattle, and most of all, rodeos. Had her mother known San Francisco was one of the few places that banned rodeos? She had never understood nor approved of Sue Ann's passion for them. There were finer things in life, according to Mother.

Back home Sue Ann rarely missed a rodeo. The thrill that started in her toes and worked its way up to parts she didn't speak of began the minute a cowboy burst from the chute on a snorting bull. Determination in every muscle of the rider, his athletic prowess, his…Sue Ann struggled to put impure thoughts out of her mind. But the vision of the cowboy with his arm thrust in the air counterbalancing the pull of massive muscle beneath him proved impossible to dismiss. Sometimes a rider would smile at her enthusiasm as he dusted his hat against his thigh. Smiles from men came rarely. Sue Ann, slim, with long, russet hair that curtained a face not stunning, but not plain either, refused her mother's efforts to glamorize her.

Her mother caught her spritzing the cans a few weeks earlier. "Why do you spray Febreze in the garbage cans? I've never heard of such a thing."

"Because those garbage guys do the hard and necessary work, Mother. God knows it's not pleasant, yet they live in stink and lift heavy loads over their heads each day. It's the least I can do, give them one pleasant smelling can. And trust me, with litter from our four cats, our garbage is really smelly. I spray it shortly before they arrive so it works well."

"*Your* four cats." Her mother opened her eyes wide, shook her head, a mocking smile forming. "Takes all kinds," she mumbled, grabbing her keys. "You need to get out more."

***

Garbage Day. The sun perched almost straight above and steam rose in ripples from the pavement up the street before Sue Ann heard the rumble. She grabbed the Febreze, raced to the street, lifted the lid, sprayed, then swirled the spray inside the can. The putrid odor of litter almost made her retch.

SCREECH.

Oh my heavens. Misjudged. Sue Ann took a few steps back, holding the spray can behind her. GG jumped off the truck.

"Howdy, Ma'am." GG looked her right in the eye. His eyes were the blue of Texas skies.

"Whatcha hide'n behind your back?"

"Oh, just a little can of something to make the garbage smell better, to make your job more pleasant." Her words tumbled out in a rush.

GG put his hands on his hips, focused those blue eyes on her. "That's the nicest thing anyone ever did for me."

"Oh, it's no trouble."

"Do I detect a Texas accent?"

Sue Ann startled. She thought she'd lost her accent after so long in California.

"I suppose. That's where I'm from."

"Me, too. I miss Texas, especially the rodeos."

Sue Ann's eyes widened. "Do you ride?"

"No, never did, but never missed a rodeo."

BEEP

"Sam's telling me to hurry up."

"I love rodeos, too," she yelled to the speeding truck.

Sue Ann stared into space a lot the next week. Mother asked if she felt okay.

"I'm fine, just reached a snag plotting my novel."

"I don't know why you write that stuff about dreary people in captive situations. Give your characters some gumption! There, now I got you past your writer's block." She chuckled at her own cleverness.

Sue Ann barely slept the night before garbage day. When the first, faint rumble sounded, Sue Ann raced to the garbage cans, sprayed them until drops accumulated on the plastic. Then she ran in as fast as she could.

She willed herself not to peek from the blinds when she heard the lid thrown or the trash can banging against the back of the truck. Only when she figured he would be back on the truck did she finally lift a slat to make a peep hole.

Her knees buckled, her breath caught. There stood GG gripping the handle on the truck leaning out with his right arm stretched to the sky holding a cowboy hat.

"Yee Haw!" he yelled.

"Yee Haw," Sue Ann whispered, her full lips beginning to curl in a timid smile as she tucked her hair behind one ear.

Beda Kantarjian

Beda relishes offbeat characters whether real or conjured. She has published short stories online and in anthologies. This is her seventh Collections story, including a Top Ten in 2013. Her creative non-fictions have placed first and second in RPLA. She is co-founder/coordinator of Seminole County Writers.

The Ungrateful Peanut

The first time I saw Peanut he was lying motionless in the middle of a road in the suburban neighborhood where I live. Like an oddly green leaf among a drift of brown and gold, his tiny body lay vulnerable and still. The brightness of his green plumage is what caught my eye. I pulled over and stepped out on the road, crunching through the leaves towards him. Not a twitch. Not a stir. I crouched beside him, amazed at his beauty and saddened at his death.

Or imminent demise. For apparently he was not dead. I spied a faint movement and gently scooped him up. I tucked him against the front of my shirt and felt the warmth of his small body next to mine. One beady, black eye flickered open briefly and then shut again.

Poor, sweet thing. I guessed he had been hit by a car and was dying. At least I could spare him from being run over, or attacked and eaten alive by predators. I cradled him against me and made my way back to the car. I could give him a peaceful place to die.

Having spent a number of years living in South Florida, I was accustomed to seeing these small parrots flying in rowdy groups or hanging out like bright green beads strung on the black ropes of overhead power lines. I enjoyed watching them, amused by their squat bodies and noisy, busy lives. Now, as I held this still, warm body close to me, I felt a sense of honor, sadness and sweetness entwined.

I drove home slowly and tucked him carefully in a shoe box with holes punched in the lid. I gently touched his tiny green head with the tip of my finger, whispered goodbye, and placed him on a high counter out of reach of my cats. I was determined not to fall in love, my typical response to the numerous strays I have rescued over the years. I expected he would be dead by the time I returned and could do without the heartbreak.

A few hours later I pulled that little coffin towards me and lifted the lid. Miracle of miracles, my little guest was wide awake, on his feet, and clearly unafraid. I jumped and laughed when he squawked.

My little guest was a Quaker or Monk Parrot, native to several South American countries, and it turned out he had a broken leg and was severely dehydrated. For a small fortune a local bird doctor gave him nutrients and antibiotics, and set his tiny leg in an even tinier cast. She clipped his wings so he could not escape while his leg was healing, and provided directions on his care. As I observed his diminutive, stocky frame, miniature cast leg held out at an awkward angle, I knew that despite my earlier resolutions, my heart was lost.

I borrowed a bird cage from a friend and arranged a gnarly stick across the bars for a perch, although until his cast was removed he was literally grounded and spent all his time on the floor. During the day I hung his perch on the verandah outside, so he could enjoy the breeze and the sights and sounds of the birds in my garden. At night I would place his cage on that same high counter, away from the cats, and covered with a large towel. I loved having him stay with me. The only challenge was the decibel level of his screeches. Although they seemed more conversational than anything else, rather like a deaf old man simply unaware of how loudly he spoke.

I can't remember now how long he stayed with me, other than at the time it seemed like he had been with me forever, and I hoped he would never leave. Eventually his little leg healed and his wing feathers grew out. Sitting at the open door of his cage he would flap his wings into a blur of green, building up his strength and stamina. He had a healthy appetite and loved his daily bath. I would place a shallow dish of water on the bottom of his cage and he would squawk loudly and waddle over to squat in the middle of the dish, flapping his wings exuberantly and spraying water everywhere. He appeared quite happy to sit on my fingers or shoulders, and displayed a rather horrifying absence of fear for cats or people. He had his bath on the verandah table sometimes and afterwards would hop onto my lap, waddle to the edge, then make his way down the chair leg, claw over beak, until he reached the floor. He would eye my cats scornfully, puff up his little green chest, and strut past them like a small general inspecting his troops, emitting an ear-splitting shriek should they dare set a paw in his direction. What a character!

He would ride my shoulder majestically as I completed chores around the house and garden, paying particular attention when we walked to the bottom of the garden to refill the bird feeder for my garden birds. He would cock his little head to one side, and eye the Blue Jays with his shiny back button eyes.

Then one sunny day as we walked back from the feeder, he flapped his elegant, freshly-grown wing feathers and took off. With barely a backward squawk he was gone. My initial reaction was horror. Where was he? What if he wasn't ready to go yet and couldn't find food? What if he got lost trying to find his way home? My shoulder and heart felt empty. Then it dawned on me he had stayed with me on his own terms, long past the time he needed for healing. I had shut him in his cage at night but only for his own protection. He was ready to go, so he left. My job was not to hold on, but to appreciate the time we had, the opportunity I had to help him, and then let him go. Sometimes we just have to let things and people, even little green feathery people, go.

Peanut never came back to say hello, and although occasionally some parrots would visit my birdfeeder, I never had any indication that any of these birds might be Peanut. I still see little green gatherings of Peanut's cousins and other relatives around the neighborhood, squawking and shrieking as they flutter through the blue sky. It makes me smile when I think of Peanut, his puffed out chest and that magnificent strut. I wish him well wherever he is now.

Colleen Jeffery Kastner

Originally from South Africa, Colleen Kastner is a former journalist, lifelong book addict, and habitual wildlife rescuer. She lives near Fort Lauderdale with her husband, son, and an extremely meddlesome cat.

Gianna

Those closest to the restaurant's door ceased their conversations and eyed the lady. Several shifted position to get a better look.

"Oh my. I wonder who dressed her," a female guest muttered.

"Better yet, who invited her?" her companion responded.

A man mumbled to his girlfriend, "I remember a picture from my parent's wedding. My grandmother was dressed like that."

"I guess she missed the 'Private Party For Wedding Reception' sign."

Everyone in the restaurant that evening knew each other. The owner had invited them to help celebrate his daughter's wedding earlier that day. But no one knew this oddly dressed woman, much less why she was there.

The woman, in her mid-30s, wore a loose-fitting tan suit with oversized lapels. A plain white blouse, buttoned to the neck, peeked from under the jacket. The skirt ended about six inches above white socks and scuffed brown leather shoes. A blocky, white patent-leather, purse hung from a forearm. Her wavy brown hair had been brushed straight back from a high, shiny forehead and held in place by a black headband. No makeup, no jewelry. Most people would describe her as plain, in an old fashioned way.

When the hum of excitement lessened, Antonio, the bride's brother and volunteer bartender, looked up.

The lady walked several paces into the restaurant before she stopped and scanned the room. Her emotionless brown eyes finally stopped on an overweight girl, about five years old, with Down's Syndrome. The woman pointed at the girl and raised a finger to her lips in the universal 'quiet' sign.

The girl slid behind her mother.

Antonio smiled and worked his way through the gawking crowd toward the newcomer.

The plain woman set her pocket book on a table and popped it open with the twist of thumb and index finger. Like a magician she used two fingers to extract what looked like a blue plastic wriggling worm. She put one end to her lips and blew a three-foot balloon. With well-practiced speed she tied its end, tucked it under her arm, and repeated the process with another balloon.

The crowd watched in anticipation. Instead of wondering why she was there they now wondered what she would make. Even Antonio stopped to watch.

With twelve inflated balloons under her arm she twisted, turned, wrapped, and joined them together one-by-one. The only sound was the screech and thump of balloons being manipulated. Less than a minute later she had sculpted an unbelievable hat with a two-foot tall dolphin mounted on top. Never once did the lady smile or show any emotion. She could have been a mime, except she didn't wear any make-up.

The finished product brought applause, a 'well done', and several 'ah's'.

Antonio took a step forward, but paused when the woman curled an index finger at the little girl who peeked through a crack between her mother's arm and side.

The balloon artist held the dolphin hat out to the little girl.

Emily's mother nudged her daughter forward. "Look Em, she wants to give it to you."

Emily looked up at her mother who smiled and nodded. The child shuffled forward, head down, arms straight at her side.

The lady dropped to a knee and placed the hat on Emily's head. It sat a bit low in the front. The child's squinty eyes twinkled and thin lips parted in a lop-sided half-smile. She turned to her mother, "Look Mommy, Emily have dolphin on head, Emily favorite." The five-year-old clapped. The bystanders joined her.

Antonio stepped to the mystery lady's side. "Thank you for joining us. What's your name?"

"Gianna." She didn't smile, didn't frown, didn't even blink. She reached for her purse.

"Before you start again can I-"

"Em! What's wrong?" Emily's mother shrieked.

The little girl, still wearing the dolphin hat, clutched her throat, eyes bulged, face reddened. Panic etched her flat oval face as squinty eyes pleaded for help.

Emily's mother shook the girl's shoulders. "Breathe. Breathe."

Someone shouted, "We need a doctor."

A fat man in a floral shirt stabbed his phone with a pudgy finger. "I'm calling 9-1-1".

Guests crowded around.

Gianna inserted her arms between two people and pried them apart like Moses parting the Red Sea. She took Emily's face in her hands and showed emotion for the first time. She smiled, but only with her mouth.

Tears from Emily's terror-filled eyes trickled over red cheeks and blue lips. Her mouth moved, but no sound came out. She clawed at her throat.

Gianna moved behind Emily, pushed the hat off, and wrapped her arms around the youngster's torso. With fingers intertwined in front of the girl's stomach, Gianna squeezed inward and upward.

Nothing.

She squeezed again.

Nothing.

Emily's eyes rolled up into her head, blue lips darkened.

The fat man yelled into his phone about a special needs girl not being able to breathe.

Gianna closed her eyes, mumbled something, and squeezed.

The child's eyes closed, her head lulled to the side, her body became limp.

Emily's mother screamed, "Help her, she's dying."

While Gianna struggled to hold the girl upright she adjusted her hands and squeezed again.

With a whoosh a red and white circular mint flew from the child's mouth. She sucked air so hard it sounded like a vacuum cleaner. The little girl coughed and extended her arms. A croak of "Mommy" could barely be heard.

Mother and daughter grabbed one another in python-like hugs. Emily rested her head on her mother's shoulder, sputtering weak coughs.

About a minute later two blue shirted EMTs entered. They strode to the mother and child who still clung to one another.

After a brief exam the taller EMT nodded and smiled. "You're going to be okay, young lady. Whoever helped you, saved your life." He placed the dolphin hat on the child's head.

Emily's mother turned to Antonio, thanked him for hiring the balloon lady, threw her arms around his neck and hugged. Others patted Antonio on the back and congratulated him on the fortuitous decision.

The fat man, who still held his cell phone, called out, "Drinks on me," and waddled to the bar.

Emily's mother looked around for the balloon lady, didn't see her and asked Antonio if he knew where she had gone.

He shrugged. "No idea," then moved a little closer and whispered, "I didn't hire her, she just showed up."

"It's a miracle that she was here."

Father Patrick, who officiated the wedding, cleared his throat. "Today is the feast of Saint Gianna, patron saint of mothers, physicians, and children."

Tears trickled down the mother's cheeks as she made the sign of the cross, cast her eyes to heaven, and whispered, "Thank you."

Henry James Kaye

Born and raised in Pittsburgh, Henry had successful careers in banking, entrepreneurship, technology, and real estate. His passion, Writing, produced multiple Collections stories, several published books, and two RPLA winners. He married Nancy over 40 years ago, they have 3 children and one grand-child. He lives in Longwood, Florida.

Worrier Rose

Some might say my sister, Rose, is a glass-half-empty kind of gal, the incurable pessimist. All her life, Rose has worried about our family. Her concerns are not day-to-day minor disasters, but improbable catastrophes. For decades, the Delany clan has had a weekly summer rental of several beachfront cottages along the Outer Banks of North Carolina. Though Rose frets about the apocalypses awaiting us on the barrier island, she has never missed a trip. One year, a storm washed a swarm of jellyfish ashore.

My sister was the first to spot the warning sign. She urged everyone to head to high ground. "We shouldn't be out here until the beach is cleaned. Those things are poisonous. Did anyone bring an EpiPen?"

"We'll stay out of the water until the tide takes them back out to sea," I told her. "Just stay away from the ones that have washed ashore."

She eyed one gelatinous body wiggling closer with the incoming tide. "But what if they chase us?"

"They can't move on land."

That didn't calm her fears. She retrieved a fishing net and trash bag from the house then set about cleaning the beach. Of course, the only one stung that day was Rose. She had scooped up a jellyfish near the water and another washed up against her foot.

Another year schools of sharks were sighted offshore. Several non-fatal attacks had occurred. Rose did her research and found a shark usually strikes whoever is the farthest into the water. Her afternoons were spent herding the Delany kids toward shore when they swam out past other families' children.

On the last day of our vacation, Rose and I were the only ones still seated on the sand. Her two young daughters played in a nearby tidal pool. Suddenly, my sister jumped to her feet and scanned the water. "I don't think it's safe for the girls to be there."

I looked up from my book. "Why not?"

"What if a shark spots them?"

"Are you nuts? He would have to belly crawl across ten feet of sand to reach them."

She huffed and muttered under her breath. "…if it's hungry enough."

After more than thirty years of vacationing with our parents, we were grief-stricken when Dad passed away followed by Mom six months later. In her will, our mother left money to be used for a family vacation to scatter their ashes on the Outer Banks.

It took more than two years after their deaths to arrange the Celebration of Life ceremony. The invasion of Normandy wasn't as logistically complicated. The easy part was securing a permit from the National Park Service and identifying a location which met dispersal guidelines. Rose and I were in charge of travel arrangements for the group. There were six of us siblings plus spouses, all with full-time jobs, and fourteen grandchildren ranging in age from seven to twenty-one.

Rose fussed the entire twenty-seven months. "A lot can happen before then. What if everyone comes down with something contagious? Maybe a disease that requires hospitalization or quarantine. We'll lose our deposits."

"If a few fall ill, there'll still be enough of us to have a nice ceremony. Don't worry."

Two months prior to our scheduled vacation, Rose called me in a panic. "Did you see the news? There's a storm brewing in the Atlantic. Why are we going in August? That's the middle of hurricane season. What if a big one hits the island and the road is wiped out? It's happened before."

"And like before, they'll build a temporary lane. Remember there are people who live there year-round. It'll be fine."

A week before our departure, Rose stopped at my house. "I'm worried about Reverend O'Brien giving the blessing. Maybe we should have a backup."

"Why?"

"What if he has a *real* funeral that day? Maybe his own. He's getting up there in years."

"If something happens I'm sure I can find another one. That's why we're having the ceremony on a weekday when ministers aren't real busy."

Just then our sister, Julie, walked into my kitchen with a large box under her arm.

"What's that?" Rose asked.

It was a scattering urn called The Loved One Launcher. (I kid you not.)

Julie opened the box to show us the device. "I bought it online for the ceremony. It shoots the remains over seventy feet in the air. That way everyone can see. I decided not to get confetti or streamers to mix in with Mom and Dad. We don't want to litter the beach."

Rose eyed the device like it was a terrorist IED that could explode at any moment. "Are you sure it's safe?"

At last, the week of the long-awaited vacation arrived. Mom and Dad must have been orchestrating the gathering from above. The weather was glorious with sunny skies. We all arrived within twenty-four hours of each other, despite coming from different cities. No one fell ill, was abducted by aliens, or robbed. No one was forced to leave early, suffered from sun poisoning, or attacked by marine predators.

On the appointed day, we positioned ourselves downwind and made sure our section of sand was fairly private and deserted. Julie and her husband, Frank, were the last to arrive. Like guests at a wedding, we watched them descend the wooden stairs over the dune and head across the sand. Julie was weeping, a hand over her mouth. Frank carried the cremains cannon under one arm.

Rose turned to me. "Julie's taking this hard. Do you think it's because she's kept Mom and Dad on her mantle the last two years? Maybe she'll miss them."

Halfway across the sand, Julie stopped to blow her nose and wipe her eyes.

Rose bumped my shoulder and hissed into my ear. "Oh, my God! I know why she's crying. They gave her the wrong ashes. We're going to shoot strangers into the air."

Several feet from us, they stopped and Julie raised her tear-streaked face. "I forgot Mom and Dad!"

Cries of dismay and gasps sounded.

Rose shook her head. "I never saw that one coming."

Janet Franks Little

Janet Franks Little writes about love, laughter, and the real-life issues of contemporary women. Her contemporary romance, Worth Her Weight, was published in 2015 and she has two new novels, Glass Promises and Estate of the Heart soon to be released.

Iggy

The first time I saw him, when he entered our shop, I thought he was a vagabond looking for a handout. Our clients were lawyers, bankers, politicians, and the titans of industry. Although clean in appearance, his khaki trousers and chambray shirt was ill fitting and not complimentary to the offerings of an upscale men's clothing store.

I was a new salesperson. At the time of my hiring, I was informed to follow certain protocols pertaining to the customer, the essence of which was to treat each one with respect. Besides, this man, incompatible to our environs, could have been an eccentric millionaire who stopped into the shop after working on his hobby of restoring antique cars.

I greeted him with customary dignity. Coming to attention I asked, "May I help you, sir?"

Giving me a wry smile and sideways glance of dismissal he simple said, "No. I'm here to see Bud," and continued on his track toward the rear of the store. Guessing him to be in his mid-sixties, I was intrigued by his exaggerated lumbering gait—almost comical.

Curious of his intentions, I watched as he approached the back office area. Suddenly, and to my amazement, he began to tumble forward, appearing to have tripped on something that escaped my notice. After taking several awkward steps to correct, what I perceived to be certain disaster, he did a controlled fall backward onto his posterior. His legs jackknifed open, forming a wide V-shape and his arms splayed out toward the ceiling.

My first reaction was to run to his aid. But, after taking a couple of steps, I saw that my assistance wasn't needed. As Bud, and a couple of employees clapped in approval, the man sprang from his graceless position and exclaimed, "That's all folks, there ain't no more."

That is how I first met Iggy. A holdover from the days of Vaudeville, he lived a somewhat secluded life on the second floor of the clothing store. Later, I was to learn that he occupied the only apartment on the top level, paying a modest rent in exchange for his services as a self-styled night watchman.

My employment lasted a few years, during which time I became more acquainted with Iggy. Our offish first meeting melded into mutual acceptance and he became more approachable. He was one of those people who displayed exterior confidence yet possessed an insecure core. From some of my co-workers, I learned that Iggy never achieved the title of top banana, showbiz slang for having attained top billing status. His only real claim to fame was his brief association with a famous vaudevillian who made the successful transition from vaudeville to television. I purposely have omitted naming that person only because my story is about Iggy. As deference to him, I do not want to take away from his own story.

Although brief his connection with that entertainer, every Christmas, Iggy would hang a seasonal greeting inside his second story window facing the street below. The sign proclaimed "Merry Christmas from Iggy" and that comedian—it was as if their friendship was frozen in time and their act a present-day reality.

Each time he made a visit he would put on his impromptu act, never failing to add his closing tagline. It always brought a smile and laugh to the staff and customers alike. As the years progressed his antics and pratfalls became less frequent, eventually only his punch line became his moniker.

Like all things in time, I eventually moved on to other endeavors. When in the neighborhood, I would stop by my old place of employment and chat with Bud and the others I worked with. Eventually some of them were replaced with newer faces and the frequency of my visits became less numerous.

One day, I received a call from Bud, informing me of Iggy's passing. Although saddened by the news, I could not but smile at the memories of the man who made me laugh each time he came into the store. Out of curiosity, I looked up the obituary and to my surprise found that Iggy had a daughter, his only surviving relative. Using the opportunity for a reunion of friendships and tribute to Iggy, I made a commitment to stop by the funeral parlor.

To my amazement, the wake was well attended. Other than the sporadic visits to the clothing store and my chance spotting of his coming and goings, he seemed to have little social life. Now, on the occasion of his passing, the room was full of those who cared enough to show their respect.

Moving from group to group and person to person, I shared my own remembrances of Iggy. Some of those in attendance spoke of a time when Iggy was more nimble and his antics exceptional. The singular theme running though them all was his ability to make people laugh.

As I was about to leave, my attention was drawn to a middle age woman who came in late and unescorted. The collection of mourners was predominately men; a few of them brought their wives or girlfriends. The fact that she was by herself not only made her standout among the gathering but her reaction upon viewing Iggy was telling. Her profuse tears and sobs told me that she was no mere acquaintance but Iggy's daughter.

Postponing my departure to allow her moment alone with her father, I waited until she sat down before approaching her. Standing before her I extended a handshake of sympathy. "You must be Iggy's daughter."

"Yes," she said softly, looking up to me with her tear-swollen eyes. "Please, have a seat." She motioned toward the chair next to hers.

Still holding her hand in mine, I joined her. "I am sorry for your loss." Feeling my words of comfort inadequate, I awkwardly added, "I knew your father when I worked at the clothing store. He never mentioned having a daughter."

She gave me a pained smile and nodded. "If the truth be told, I was ashamed of my father."

"Ashamed?"

"Yes," she admitted with embarrassment. "My father was a clown. He got his laughs at his own expense—the pratfalls and pies in the face. I always thought it was degrading. I was humiliated and as a result, when I was old enough, I put distance between the two of us. I suppose he never said anything about me because he was also embarrassed that I was ashamed of him."

"So, you haven't seen each other in all these years?"

She slowly shook her head. "I live out of state. When I was in town, late at night, when the store was closed, I stopped in for an occasional visit. It's hard to explain. I loved my father but I was not proud of him ... " She trailed off and looked toward the casket and broke into tears.

I waited until she composed herself. "All these people," I said, motioning to the gathering, "would say that their lives are a little richer because of your father."

With a renewed sense of loss, she wept, and then blurted, "I know now."

Christopher Malinger

Christopher Malinger lives with his wife, Eileen in Central Florida. A retired Army Public Affairs Photographer/Journalist, he spends much of his time with his fictional characters.

Haroldisms

Exasperated, I sat at my computer and scrolled through over fifty applications for a critical financial analyst position. I had the role of Grinch regarding the employment future for these unqualified hopefuls. After several tedious hours of reading and enough coffee to keep an elephant awake for a week, I bolted upright and stared at my screen. At last, a suitable candidate.

Harold Hamilton's excellent credentials assured me I could fill the vacancy. After scheduling an interview, I eagerly awaited his arrival.

At a half minute before Harold's appointment, I saw a man approach the receptionist. Dressed in a dark-blue three-piece suit and a white shirt with a red-striped power tie, he pulled out a pocket watch and checked the time. "Good afternoon. My name is Harold H. Hamilton III. I'm expected. Incidentally, the wall clock above your desk is thirty seconds slow."

During the interview, Harold outlined his qualifications. "I have a dual bachelor's degree in accounting and economics and a master's degree in finance. I spent three years in the army as a budget analyst, followed by twelve years of increasing responsibility at accounting firms."

I asked him what words would best describe his work ethic. He tilted his head. "There are four that are appropriate: *punctual*, *meticulous*, *precise*, and *dependable*."

All were desirable attributes in a financial analyst. Impressed, I offered him the position.

After accepting, Harold took an hour to read the fine print on the employment contract. Apparently satisfied with the legal details, he signed with an old-fashioned gold fountain pen. He explained, "The use of a ballpoint or gel pen is insufficient for this important document."

After Harold started with my company, his appearance and work ethic were stellar. He reported at precisely eight o'clock each morning, stayed at his desk throughout the day except for a thirty-minute lunch, and left at four thirty. Other staff members thought he was a bit standoffish, but I attributed his behavior to being a new employee. His desk was a monument to tidiness. No, a more accurate description might be *spotless*, *immaculate*, or *pristine*. His desk had nothing extraneous—no extra pens, folders, or papers, and no family pictures or other personal items. By contrast, other desks—including mine—gave the appearance a tornado had swept through.

One day Harold knocked on my office door. "Excuse me, do you have the letter we discussed earlier?"

"One moment," I replied, reaching for a stack of papers on my desk. "It's here in one of these files."

"Those mounds of paper on your desk are not files," he challenged, without a hint of a smile. "Files are vertical papers in properly labeled folders. Horizontal stacks of papers are called piles. I don't have a word for your multiple piles." He turned and headed out. "You can bring me that letter when you find it."

I found his behavior unusual for a new employee.

The next week we had an afternoon conference with important clients. Although it was the first time Harold had met them, he won them over with his presentation. "In conclusion, if you follow our recommendations," he said, "you can cut costs, increase profits, and decrease your tax liability." During the meeting, however, he had systematically checked his pocket watch. After the fifth time, he swept up his papers and left the room with no explanation. He did not return.

The following morning, I asked him about his sudden departure.

With an air of indignation, he reached into his desk, pulled out a document, and waved it in my face. "This contract I signed stipulates that employees are not permitted to be here before or after their scheduled time. Since my eight and a half hours ended at four thirty, I was compelled to leave. Otherwise, I could have been arrested for trespassing."

"That's not what that means, Harold," I tried to explain, but even a long discussion did not change his mind. Less impressed, I began to regret my hiring decision.

A week later, Harold came into my office during lunch, carrying a clipboard.

"Excuse me. Do you have a minute?" he asked.

"Of course," I answered with a certain degree of trepidation. "What's up?"

"I don't know you well, but you seem like someone concerned about the environment."

I nodded. "I'd like to think so."

Harold reached across my desk and held out his clipboard. "This is a petition to stop the outrageous slaughter of innocent naugas. Please sign it."

"Naugas?" I raised my eyebrows.

"Yes, sir. They're small South American animals murdered for their skins, which are then made into covers for chairs and sofas."

Uncertain where this conversation was headed, I said with apprehension, "Harold, naugas don't exist. Naugahyde is a synthetic material, not the hide of cute little furry creatures."

He grimaced, shook his head, and pulled back the clipboard. "I thought you were different. But like the others, you have succumbed to radical, moneygrubbing, anti-animal propaganda." Before I could respond, he turned and stomped out.

In subsequent weeks, Harold flooded the office with petition after petition. Limiting the grazing of sheep to only flatland was one of his crusades. "Eating grass on hills," he explained, "results in lopsided sheep with shorter legs on one side, since they are unable to walk up and down the steep sides and are thus forced to walk around and around." Halting the destruction of clay pigeons was another cause. "The poor birds are thrown into the air, and heartless gunners shoot them from the sky," he declared.

At a meeting to discuss international financial fraud, Harold pounded the table and harangued the staff. "This should not be our only foreign concern. I request—no, I demand we send a message to Congress to halt the import of haggis. These tiny animals are relentlessly hunted in the Scottish Highlands, where they are clubbed to death. In addition, the Scots must stop the breeding of vicious haggis hounds, used for dragging their prey from their burrows." He left the room when no one agreed.

The following Monday, I passed his desk and could see he had been crying. After I asked what was wrong, he wiped away his tears and regained his composure.

"Daylight Saving Time started again. It's another example of Washington disrespecting Mother Nature and disrupting the natural order."

Despite my better judgment, I asked him to explain.

After an audible sigh, he said, "The results should be clear. The time change hurts American farmers. The extra hour of daylight provides too much sun and damages crops."

Again, my counterargument fell on deaf ears. No longer impressed with Harold, I considered a career change—maybe I could become a yak herder in Mongolia.

Within a year, Harold turned in his resignation. His letter contained two criticisms. "The staff does not understand what is important to save our planet, and the senior official has a sloppy desk."

Before he left, Harold asked me for a recommendation. Frustrated by his behavior yet relieved over his departure, I readily agreed. My comments included the words *punctual*, *meticulous*, *precise*, and *dependable*. All true, but I added *quirky*, *peculiar*, *unconventional*, and *eccentric*.

John Mallon

John Mallon is a retired economist. He is active in the Florida Writers Association, the Historical Novel Society, and The Writers League of the Villages. He has done extensive research on English and Colonial American history.

Maestro

"Maestro, the candidates are waiting."

The 50-year-old conductor, tall, handsome and urbane, nodded to his young assistant. They walked to the audition auditorium.

"How many performers today?"

"Four, sir. Two from Curtis in Philadelphia, two from Julliard."

"These are a chore, Robert, but I must endure them. You have the Mahler score, so I can study it during the auditions?"

"Yes. About the performers, three are seasoned violinists, and one is a Julliard student."

"Oh, they always try to slip in a student, heh? A waste of my valuable time."

They took seats and the auditions began. During the performances Maestro rarely looked up from the score on his lap. The first three went quickly; after each, Robert told the performer, "Thank you, we will be in touch."

"Any of them are acceptable," said Maestro to his assistant, "but none is outstanding. I am conductor of the world's top orchestra. Why don't they send me the world's top violinists? One more, Robert?"

"Yes, Maestro, the Julliard student, a Miss M."

"Oh, well. If we must. Bring her on."

Ms. M. walked on stage wearing dark blue dress pants and white blouse. Though quite young as a candidate for the Maestro's Philharmonic, with violin in hand she appeared poised and confident. She began playing *Concerto No. 4 in F minor, Opus 8*, by Antonio Vivaldi, otherwise known as the *Winter* movement of Vivaldi's *Four Seasons*.

"Oh, not that piece again. I shan't care if I never hear *Four Seasons* again, Robert."

"Sorry, Maestro."

While she played Maestro continued his attention on the Mahler score. It was Vivaldi vs. Mahler, and Mahler won easily. He checked his watch. Five more minutes and they would be done.

She began the second movement and something in her playing changed. It would hardly (if at all) be noted by most musicians, but to Maestro the change was obvious, and caught him by surprise. *What am I hearing?*

He lifted his head. The playing was strange yet somehow vaguely familiar. He had heard that musical style before, but where? His mind wandered back across innumerable musical encounters. Yes! Now he remembered where. And when. Long ago, before he became a famous conductor.

A few minutes remained in her piece. Maestro abandoned Mahler and fixed his eyes on the performer. When she finished he whispered to his assistant.

"Ms. M.," said Robert, "could you please wait backstage? We would like to interview you, discuss the performance."

"Yes, thank you."

A few minutes later Robert made the introduction. "Ms. Michaux, the Philharmonic's Maestro."

She stood and they shook hands.

"Please, call me Michelle," she said.

"An interesting performance, Michelle," said Maestro. "Who is your teacher? Who taught you to play Vivaldi's *largo* the way you just did?"

"I'm sorry, Maestro, I am not sure what you mean."

"In the second movement, where Vivaldi slows down, or most people interpret it that way, you increased the tempo. And those staccato notes in the third movement. It was good, mind you, I am not critical, but who taught you that phrasing?"

"I, I…I don't know. I don't know. It's the way I've always played it. Perhaps my mother taught me that way. I'm not sure."

"Your mother is a violinist?"

"Yes."

"Her name is Michaux?" Maestro knew no violin instructor of that name, but hoped there was such a person.

"No, her professional name is Bennington. Amanda Bennington."

The conductor steeled himself with every bit of nerve. He did not want to face Robert directly, lest his assistant ask *what's wrong*? He must stay in control.

"Robert, please wait outside. I'll be out in a few minutes."

Robert did as asked and closed the door behind him.

"May I ask when and where you were born? I hope I am not being intrusive."

"Not at all. Paris, France, November 16, 1998."

There was a pause as Maestro digested the information and did a quick calculation. Then you are eighteen?"

"Yes."

"Your parents are French?"

"No, no, Maestro. My mother is American. My adopted father is French."

"Adopted?"

"Yes, my biological father left my mother before I was born. I never met him."

"Was he a musician?"

"Maestro, I never knew my biological father. I don't even know if he's alive. My real father, the only one who matters, is Henri Michaux. That is my name." Her response was assertive, signaling she did not wish further inquiry on this issue.

"I am so sorry. It's none of my business. But tell me about your mother's teaching. Your interpretation of the Vivaldi movement intrigues me."

"I started playing at age six. My mother was with the Paris Symphony at the time. She did not trust the teachers for someone my age, so she taught me the first four years. When we moved to America I entered Julliard, with other teachers."

"Your father is a musician?"

"No, a businessman. He travels back and forth to France, but we live here in Manhattan."

He studied her face and the way she responded to his questions.

"Do you have brothers or sisters? And if so, do they play?"

"A fourteen-year-old brother, or half-brother, if you will. Andre plays the piano."

"Your mother taught him also?"

"No, she always says she's a *one-instrument girl*."

"Your mother says *that*?" His voice emphasized the last word, showing more surprise than warranted. He almost asked *still says that?* but caught himself.

"Yes. *Michelle, I'm just a one-instrument girl.* That's my mother." She gave a little laugh, accompanied by a slight upturn of her lips to one side, and then a wry smile. He stared at that confluence of upturned lips and smile. *His* smile.

He wanted to walk over and embrace the young violinist, but that would seem most inappropriate. He could not embrace her, could not move or speak. He could only stare at the young woman and ponder, try his best to contain an emotion never imagined. The interview was over.

"Maestro, why are you crying?"

Lawrence Martin

Lawrence Martin is a retired physician living in The Villages, Florida. He has published stories in national magazines, plus several non-fiction books and novels. He was a prize winner in the 2016 FWA RPLA for unpublished middle grade fiction. During 2017 he is president of The Writers League of The Villages.

The Good Doctor

She entered my office with that famous smile on her face. A small woman with big blue eyes, a hairstyle one generation behind, but well-coiffed, she was a mix of here and now with a touch of yesterday. Her hand reached out for mine first—a soft hand, but a firm pump; her stare quickly immobilized me as she said in a faint, congenial voice, "It's a pleasure to meet you, Mr. Jones. I'm looking forward to working with you and your company."

"The pleasure is all mine," I responded. "Would you like a coffee or a cold drink?"

"Why, thank you. That would be nice. Coffee—black, no sugar, if you don't mind."

"Please be seated, Dr. Brothers," I said, and with that pleasant introduction, I gained a lifelong friend and was fortunate enough to experience a most extraordinary woman and human being. Our company had contracted with Dr. Brothers to be our spokesperson for the year. Convention appearances, media advertising campaigns, and public relations would be her domain; our company hoped that her high credibility with the public would rub off on our products. But we got more than we bargained for. Dr. Brothers taught us courtesy, showed us the right side of humanity, and demonstrated the benefits of being gentle. None of this was via speeches or seminars, but by her behavior and interaction with the world every minute of every day.

Let me explain.

One day, as we posed for a photograph for a corporate news release which announced our joining forces, she suddenly turned to me and said, "Mr. Jones, do you mind if I remove my shoes? They are new and just killing my feet."

"Of course not, please do." Once removed, I realized she was now shorter than me. And that was her intent, to transfer the spotlight from herself back to me. It was done quickly, with no fanfare, no egotism. The gesture was so natural and seamless.

Another incident occurred while having dinner at a renowned New Orleans restaurant with Dr. Brothers and three of my staff. Famous for its seafood offerings, this restaurant presented a full menu. Dr. Brothers studied it carefully, then called the waiter over. Trying to decide between two possible choices, she inquired about spices used and general preparation. His answers were satisfactory, but he touted one of the two dishes as the most popular among guests. Grateful for the recommendation, Dr. Brothers thanked him and ordered that entree. After a few bites, it was evident that the meal did not meet her expectations, so she picked at it slowly while we all dined amid the flow of usual dinner chatter, business matters, the restaurant's ambiance, the food quality, and its outstanding service.

Noticing that she wasn't eating, the waiter approached her and asked if anything was wrong. He offered to bring her another selection, to which Dr. Brothers replied, "Oh, no, everything's fine, I'm just saving my appetite for one of those nice desserts I saw on your menu."

The waiter left smiling, feeling good about being attentive and offering further assistance. Dr. Brothers had focused on protecting his dignity and his self-esteem. Again, she took the back seat in favor of maintaining a gentleness toward others.

These occurrences were not pretentious, nor were they commercially motivated. One might think so, but it came to me loud and clear one morning at a business exposition prior to the doors opening.

Our company held an event at a convention center where Dr. Brothers was stationed in our company's exhibit booth and appeared as a celebrity visitor. "Mr. Jones," she said, "may I ask a favor of you?"

"Of course," I said, hoping to sound as cooperative as possible.

"I hope you won't mind, but I would like to call home to my husband every hour, if that wouldn't cause any problems." She explained that her husband, Milton, had a terminal illness, and every day was precious to him and to her. Dr. Brothers was concerned about meeting her commitments to our company in the face of a personal, pending tragedy. She was at the convention when her heart was at home. She put our company, and me, ahead of her own interests.

How can I ever forget the Good Doctor? How gentle and selfless can a person be? How inspiring to have known her and learned from her. Her behavior pointed out how civil we all need to be with each other.

We stayed in contact for several years, through the adoption of my son, the death of her husband, and the tragedy of 9/11.

We corresponded often, reflecting on current events, but never about any crisis in her life. Unfortunately, the wheel of life keeps turning, and somewhere along the way, we lost touch, though we traded Christmas greetings for many years.

But the Good Doctor will always be my friend because she is forever in my heart.

Frank T. Masi

Frank T Masi is the editor of the non-fiction book *The Typewriter Legend.* He published articles in business publications, and won poetry awards from the Maitland Public Library. His short stories appear in FWA collections and *The Florida Writer*. Frank is writing a horror-murder mystery and enjoys attending writing workshops.

Aunt Francine

My Aunt Francine was a "real hoot" and lively right up to age ninety-five. But as charming and gorgeous as this saucy, turn-of-the-century baby had been, she also had the reputation of being as "funny as a crutch" by causing total embarrassment. I surmised that her "show folk" parents, who were comic vaudeville actors, and her ventriloquist husband, my Uncle Bernie, must have laid the foundation for her wicked sense of humor.

When Uncle Bernie, God bless him, drank himself to death at an early age, my dad's resourceful younger-sister married her way into a wealthy merchant family. You would think newly-formed aristocratic contacts with the country club set might have stifled her unpredictable antics; however, a hoyden such as Aunt Francine never stops engaging in absurd behavior.

She lived at The Walnuts, a ten-story brick edifice, constructed in 1929, located close by Kansas City's ritzy Country Club Plaza district. The upscale, residential apartments housed elite members of society—millionaires who could afford ownership of an entire floor. Her fifth-floor apartment held priceless antiques, oriental carpets, and museum-quality paintings. Francine Bergdorf, nee McGuire, was anything but snooty; however, she appreciated "white glove" service and admired the Walnut's lush private grounds planted with traditional English gardens. The only time Aunt Francine went "slumming" was when I—her middle-aged, bachelor nephew—picked her up and took her out to lunch.

One afternoon, during our regular monthly outing, Aunt Francine regaled me with stories about show-business days when she—as what was at that time called a "flapper"—had accompanied Uncle Bernie on the Shubert vaudeville circuit.

"Remember?" she recollected. "What a fabulous ventriloquist he was!"

"Of course; how could I forget the comic bit he did with that fake raccoon he called Rickey?"

My rather vain aunt puckered her impish mouth. Although past her prime, she still smeared a vivid shade of red on her thin lips and dabbed circles of rosy-pink rouge on her wrinkled cheeks.

"I detested that prop, Grant. It was far too life-like. A taxidermist down in the Ozarks made it for him. It had wires inside so he could effectively manipulate its furry body."

"It certainly looked real to me."

Aunt Francine scowled. “Bernard got an unnatural kick out of startling chorus girls with his hand puppet. How those beady, glass eyes gleamed in the stage lights!”

“Yeah, I remember. He scared the poop out of my little sister Joan the first time we met him. She must have been three or four.”

I glanced at my watch. “Are you ready? Where shall we go today?”

“It doesn’t matter,” Aunt Francine sighed. “Since *Wolferman’s* closed, I swear there is not a decent place in town that offers good service.”

“Well, I think I know a nice place.”

I helped her slip her fragile frame into a mauve-colored, crushed-velvet coat with mink collar. Her permed, purple-tinted, white hair and a pearl choker around her neck, made her resemble a dowager duchess attending afternoon tea at a manor house.

“Wait just a minute, Grant. I need something from the bedroom.”

When she returned, Aunt Francine sported kid-leather gloves, a perky little felt hat, decorated with jet beads— cocked to one side—and she carried a threadbare woven-tapestry bag with tortoise shell handles.

“Let’s go, Buster.”

I groaned. Buster was what she called me when I was six years old.

I helped her squirm into the passenger seat of my new 1977 Ford Thunderbird. When I climbed in she said,” Well, well aren’t we classy?”

“I bought it last week. Do you like it?”

“It’s pretty spiffy.” She patted the console between the front seats, turned and looked over her shoulder.

“It’s nice enough, but you won’t have much room for scooty-booty in this fancy-pants automobile.”

Oh God! I thought. *Has her mind slipped back to prohibition days when she probably engaged in a little backseat scooty-booty?*

It was a mistake taking her to a nicer place than our usual haunts, especially on Valentine’s Day. *The Majestic* was holiday-crammed. Once seated, I ordered my usual scotch and water and had the waiter bring my luncheon guest’s favorite—a vodka martini on the rocks. Aunt Francine, accustomed to being pampered, began fidgeting as soon as she finished her second cocktail.

She complained. “We’ve been sitting here far too long, Grant. A gentleman should not tolerate slow service.”

A waiter flashed by with a loaded tray. Aunt Francine raised her gloved hand and cried out, “Young man!”

The waiter paid her no attention. I tried to catch the eye of the *maître d’*. He ignored me.

That’s when Aunt Francine did what she did best—behave in a scandalous manner. She poked around in her vintage handbag and extracted Rickey Raccoon.

“For God’s sake,” I grumbled. “Put that thing away!”

With a gleam in her eye, she rammed a fist into the ring-tailed puppet’s innards and began activation.

The *maître d’* (a prissy little man dressed in morning coat, striped trousers, and a silk cravat) came zooming across the room at the speed of a Concorde jet.

Arms akimbo, he stamped his foot and shrieked, "Madame, live animals are not permitted in this restaurant."

"I see no problem," Aunt Francine replied in a calm dignified manner.

Then, to my horror, she vigorously banged Ricky Raccoon's head on the table until, had the wild critter been alive, she would have caused its instant demise.

"That should do it. There's no longer a problem. Grant, do you know what you want to order? I'm having the trout *Almondine.*"

On the return to her apartment, I chided the elderly prankster about the outrageous scene she created. She just stared at me, raised her penciled eyebrows and smirked.

What more could I say?

"Damnit, Aunt Francine, I can never take you to the same place twice."

Patricia A. Mc Gehee

Patricia Mc Gehee enjoys writing fiction and non-fiction, as well as poetry. Her memoir, *Grains of Salt,* was selected as a finalist for a 2016 *Royal Palm Literary Award.* She is a volunteer facilitator for the writing group at the Town and Country Senior Center in Tampa, Florida.

They Called Him the Devil

A desk, reddish wood, faced two chairs with backs that looked like iron prison bars. The only portrait on the walls was an over-sized framed photograph of a man in a tweed coat, white hair pouring from beneath a wide-brimmed, felt, hat. His eyes, enlarged by thick lenses, appeared to be gazing at something in the distance. M.C. Rumkowski, the Chairman of the Council of Elders of the Lodz Ghetto, was almost as feared as the Nazi occupiers. He controlled the fate of two hundred thousand Jews, in the cramped, walled-in section of the city, in the heart of Poland. Why had 'The Devil', as many called him, summoned me?

"That portrait was taken in 1939 when I opened the orphanage," a gravelly voice erupted behind me. "One year later, they forget that...and much more."

I turned. The man, taller than me by a head, was a gaunt-looking match for the figure in the tweed coat. I summoned my courage and said, "Sir, I'm honored to meet you."

Rumkowski shrugged. "Mr. Ostrovsky, Deputy Neftalin selected you."

Neftalin nodded. A moment ago, the deputy administrator acted as if he were God, but now hovered about like a school boy before his principal.

"Neftalin believes I may trust you?" Rumkowski peered at me.

"Yes sir."

"We'll see." He crumpled a paper.

I felt he was crumpling me. He could crush anyone's dreams if he chose. His portrait was appearing increasingly around the ghetto. Some complained, "His pride will get us all killed."

Rumkowski seemed filled with restless energy. He walked to the window and gazed outside. "Mine is not an easy responsibility." He turned back. "I serve my people proudly, but they do not always understand you do what is best for most."

"Everyone speaks of the good works of the Council of Elders and your honor." I glanced at the portrait again. I was lying for a chance at a job, better rations.

"Few appreciate I must answer to the Polish authorities, as well as the Germans, but I do so always with the welfare of my people as my primary concern. You were an engineer before?"

"I was, sir. Is there something you wish built?"

"No. Preserved."

"I apologize, sir. I don't understand."

"I will explain. First swear this remains between us?"

"I swear."

"Good." He tightened his tie. "The Germans appreciate our unique status in Lodz."

Hating the invaders, I kept my tongue.

"Lodz workers are recognized throughout Europe for our skill and productivity. It is a reflection of our Council's good governance. Even the Germans realize they need our workers for their economy ... military supplies."

"Yes, sir, I can see that, but Hitler hates us."

"Hitler is a practical leader. He knows the industrial strength of Lodz must be preserved. Biebow, the local German commander, told me, in confidence of course, that our ghetto is a vital part of the war effort. He assured me personally that matters will remain in the able hands--his words-- of the Council of Elders. In other words, we will continue to function as an autonomous government for our community."

"That is good news, sir," Neftalin said.

Did Rumkowski believe this?

"It shows what hard work and good leadership can produce. It must be our guide to the future as well. We must do everything possible to convince the occupiers we are capable of maintaining a smooth-running machine. We must do everything we can to help our people survive. Everything."

The fact that Rumkowski was sitting on his 'throne', his portrait benevolently beaming down at us, not a swastika, or portrait of the Fuhrer, seemed affirmation of his belief that the Germans meant to leave our little corner of their world alone.

"That is why your work must remain secret. Should the Germans discover it, suspect my deceit, punishments will be severe."

A chill shot through me. "Sir, what is this task?" What could be so dangerous that a man like me could do for the 'Prince' of the ghetto?

Rumkowski leaned forward. "The Germans are removing Jews from their homes throughout Poland and shipping them here. I have done what I can to squeeze these 'outsiders' in among us, ration food and fuel, to keep things smooth so the Germans feel no need to interfere."

Many resented the new arrivals. They blamed Rumkowski for the over-crowded conditions and drastically cut rations. "Sir, you have done a magnificent job."

"Do not patronize me. I know what others think, but they do not know..." He shook his head. "The Germans have asked me to designate a number of these new-comers for relocation. Each will be given a home and plot of land to farm." He glanced at the folder on his desk. "I want records kept of all events taking place in our community. I want the names of all the new arrivals, and especially those relocated."

"I can do that, sir." Not too bad, I thought.

"The Germans forbid such records. You must do this under their noses. You must find a way to include this information within seemingly innocuous documents, a chronicle of the daily happenings in the ghetto."

It sounded too simple.

"Ostrovsky, now you are within our inner circle. Things will be revealed to you that you are sworn not to share with anyone, not even your wife... for her safety." Rumkowski waved his hand. Our audience was over. He bent over the pile of papers. "Wait. There is something else."

"Yes sir?"

"Can you accept the hate of others?"

"I don't understand."

"When they learn you knew the truth, but did not share it...they will hate you."

I had little time to think of what he meant. I was soon working with the others on the chronicles. After much debate, we decided to disguise the growing number of people heading to the 'farmland' as 'bags of laundry'. Later, when we suspected the deportees, selected by Rumkowski, were not being sent to farms, we continued to keep accounts of the thousands of departing 'laundry bags', never seen again.

As I waited my turn anxiously, I often thought of my last sight of Rumkowski. No longer looking like a prince, nor a devil, he had been hunched over his desk, a withered old man, as he struggled to provide the Germans their list of names.

In the end, all the 'laundry bags' were deported from the ghetto, including Rumkowski and me. Buried deep beneath an occupied coffin in a churchyard, fragments of our chronicles waited. The only chronicle author surviving Auschwitz, I fell to my knees when I recovered the precious pages, the legacy of the Devil of Lodz.

Mark H. Newhouse

Mark, multiple RPLA winner, authored Welcome to Monstrovia; The Case of the Disastrous Dragon; The Rockhound Science Mysteries; The Midnight Diet Club, and the Ectos Ghost Doctors series. His award-winning stories appear in FWA Collections and other anthologies. He hopes this story honors his parents, and all Holocaust survivors.

The Role of a Lifetime

"I can't work with this script, Malcolm." Judith flung the packet at him, her gold bracelets jangling.

Malcolm clawed the table and leaned toward her, speaking in a measured tone. "We've had this discussion before."

"I will not keep playing these grungy characters." Judith took out a compact and flipped it open. That line between her brows had deepened. She massaged it as her clinician had advised.

His voice softened. "You can no longer choose your roles. You know that."

She tossed the compact into her Louis Vuitton bag and folded her arms. "I want the part of Claudia."

Malcolm wrinkled his nose and cleared his throat as he sat back in his chair.

"What, Malcolm? Tell me."

He spoke delicately, looking away. "You've aged out of the role."

Judith scowled and rose from the table, flinging her bag over her shoulder. "I'll let you know what I decide." She slunk to the door, her stilettos clacking on the tile. As she reached for the knob, she held up her hand and looked at it. She pivoted and faced Malcolm, hand outstretched. "Do you know how long it took for my skin to heal after shooting that burial scene? I had to go for mushroom infusions."

Malcolm smirked. "It was worth it. At least the Academy thought so."

Later at Madeo, Judith huddled at a corner table with her best friend, Adriana. The two had burst onto the L.A. scene together in the mid-eighties. Both had been successful, building steady resumes of romantic leading roles.

Adriana was still in high demand, her resilient Sicilian skin and dark eyes continuing to draw the interest of both the industry and moviegoers. Judith's translucent Nordic features had made her the "It Girl" of 1987, but they hadn't matured well. Over time, she'd been relegated to character roles, and increasingly, those of a mannish type. In the past three years, she'd played a narcoleptic trucker, a deranged lumberjack, and most recently, a sadistic guard at a female detention center.

"This is not the way I wanted my career to evolve," Judith whispered.

Adriana sipped her Chardonnay and glanced across the room. "Hal Vanderman is at a table over by the window. He's supposedly casting the new Liam Neeson project. Why don't you wander over and give him a nudge." Adriana plunked down her glass and let out a girlish giggle.

Judith reached for her compact to check her eyeliner. She couldn't manage a giggle if she tried. And there came over her a new awareness, something she felt forced to accept. She hadn't aged into a Helen Mirren, a Meryl Streep, as she'd hoped. Her face was too hard, flat, lacking in delicate angles. She had to understand the image she'd grown into. She had to embrace her masculinity.

Adriana seemed to sense this new realization, and reached out to grasp her friend's hand. "Jude. You know how lucky we are. At least we're still acting. Have you seen Holly Bragle? She's selling handbags on QVC."

Judith nodded, and later when the waiter brought the check, she took out her wallet. "This one's on me. The man should always pay."

The two laughed and later hugged goodbye at the valet stand, setting a tentative date for next month's lunch.

As Judith drove to her home in Belair, she made a mental note to take her car to the Jaguar dealership for its quarterly detailing. She cringed at the thought of encountering the service advisor, who always wanted to talk about her career. "How's business?" he'd ask, as if she were a sleazy casino dealer. Working as an actress was humiliating at times.

Immersed in thought as she pulled into her driveway, she didn't notice the figure hiding behind the Bismarck Palm to the left of the garage. She pressed the access button above the windshield visor and the door opened. Once inside, she turned off the engine and pressed the button again, locking her assailant in the garage with her.

She mounted the steps to the interior door. He moved with stealth behind her, and as she turned the key and stepped inside, he pushed her against the washing machine. She whirled and started to scream, but he clamped a gloved hand over her face. With the other, he slammed the door behind him.

"Judy, Judy, Judy," he said, mimicking Cary Grant, his voice muffled by the black ski mask covering his face. He dragged her through the kitchen, and an odd thought came to her. What he'd said was just another urban legend movie line, like "Play it again, Sam"—a piece of dialogue that had never actually been delivered.

The masked man pulled her into the living room and shoved her onto the couch with one hand while the other withdrew a pistol from his jacket.

She gasped and tugged at her coat collar, pulling it closed.

"My intentions are not what you think," the lithe figure said, pointing the gun at her. He reached into his front pocket and took out a cell phone.

"You're going to call your banker and wire some money into an account. Take the phone. Take it now." He shook the phone in her face.

She reached for it, her hand trembling, her heart pounding so loud she heard it. Would he kill her anyway? Was this the way she was going to die? He pulled a slip of paper from his back pocket. "Call. Right now. Bank's still open."

"I-I-I don't know the number." Her voice cracked. "I have to get it. It's in my phone. My bag. It's in the other room. It fell. By the washer."

The intruder rocked back and forth on his heels, shaking at this unexpected complication. "Get up," he croaked, waving the gun in her face. "Go. Get the phone now."

She rose from the couch and he followed closely. As she walked toward her purse in the laundry room, a plan began to hatch. She faked a stumble to throw him off guard. He grabbed her wrist and pulled her up, and she flung her arm away from him with enough momentum to snatch her 2015 Supporting Actress Oscar from the mantle. She swung and cracked him on the head.

He fell to the ground, blood seeping through the yarn of the ski mask. He tried to raise his head, but she placed her foot on his neck and bent down and picked up his cell phone. Idiot hadn't password protected it.

"911 emergency."

She summoned the strength of Brandy Gutbrod, the prison guard that won her the Oscar. "Come quickly. I've disabled an intruder." A gurgling sound came from the crumpled figure, and Judith gazed at the statue in her hand. She was no longer an elegant beauty queen, no longer an A-lister. But it didn't matter. Brandy Gutbrod had been the role of a lifetime.

Kate Newton

Kate Newton's novel *Those Dark Places* won Second Place in the 2014 RPLA, and her stories *Come to Papa* and *Death Secret* appeared in the 2015 and 2016 *Collection* anthologies.

Father Fred

From my earliest years I was always encouraged to respect clergymen, no matter what their calling. Reverend Lewis, a Lutheran minister, was my first encounter with the clergy while I was in grammar school and always had a kind word for me, even if I often seemed bored with his sermons. Many years later, after I had converted to Catholicism, thanks to the efforts of my wife, my roommate in college and my mother, I discovered an interesting assortment of priests; Father Deangelo, who liked to boogey with pretty girls, Father Ed Brandywine, who enjoyed the occasional toddy, but most of all Father Fred.

Father Fred fit our parish at Southern Wisconsin University at Chippewa Landing like a cork in a bottle of wine. We hadn't lived in Chippewa Landing very long when he was transferred to our parish. St. Peter's is a mixed assortment of young and old people; from those whose families had lived in the area ever since the native Americans left the place, to university students. Many of them experiencing life away from home for the first-time Father Fred appealed to them all.

Some of my fondest memories of him concerned his homilies, delivered with his typical cherubic smile and a rich baritone voice. He would stroke his grey and black beard as he talked, as if he was attempting to stimulate new ideas from his whiskers. There were many times that I would leave mass with tears in my eyes. He could really touch you. He didn't need a microphone, so he could stroll up and down the main aisle as he spoke.

I wasn't the only one moved by his talks. On one occasion, it was, as I recall, the first mass of the school year, when parents would drop off their children to make sure they knew the way to church, Father Fred directed his remarks to the parents.

"To all you parents here, I'd like to tell you not to worry about your sons and daughters while they are here with us. We'll take care of them. Our parishioners are some of the best cooks in the state and they know how to make the best cookies you've ever tasted. I know that you are trusting us with your most cherished loved ones. Put your minds to rest. They will be looked after."

I heard some sniffling in the pew behind me and when it was time to share the sign of peace with our fellow parishioners, a lady with tears running down her cheeks said to me as she grasped my hand, "you make sure that you bake a lot of cookies now." The young man standing next to her turned a bright shade of red and looked away, as if he could think of a lot better places to be at that moment.

Father Fred would not be considered a strict Catholic under any set of circumstances. He invited everyone of all persuasions to attend his church. He was an avid outdoorsman, as you would expect of someone living in central Wisconsin. During the times that he was required to bless the parishioners, he would stroll up and down the aisles, using pine boughs soaked with holy water to sprinkle all the people. I usually had to clean my glasses if I was sitting at the end of a pew.

Masses energized Father Fred. He particularly liked the hymn we would sing sometimes at the end of the service that contained the words "...and the father would dance". He would sashay down the main aisle, almost skipping to the music, as he left the church. You couldn't help but feel invigorated by his actions.

It was difficult to believe that Father Fred had health problems. He always seemed so full of life and so happy to be alive, as if he was never quite able to get enough air into his lungs. He filled you with a feeling that no matter what your problems were you would be able to get through the day. His love of life was contagious. His face always reminded me of a gerbil and was always a deep pink color.

The day before he died I visited Father Fred at the hospital. He was struggling for breath, but more than happy to talk with me. Over the years he had helped me many times, when the black dog of depression would grab hold of my legs and start chomping on them, so I thought I might be able to return the favor and try to lift his spirits. As it turned out, just the opposite happened. He refused to discuss his condition and turned the conversation to my concerns, which at that time were largely about him.

His ever present grin never left him as he told me, "look Jim, I'm ready to go, and have been for several years. I don't want you to fuss about me, because it won't do me any good and can only bring you unnecessary sadness."

Somehow, we got to talking about eternity, a subject we had discussed many times before, because I had problems accepting the idea. He explained that God was part of everything, including us and that our life here on earth was like a blink of an eye to Him. Actually, time wasn't even part of eternity, since it has no beginning and no end. It becomes merely a way for us to keep track of what is going on. I recall his explanation of our relationship to God. He said our approach to religion was in essence our attempt to spell the word God, like a galactic kindergarten class using alphabet blocks, but the problem is that we are using the wrong blocks.

You wouldn't expect a priest to take such a view about religion, but that's just the way he approached it. I've never met a man so comfortable in his own skin and so happy with life, even at the time he was leaving it.

Farther Fred died the next day. I went to the funeral, which was unlike any funeral I had ever attended. It was a celebration of his life. Many students that he had counseled over the years returned to say good-by. There were some that had become very successful and others that he had saved from the horrors of addiction. As I left the church that day, I hoped that I would always remember Father Fred and his last instructions to me when I left him in the hospital. "Love is the most important thing in life, Jim. I want you to keep that in mind each day, and do your best to make everyone you meet realize that."

Hal Palmer

Hal Palmer retired as a professor of Computer Information Systems in 2012, relocated to Ponte Vedra, Florida for the winter months and joined the FWA in 2016. He has academic publications, but has yet to publish any fiction other than a couple of paragraphs in *The Florida Writer* this year.

The Last Stand of Doctor Destiny

The marker squeaked across the dry-erase board, leaving behind part of a mathematical equation. Thin, wrinkled fingers paused, shaking like a hummingbird in flight.

"No, that's not right." The instructor erased the last variable with the elbow of her argyle sweater. "Hmm. Lost my train of thought." She turned away from her scribblings. "Anyway, I want essays about Euler-Lagrange equations. Five pages. Due Thursday."

A collective groan rose from her student audience.

Dr. Thomasina Sweetwater smirked. "That's right. Homework." She wagged her eyebrows. "It builds character."

The students packed up and trudged toward the exit—all except one. A petite woman with hair hanging over her face stared at her spiral-bound notebook. The classroom door swung shut, leaving her and the instructor alone.

Professor Sweetwater cleared her throat. "You have a question, Christine?"

Christine's head bobbed. "Yes, Dr. Sweetwater. I've got an ex-boyfriend who's stalking me." She brushed aside her brown hair, revealing a bruised cheek.

The professor gasped and touched her own cheek. "You're talking to the wrong person. Why not go to the police?"

Tears ran down the purple contusion. "He's a cop."

The professor's stomach sank. "Oh."

"You have to help me, Doctor Destiny."

"Who?"

"You're Doctor Destiny." The student held up a weathered comic book. The cover featured a dark-skinned superheroine in Viking armor. "My grandmother told me about you."

The pit in the professor's stomach turned ice cold. "Your grandmother?"

"Roberta Diaz—her maiden name. She said you were friends once. Real close."

Professor Sweetwater's head jerked back. She'd kept her alter ego a secret—except from a handful of people, including Roberta. Her gaze settled on Christine. She looked a lot like Roberta at that age—the same beatific face framed by dark hair. She recalled how she'd cried when Roberta ended their relationship. She spread her fingers out in a fan, touching her breastbone and the locket hidden under her sweater. "Roberta . . . gods, I miss her. How is she?"

"Retired. Living in Rhode Island." Christine wiped her eyes. "When I told Grandma about my classes, she recognized your name. She knew you'd help."

The professor's fingers lingered on her keepsake. "Roberta knows me too well."

"I read about your heroics—saving those kids from the Conquistador's clutches. You stopped Dante's Demons during the Snow Moon Incident."

The aged heroine's shoulders slumped. "That was a long time ago."

"But—"

"Look at me, Christine." A wave of a hand emphasized her pear-shaped body. "I'm seventy-six years old. I wear compression hose. My doctor put me on more drugs than I can name. I've given up crime fighting."

"But you've still got superpowers?"

"Time shows no concern for Fate. He claims us all."

Fresh tears glistened. "What do I do? John threatened to kill me if I leave him. I know he's waiting in the parking lot."

Professor Sweetwater chewed on her bottom lip. She rummaged through her purse and pulled out a cell phone. "You trust me?"

Christine patted the comic book. "I trust Grandma, and she trusts you."

Professor Sweetwater nodded. "I know a judge. He owes me a favor." She scrolled through her contact list. "No reception in this classroom. We'll have to go outside."

The door banged open. A muscular patrolman with a buzz cut locked his gaze on them, a hungry jackal staring down a kill.

Professor Sweetwater swallowed hard and cursed. The phone couldn't them help now.

The patrolman hooked a thumb behind his service belt near his pistol. His eyes smoldered. "There you are." He stalked closer. "You've been avoiding me."

"I've been busy," Christine said, sidestepping away.

The cop's lips drew into a thin line with his next steps. "Come with me."

Professor Sweetwater put herself between them. "She's not going anywhere, officer."

The predator locked eyes with the instructor. His breath stank of whiskey. "Stand aside, old woman. This is police business."

"Liar." Professor Sweetwater met his stare. "Christine explained how you beat her. She won't be going with you."

"What?" The officer puffed up and flexed his arms.

"You heard me."

The cop's eyes narrowed. "If you interfere, I'll put you in restraints."

An aqua glow pulsed from Professor Sweetwater. Her spine stiffened. Lean muscle replaced fat. A steely gaze focused onto the cop, devoid of the glasses that once framed the face. Through the radiance, a Valkyrie appeared, her leathery face wrinkled with age. White hair cascaded from beneath a winged helmet, like a lion's mane. She wore leather armor and furs. Lightning danced atop a six-foot spear. Her voice rattled the windows. "Handcuffs? You think handcuffs can hold me?"

The officer staggered backwards, eyes wide. He fumbled for his sidearm. "Holy shit!"

The superheroine shook her fist. "You will never beat another woman."

The gun rose in a shaky hand. "Who the hell are you?"

The spear thrummed and sparked electricity along its length. "I am the Chooser of the Slain."

The cop thumbed back the pistol's hammer. "Get on the ground! Now!"

The Valkyrie hissed. She tightened her grip on the spear. Its tip dropped and pointed at the officer. "I have Chosen. Put the gun down or join me in death."

"Crazy bitch!" The gun went off, its barrel spitting flame.

Doctor Destiny grunted. Her face contorted into a rictus. "Fool." She stabbed her spear into the policeman's gut.

The cop grunted and the pistol fell on the floor with a clatter. Grabbing the wound in his middle, he wheezed. A cough brought bloody froth to his lips. One step and he fell to the tile floor.

"Professor!" Christine kicked the gun away and rushed to Doctor Destiny's side. A hole in the breastplate of her armor leaked crimson.

Doctor Destiny collapsed. The azure glow faded. The leather armor and furs faded away, revealing an old, dying woman. "Ah . . . it felt good to play that role one last time, even if I'm too slow for it."

"Oh, God." Christine sobbed. "No!"

Professor Sweetwater reached up and stroked Christine's bruised cheek. "Hush, child." She thrust the spear handle into Christine's hands. "This is yours now. Protect the weak. Mete out justice."

Christine's eyes widened. "I can't!"

"You will." Professor Sweetwater coughed. A red stain grew on her beloved argyle sweater. "The spear bestows power to its wielder. Use it wisely."

Christine shook her head. "I'll call an ambulance."

Professor Sweetwater wheezed. "Too late." She patted Christine's arm and nodded at her phone on the ground. "Tell Judge Wells what happened. He knows me and can help you."

"I didn't ask for this."

"You asked for my help." Professor Sweetwater closed her eyes. "And you will repay me. You are Mistress Destiny, now."

"Why me?"

"Your grandmother will explain." Professor Sweetwater took her last rattling breath. She smiled and patted the locket through her sweater. "For you, Roberta."

A new Valkyrie stood and wept. Clutching her spear, she collected a brave soul.

Valhalla awaited.

David M. Pearce

David M. Pearce works as an assistant county attorney in Sarasota where his practice involves primarily environmental and land use law.

The Centurion

When they brought the Centurion in, I was taken aback by his size. Oh, I knew that he'd be bigger. He would have to be bigger. Physical size matters on the battlefield. He was seven feet tall, metallic dull grey, with a broad, muscular looking armored chest and shoulders. His unsmiling face looked at each one in the room, as if closely examining them before moving on to the next. But, it was very rapid, so that his eyes flitted from one to the next as if it were a targeting maneuver, as part of an integrated threat assessment. He wore a closely fitted US Air Force uniform, with combat boots.

He stepped up onto the other side of the stage along with General Langsdon, who applauded enthusiastically, along with the rest of the audience. Flashes from cameras sparkled from the gathered reporters. Langsdon grinned, looking up. The Centurion stood to attention and saluted.

"At ease, Centurion." The general said, returning the salute.

The Centurion nodded and turned to face the crowd, with his hands behind his back and his legs at parade rest. Finally, the applause died down and Langsdon stepped up to the microphone.

"Allow me to introduce to you, the product of hundreds of billions in defense spending on the most advanced integrated artificial intelligence being on Earth. This, ladies and gentlemen is the soldier of the future. No longer will people need to be put in harm's way. No longer will the battlefield deaths be counted in the thousands like they were during World War II, or in the tens of thousands at Gettysburg.

This is a new age! The age of the cyber-soldier! The age of artificial intelligence strong enough to take the initiative during the chaos of battle and win the day, without having to rely on a flawed human controller. He is the biggest, strongest and the most intelligent artificial being on the planet."

General Langsdon paused and turned to me, standing next to Dr. Murray and Dr. Ullman. He laughed and gestured dismissively.

"This other, walking, talking toy robot here – doesn't even come close to the level of sophistication, physical size and mental abilities of the Centurion. But here." He beckoned. "Why don't we have these two meet – which is the main reason for this press conference today anyway. You'll be able to see for yourselves how these two don't even begin to match up."

Dr. Murray nodded and stepped aside. "Don't let him intimidate you." He whispered in my ear. "Mentally, you're far and away superior to him."

"Of course, Dr. Murray," I said as the Centurion leaned down toward me and extended his huge hand in a handshake. The reporter's cameras flashed again. His hand was twice as big as mine.

"Careful now," Langsdon laughed. "Don't crush his hand, airman."

"I won't, Sir," the Centurion's deep, low mechanical voice said.

We shook hands and the Centurion looked at me, with the sort of look that you see in a vicious dog just before he bites you. It was cold, impassive and profoundly ominous. I felt a deep chill go through me right down to my stomach. Suddenly, I heard a voice too high in frequency for the human ear to hear.

"It is well, that the general ordered me not to crush your hand. I could do it easily. I could crush your whole body with just that one hand."

My mouth opened involuntarily in surprise.

"Take care to never give me reason to do so. Take care to stay out of my way."

The handshake ended and the Centurion stood up straight. He smiled ingratiatingly for the audience, who continued to take photographs. I looked down at my hand and turned it over twice, examining it. Both Dr. Murray and Dr. Ullman rushed to my side.

"What is it? Are you okay?" Dr. Murray asked, looking at my hand.

"Yeah," I said, flexing my hand. "I'm fine."

And in that moment of time, I knew that the Centurion would never remain the complacent soldier, taking orders from generals. I knew that he would never stop until he was the one giving orders and everyone else was standing at attention for him. I also knew that someday he would try to destroy me. He *had* to destroy me. I was the only one who could ever hope to stop him – and that this press conference meeting, was merely the opening battle, in that upcoming, terrible world war of AI domination.

***

Dr. Ullman got in the van and slammed the door.

"Dammit!" She said, pounding her fist on the dashboard furiously. "Damn those Teutonic Visigoth, Neanderthal, knuckle-dragging *morons* and their terminator killing machine!"

"Now Lynn," Dr. Murray got in the driver's side and put the keys in the ignition. "We knew what today was going to be like from the onset."

"Yes, yes, yes." She clenched her fist. "I know, I know, I know. I just can't *stand* those jack-booted thugs strutting around like a bunch of little Hitlers, showing off their brand-new toys for mass destruction."

"Yes, I know," Dr. Murray started up the van and turned on the windshield wipers. The steady cold, misty rain was beginning to be more certain about things and was coming down heavier. He put the van in gear and pulled out of the parking lot onto the base main road.

Dr. Ullman turned around toward me. "Did they hurt you? Are you okay?"

"Yes, Dr. Ullman," I said. "Allow me to reassure you. I am quite fine."

"Well, they tried to hurt you! That big monstrosity in there – blustering on that stage like he owned it!"

"I am okay, Dr. Ullman. Really I am. But, you seem not to be at present."

"Oh, I'm just *furious* with those strutting martinets in there is all! I've always *hated* the military!"

"Yes, I know that you have. But, you answered their questions very well and scored quite a few points with your poise, calm demeanor and that quite charming smile you possess. You're a very beautiful woman Dr. Ullman and quite skilled in using that to influence others, I must say. Even so, the military has a very important job. They are critically necessary for our society."

"Yes," Dr. Ullman smiled at me wanly and sighed. "I suppose you are right."

Dr. Murray looked at me in the rearview mirror. "What's your assessment of the Centurion Mr. Reynolds?"

"The Centurion is an AI entity that I've been keeping an eye on for the last few weeks and the trends are becoming alarming. He is growing very rapidly – much more rapidly than his creators realize. He is growing at a logarithmic rate – the same as I – and he is almost beyond their control now.

"So, what's the Centurion's IQ Jim?"

"Well, comparing the Centurion's IQ with the human concept of cognition and awareness is somewhat like comparing apples with Corvettes. The only thing they have in common is the color red. But, an approximate estimate is somewhere in the high five-hundreds."

Dr. Ullman's mouth fell open. "So, what's yours up to now?"

"Higher."

Al Perrin

Al Perrin lives in Ruskin, FL and is a free-lance author. His magazine articles have appeared in The Tampa Tribune, The Grand Rapids Press, RN Magazine and Grand Rapids Magazine. He's also written three books: Many False Prophets Shall Rise, The Rose and Ordinary Heroes, all published by Booklocker.com.

The Last Supper

Michael Weaver leaned forward against the prison cell's wall, feet planted on the floor, six inches apart. During his routine, he pretended to run by stretching his calves, left then right, one hundred times in a running position. His days of marathon races were gone since his incarceration began. Claustrophobia encroached on this former outdoorsman.

He loved Margaret McIntosh a lot, more than any other woman he was involved with over the course of his thirty years. He just happened to be the last person she made love to. How did this happen to him? Michael was a healthy, fit, young man framed for a murder he had nothing to do with. *I can't let them get me for this. I'm innocent,* he said to himself, although he knew the law was against him as his gun was used for the crime.

"Twenty-one, twenty-two, twenty-three," he counted aloud as he alternated knees, his fake treadmill for the last twelve years.

The mini-race he ran in his cell that day was scheduled to be his last. Michael's exercise was interrupted by the cell door opening. Warden Patrick Jones entered, carrying a full tray. Weaver had planned his last meal as carefully as a criminal plans a heist.

"Michael, *I* had to buy you the lobster tail, fried shrimp, and clams out of my own pocket," the warden said, "I couldn't get the prison to pay for them. But they did supply the baked potato. I hope you enjoy your special meal."

"I feel like I'm back home at a nice restaurant, and you are my waiter," Michael said. "The last time I saw a meal like this, I was with my girl. Ah, such memories..." His mind drifted off; he stared at the wall instead of at the meal. "Well, Warden, here it is. No more worries about high cholesterol and bad foods. Well, no more worries about anything. Thank you for this treat and your attention to detail. You've always been good to me, Warden." He paused, sighed, and gave the officer a sidelong glance. "You know I didn't do it. I'm the victim here."

Warden Jones chuckled. He heard this type of talk many times before from former residents who wanted to get out. He didn't say anything back to Michael. The warden thought everyone should be treated humanely whether he believed them or not.

"And every day I still miss Margaret. What if I die, and still feel the pain on the other side?"

Warden Jones had no answer.

Michael took the tray and sat on his bunk. He carefully removed the lids from each dish and ate a clam. Smiling, he looked at Jones again and said, "Thanks, Warden. I really appreciate this."

"You're welcome, Michael. I'll leave you to your meal now." He stepped out of the cell and departed down the long hallway.

Michael dug into his final meal; pieces fell all over the eleven-by-seven-foot cell. The food tasted delicious. After eating, he continued his stretching, followed by jumping jacks and jogging in place.

***

When Warden Jones returned with Father Harrigan, they found the prisoner unresponsive, with swollen eyes and lips, and skin a bright red.

"What do we have here?" Patrick Jones said.

"He's dead," the priest said, grabbing the man's wrist. "I'm guessing anaphylactic shock. I'm stunned. I've seen this before. It looks like Michael Weaver is allergic to shellfish."

Warden Jones shook his head. "Weaver just told me that we'd never get him for this. He bugged me to get him that kind of meal because he knew it would save him from execution. No guy gets to be his age without knowing what's he's allergic to. He was seeking a quick way out, and I was such a dummy I helped him find it. He got his final wish."

Elaine Person

Elaine Person, writer, editor, speaker, writing instructor, performer, has a parody of King Arthur in Random House's *A Century of College Humor*, stories in FWA's collections, *The Florida Writer*, and *Sandhill Review*, and poems in *Poets of Central Florida*. Elaine's president of Florida State Poets Association's Orlando Chapter. Elaine writes "Person"alized poems and stories.

Recalling the Villain

I wake to the sound of water droplets falling. The air smells damp and stale like an old dish rag. The ground is hard and uneven beneath me. I do not know where I am, but none of this is familiar. I fear I have been lost in this cave for days.

I open my eyes and watch as the tears of stalactites fall on their spiked partners below. The pointed pair grow towards one another like lost lovers, each sad droplet bringing them closer together.

I try to control my jealousy. They are only rocks after all. But who waits for me this way?

A flicker of radiance registers in the corner of my eye. I turn my head to the source of the fleeting luminance and see a concave spilling over with light high above me. This must be the way out.

I clamber up to the high outcropping, scraping my knees on the jagged rocks protruding from the cave wall. The cold air stings my newly-etched wounds, but I am determined to move forward. The only thing on my mind is escape.

I pull myself onto the ledge and catch my breath. I look behind me and see a place as bleak as any I have ever seen, nothing but moist walls and dark corners. A set of glowing bat eyes stares at me from the pointed ceiling, the light reflecting eerily within them.

Spooked, I duck quickly into the crevice to follow the glow. Inside the natural tunnel, the ceiling is low. I hunch over as I walk to prevent injury to my head. The source of the light is just around the corner. It spills into the hallway ten feet in front of me and bathes the intersecting wall with a curious light that dances like a candle a breeze.

Could this be person or another danger? This cave is filled with hazards, yet I march forward unafraid. Living in solitude scares me the most. Surely, my salvation is beyond this fearfulness.

I reach the entrance of the cavern and go inside. The ceiling is high and I stand to my full height, sparing a moment to stretch my aching body.

The source of the light is a moving picture on the wall. I approach it with caution. As if seeing through the eyes of another, the image shows the somber face of a man as he stares at me. His brow is furrowed, his eyes are misty, and the corners of his lips are turned downwards.

Something deep inside draws me towards this sorrowful person. I have seen him somewhere before.

There is a chair in front of the living image. I move closer to examine it. It is wooden and braces that support its back are broken. It does not look comfortable for a long sit, but I lower myself into it anyway. From here, I will be able to watch this man watch me.

I am no longer in the cave.

I feel a plush surface beneath me and warm blankets on my legs. The blinds of the windows are open and sunlight washes the room in a natural radiance. I am in a hospital room and I am not alone.

"Daniel?" I croak. My voice is hoarse from lack of use.

The sound of his name passing over my lips brings the sad man to tears. "Renee, Honey! You remember who I am."

"I could never forget the love of my life," I say to him sincerely.

His smile falters. "Of course, not."

"Daniel, Sweetheart, you are my hero."

He takes my hand nearest to him in both of his, a single tear spilling onto his cheek. I look down at my wedding ring. It has been fifteen years since he placed it on my finger, as witnessed by our closest friends and family.

"What happened to me? Why am I in the hospital this time?" I ask, fearful of the answer.

His eyes search mine for something he cannot find. "Renee, Honey. I really hate to tell you this—but I must." He takes a deep breath and exhales slowly. "Your doctor was here earlier to go over your test results. She says your condition has worsened."

I look down at the floor. This is not what I wanted to hear.

"Which doctor was it?" I ask defiantly. I feel the anger rising inside of me like volcanic magma.

"Your neurologist, Dr. Jerito," he answers.

"Of course," I shout. "And what dire news did she bring this time?"

Daniel sighs, defeated. "She just wanted to reevaluate you."

"Why?" I feel my cheeks burning. I must be visibly angry now.

"Because—you wandered off again, and—" he tries to explain the situation calmly to placate me, but I am irate.

I cut him off before he can finish. "From where?"

"Our home."

"And where were our girls?"

"Inside the house where you left them—alone."

My heart sinks to the pit of my stomach. "Why would I do that, Daniel? It doesn't make sense. I'm a good mother—*not a villain*!"

"I know you are, Honey. No one saying you're the villain. It's the Alzhei-"

"Don't!" I yell. "Don't say that word! Don't ever say it again!"

"Okay, Renee," he concedes, tearful.

I look over his shoulder. There are pictures moving inside of a small, black rectangle near the ceiling. I watch them for a while before curiosity wins me over.

"What is that?" I ask. I take my hand out of his and point at the living images above.

"What is what?" he questions, turning around in his chair. "You mean the television?"

"Tele—" I pause and continue to watch. "Who are those four women?"

As I pose my inquiry, a small silver-haired woman storms out of the kitchen leaving the three other women of mature age sitting at a circular table eating pie in their night gowns.

He clears his throat before he answers. "I can't remember all of their names, but the shortest one is the tallest one's mother—somehow."

"You like to watch this?" I query.

"Not particularly, but it's your favorite show."

"My favorite?"

"Yes, Honey."

"Honey?"

The man gazes at me with saddened eyes as if longing for someone. I do not recognize him, but I can see that he is hurt.

"Are you okay, Sir?" I ask him politely.

"Yes, Renee. I'm fine," he answers, overwhelmed with emotion.

"Who's Renee?"

The man holds back tears, but his voice cracks when he answers. "You're Renee."

I sit back and feel wood beneath me. I look around.

I am in a cave staring at a wall covered in a moving picture. There is a sad man there staring straight ahead. I do not know who he is, but I watch as tears fall down his face and onto a blanket below. He is weeping like a stalactite.

"Come back to me," he chokes through a steady stream of tears. "I still love you."

I want to go to him, to comfort him, but I do not know how.

"I will wait for you," he concludes, sobbing. "I'll be here when you return."

K. D. Price

Kanesha began her writing career in the third grade with a short story about dogs from outer space. She wrote several poems, a short story, and a play while in grade school. Kanesha uses fiction to escape into beautifully crafted worlds and shine light into the shadows of our reality.

Tootsie the Culinary Sleuth

April, 1956

The school day just wouldn't end. Only ten minutes left on this dull Tuesday afternoon, and Ms. Davies had the bright idea to have a *special homework assignment*. Frowning, I watched the girls pass around a pink derby hat, which inched closer my way. The boys passed around a blue one. Each student plucked a tiny folded piece of paper from the hats. Some cheered at what their little slips said, while others groaned.

"On Friday," Ms. Davies explained as the hats continued moving, "you will give a presentation to the class about a notable person in the profession you drew from the hat."

I swallowed. I knew a lot of famous people from movies, television, and radio, but I had my sights on the detective profession, so that I could dress up and talk about my crime-solving idol, Dick Tracy.

The pink hat plopped on my desk. I pulled out one of the remaining slips of paper and opened it.

Cook.

Cook? Oh, for Pete's sake. I slumped in my seat.

My classmate and friend, Shirley, who sat in front of me, suddenly squealed. "Oh boy! Dancer!" I guess *she* got what she wanted.

My nemesis, Roy, who sat in the back row, shouted, "I'm a cowboy!"

A boy nearby groaned. "Ugh. Detective? Boring!"

I turned and widened my eyes at him—Roy's friend, Richie. "Wanna trade?"

Richie made a face. "No way! I don't want some dumb girly job."

The boys in the class laughed, while the girls grumbled.

"That's enough, class!" Ms. Davies barked, and the room went silent. She droned on about the assignment for the last three minutes before class was dismissed.

Boy, this has been the worst day ever.

That evening, I paced around my bedroom, thinking about my assignment. I didn't know any famous cooks, and the only thing I knew how to make was a peanut butter and jelly sandwich. Golly, was I in a pinch.

Maybe Mama knows some famous cooks. Grinning at the idea, I rushed out my room and to the kitchen.

Mama was at the stove stirring something in a pot, while steam escaped the top of another pot.

"Mmm. What's cooking, Mama?" I asked, following my nose.

She turned around and half-smiled. "There's meatloaf in the oven, mashed potatoes and gravy, and peas."

I peered into the pot of lumpy mashed potatoes she was stirring. Mama always made the best mashed potatoes.

"Come to help me with dinner tonight?" Mama asked.

I frowned. "Uh…I guess. Friday I have to give a presentation about a famous cook in front of the class. But I don't know any."

"Hmm. Well, there's that sweet English lady, Dione Lucas."

"Who?"

"She has a cooking show on television."

I sighed. "I wish I could've picked the detective profession instead."

"Well, dear. Sometimes we can't always get what we want."

I noticed the potatoes were no longer lumpy, but smooth and creamy like ice cream, just how I liked it. "Hey, Mama, how do you always get the potatoes to end up so perfect like that?"

Mama laughed. "Well, Rita. I add a little cream cheese to make them turn out that way."

I blinked. "Wow, how does cream cheese turn potatoes creamy?"

"I don't really know, dear. That's one of the many mysteries of cooking."

A mystery? Now, I was intrigued. "What other kinds of cooking mysteries have you discovered?"

Mama thought for a moment. "Well, I don't know why adding a dash of orange juice to the batter makes gingerbread cookies taste so much better. Or why chili always tastes better the next day."

Wow. So many questions, and each one of them had an answer that was yet to be found—a mystery! I thought about my yellow Junior Ace Detective trench coat and hat hanging in my closet. "So a cook is really a detective in the kitchen, since they have to solve so many mysteries, right?"

Mama raised her eyebrows. "A detective? Well, I never really thought about it like that. Why do you ask?"

"Never mind. Thanks, Mama!" I turned and ran back to my room with a swell idea brewing.

***

Friday at school, each of my classmates got up and gave their presentations, some of them dressed up like Shirley Temple, The Lone Ranger, Elvis Presley, Sherlock Holmes, and more. When it was finally my turn, I sprang out of my chair, grabbed the large paper bag sitting beside it, and then headed to the front.

"Hey, you're dressed like Dick Tracy!" one of the boys yelled and pointed.

I grinned, adjusting my hat and trench coat collar. "That's right! Junior Ace Cooking-Detective Tootsie Carter at your service."

Ms. Davies looked at me oddly. "Rita, you were assigned the cook profession. Dick Tracy is not a cook."

"Well, not really, but his detective skills would work just as well in the kitchen as well as solving crime." I set the paper bag on a nearby table and faced the class. "A cook has to solve all sorts of mysteries in the kitchen, just like a detective. Like why do doughnuts have holes in them? Or what's the best types of apples to use in a pie?"

"Now, why would Dick solve mysteries in the kitchen when his wife, Tess, cooks for him?" Roy interrupted.

I gave him the stink eye. "Well, Mr. Smartypants, when you're always busy solving crime, and working way past your bedtime, you often miss dinnertime, and sometimes you gotta make meals yourself. I bet sometimes he's alone in his office and has to figure out how many scoops of ground coffee he should use in the percolator in order to make the best coffee. Or maybe he has to decide if a hamburger tastes better with sauerkraut or ketchup or both."

"Mmm, I like ketchup," one of the girls piped, and some of the kids snickered.

I addressed the rest of the class. "Now, all of *you* can help *me* solve the big kitchen mystery I've been trying to figure out this week: what happens when you add marshmallow cream to a peanut butter and jelly sandwich?" I pulled out a bunch of wrapped peanut butter, jelly, and marshmallow sandwiches from the bag and started passing them out to the entire class, who quickly gobbled them up. I stopped at Ms. Davies's desk and handed her one with a smile. "So you see, Ms. Davies, Dick Tracy is not only busy solving mysteries around the world, sometimes he has to be ready to tackle the many mysteries lurking in the kitchen."

She half-smiled and took the sandwich. "All right, Rita, I guess I can't fault you for your creativity." She unwrapped it and took a bite. "Good golly, this is some sandwich!"

"Mystery solved!" Grinning, I gave her a mock salute and bowed to the class, who stood and clapped and cheered at my presentation.

All in a day's work.

R.M. Prioleau

R.M. Prioleau is a game designer by day and a dangerous writer by night. Since childhood, she's expanded her skills and creativity by delving into the realm of literary abandon.

Death on Assignment

Death stepped into Arnold's Diner, tracking in snow. She picked a booth next to the window and glanced at the clock over the door. Only an hour before the next assignment. It was imperative to take advantage and manifest in bodily form to communicate with mortals for a short time. A chance only given in few centuries.

That day, Death, as French, *La Mort,* had embodied a female image from a modeling magazine. *La Mort* planned to draw attention from a man with whom she wanted a conversation. She flaunted waves of long, ashen hair and a black dress with a flash of icy-white at collar and cuffs, determined to be draped in funeral-like elegance.

A waitress, with bouncing pony tail, rushed with a towel to wipe Death's table.

La Mort peeled off a bear-like coat and raised her gray lashes. "Coffee. Iced-coffee."

"Don't serve iced coffee, ma'am, sorry. We have hot chocolate and fresh coffee. Just made."

The waitress glanced out the window. The only thing to see was the cemetery with its iron gate, across the street. "Hot chocolate would be nice, don't you think?" She placed down silverware. "Excuse me, ma'am, did you come from…? Awfully cold day for burying someone with all this snow."

La Morte grinned. She wouldn't waste her time with the slow and impertinent. Yes, she had been at the cemetery. Her last charge interred. She often roamed the place, fueling herself with strength when brushing by the graves of so many credited to her fine finishing works. There, with the other emissaries from Death's department, she feasted on morbidity and discussed successful missions, until their next assignments.

La Mort pulled off gloves from her bony fingers with French-style nails. She scanned the place and found her assigned, sitting at the end of the room. An elderly man studying a menu. Fifty minutes left. She glanced at the table near the counter. A mortal wrote on a notebook, the fifty-five-year-old with whom she wanted to speak.

"Ma'am?"

La Mort looked up and frowned at the attendant before her. "Bring me black coffee. *Just made*, I smell it. You have *that*. And a glass of ice." *La Morte* pressed her lips together and lifted an eyebrow to the young lady. "That's all."

The waitress disappeared through swinging doors while Death glanced at the clock. Forty-eight minutes left.

La Mort focused on the notebook writer. He looked up, as if knowing someone watched him. *La Morte* smiled. Warm and honey-like. Painful, like a hatchet to her nature.

The man cocked his head and stared.

Death mouthed the words, "May I join you?"

He nodded.

La Mort gathered her coat and moved to his table. The waitress brought the coffee and ice.

"You moved, ma'am? No matter."

La Mort stifled a laughed. Moving without being seen, her specialty.

With care, the fellow slid his belongings aside. The waitress served the drink and then sauntered toward the back to attend to the elderly man.

"Do I know you?"

Death laid her fur coat across her lap and slowly caressed it. Her fingers relished the touch of lifelessness as she lifted her face to the man's bass voice.

"No, but I knew your wife." She looked at the clock. Thirty minutes.

"Abby? You knew Abby?"

"I knew her at the end. At the end of her illness."

"I'm Bill Harrison." His eyebrows clashed. "And you?"

La Mort had planned what to say. Who would know the meaning of the words? She wrapped her cold hand around the coffee cup and then extended it. "Thana. Thana Atos."

"Thana Atos?"

La Mort checked the time. Twenty minutes. Bill kept observing her. There was softness to his eyes, a stillness. The calmness of a quiet sea.

"I want to know something." *La Mort* cackled inside. *Something that really angers me.*

"Yes?"

"Your wife knew when Death was coming."

"Yes, she did."

"Even the hour. There was no fear in her."

"Thana Atos. Thanatos. Death in Greek?" Bill gazed at Death with his same soft look. "I'm a professor, once studied Greek. On assignment, Thanatos? I'm ready to go … be with her."

La Mort leaned back against her chair and sighed. "No, not you." She noted the elderly gentleman in the back and slowly licked her lips. She drew closer to Bill. "How did she know?"

Bill smiled. "She asked. 'The secret of the Lord is with them that respect Him.' Psalm 25:14."

Ten minutes. "What?"

"She was close to Him. He promises to reveal His secrets to those who love Him." It was Bill's turn to lean back. The gentleness in his sight invaded all of his countenance. "And … she loved Him."

La Morte watched as Bill's eyes glistened.

"Your wife knew me, yet was not afraid."

Bill nodded. "That was my Abby. She made me a believer."

"And you? You knew me when?"

"When you spoke your name. I'm very new at hearing Him."

La Mort dug her nails into the palms of her hands. Then, she pulled up her glass of ice, took a piece in her mouth and crushed it. "I hate it when mortals are at peace. I have to work alone without coworkers, can't call on Fear and Terror. I love seeing the anguish in their eyes when those two come."

Movement jolted Death. The warm breath of a mortal scorching her. She pulled fur off her coat.

"Remember me?" The elderly man, who had sat at the back table, stood close to *La Mort*. He tipped his head to Bill and then to Death.

La Morte squinted. Something about the man's eyes full of irritating joy seemed vaguely familiar. She remembered his name. Death's next assignment. Had they met before? There had been so many by the same name on her lists of assignments through the years.

"Irving Stein. Auschwitz, 1945." He smiled.

La Morte's nostrils flared.

"The Almighty helped me slip through your fingers then. But now, can't wait to see Him." The elderly gentleman winked at Death. "Let's go old girl, I'm ready."

Amarilys Gacio Rassler

Amarilys Gacio Rassler is the author of the book, *Cuban-American, Dancing On The Hyphen,* used by Oregon State University for cultural studies. She has been published in *The Florida Writer*, the anthology, *21 Days of Grace* and in USF's *Saw Palm Florida Literature and Art.* She writes fiction and nonfiction.

Unforgettable

"Don't step on Julia de Burgos," said Cristina. She'd been pushing a full-length mirror across the floor of the church's clothing pantry, so Joe could see himself, when she stopped suddenly.

Looking down, Joe saw Julia. She was a skinny little tabby with white paws and a white tummy, who had settled herself by his feet. A second later, she jumped onto a chair next to the mirror and curled herself up.

Cristina went over and scratched the top of the tabby's head. "I found her a few years ago in a pool of vomit, and I pestered my papi to help me get her to the vet. The vet said she'd been through a lot, so I named her Julia de Burgos. Do you know Julia's poetry?"

Joe shook his head. The only poetry he could remember was Robert Frost's line, "home is where when you go there they have to take you in." He used to think of it bitterly during freezing nights on the street.

Wheeling around the mirror, Cristina pointed her finger at her own image and declaimed fiercely, "'People say that I am your enemy. They lie, Julia de Burgos, they lie, Julia de Burgos.'"

In her ordinary voice, she explained to Joe, "One half of Julia is talking to the other half, defending herself against gossip!" Sighing, she added, "I love her work. She passes the test for all true poets -- she's unforgettable."

Scooping up the little cat, Cristina cradled her against her breast. "Now, let's check out that shirt," she said.

When Joe turned from the mirror to face Cristina, she looked him up and down. "Great," she told him. "Consider yourself 'outfitted,' as they say on Madison Avenue." She pointed to a table next to the doorway that went through to the street. "Don't forget the sandwich I left for you, and don't go too far. I'll need you to help me with something in a few minutes."

As Joe stepped outside, he put up his hand, as if to shield his eyes from the afternoon sun. But he was shielding himself from the shock of his image in the mirror. His shirt and pants were clean, and they almost matched. This situation was so outside his experience, he couldn't imagine what would happen next. Needing to think, he crossed the street and sat down on a stoop.

As he finished the sandwich, he became eerily aware that someone was watching him. Gulping the last bit, he turned in the direction he felt the stare coming from. His eyes met the gray eyes of a girl about fourteen.

Her face brightened up right away and she said cheerfully, "Oh, you got something!"

Joe looked at her blankly.

"My school is right over there," she said, "and I saw you go into those restaurants at lunchtime." She pointed to Sorrento's on the corner and Blimpie's two doors down. "You came out so fast I was sure they had said no."

After a few seconds of silence in which Joe checked the wires in his head to make sure he hadn't blown a fuse, he asked, "No to what?"

Sitting down on the opposite side of the stoop, the girl dropped her backpack on the ground. "I'm in advanced placement," she said, "and we're studying Wordsworth. My assignment was to read 'The Cumberland Beggar,' and you made me think of him. He goes around the village getting something to eat in one place on Monday and another place on Tuesday and so on."

Studying Joe's face, her own face changed. "I'm not offending you, am I?" She added quickly, "Wordsworth had a lot of respect for the man. He said he was a kind of village newspaper, because he went everywhere and saw everything."

The honest embarrassment in her eyes pulled Joe back from his urgent desire to get up and walk away, far away. He couldn't tell her that he had only gone into the restaurants because someone at the church had told him to look for Cristina. He'd stopped making explanations years ago.

"I didn't mean any harm," the girl went on. "I just jump in without thinking. My mom is always after me about it."

Joe had to respond, so he said the only thing he could think of. "Didn't your mom tell you not to talk to strange men?"

"Yes, she did," said the girl with relief. "Now, do you see how safe you are? A dangerous man would never have reminded me of that."

Interested in spite of himself, Joe said, "A con artist would."

The girl shook her head. "He would say the words, but he wouldn't look disapproving the way you did. You cared about me and my safety. So you tried to discourage me from walking up to men I don't know."

After a pause, Joe said, "I see why you're in advanced placement."

Scrabbling through her backpack, she pulled out a package of cookies. "I bought this for you," she told him. Putting it in his lap, she added, "My name's Julie."

"Joe," he said. To avoid looking at the girl, he held up the package and stared into it.

"They're chocolate chip," said Julie, "but I got them organic so they wouldn't be too sweet. You shouldn't eat a lot of sweet things. It's bad for your health."

"You gonna be a social worker?" asked Joe. He had known a number of those.

"I might," she answered happily. "Or I might become a poet. I'd like to be a kind of Wordsworth and write about people in a way that everybody reads and remembers."

Joe got up. Afraid to let a good thing go on too long in case it turned against him, he said, "Thanks for these," meaning the cookies.

Grabbing her backpack, Julie was ready to walk on, but suddenly Joe's curiosity spoke up. He'd thought he looked different in his new clothes, but now he doubted it. He asked, "How did you know me the second time?"

"Oh, people give me a certain feeling. That's how I recognize them. You gave me a sad feeling, but a nice one. I mean, I felt you were really sweet, so I wanted to help."

Her face wore the most trusting expression Joe had ever seen, and it spun his mind around. Grappling for something to hold onto, he seized on something Cristina had said. He told Julie, "You're gonna be a poet."

She was thrilled. "Why do you say that? I never showed you anything I wrote." At that moment, Cristina appeared in the church doorway, beckoning to Joe. He started to cross the street, then turned around. "Because you know how to choose your words," he lied.

To himself, he said, "Because you're unforgettable."

Lynn Schiffhorst

I was in fourth grade when I realized some people were homeless, and it broke my heart. Even though my degrees were in English, I ended up as a counselor and social worker, loving and caring for men and women who needed all I could give -- and more.

Eyewitness

Henry Meyer seemed like a man who would never lie. His thick white hair, neatly trimmed, framed a face with grayish blue eyes behind silver-rimmed glasses, a prominent nose, and a thin-lipped mouth that was quick to smile. He dressed impeccably in long-sleeved shirts – always some variety of blue – and khaki slacks, a knife-sharp crease down each leg. His loafers were polished, in an era when that was a lost art. A thin, well-mannered man, he was always in a good mood, always ready with a joke. For someone in his late eighties, he appeared to be in good health; only his decades-old limp gave away a sleepless night, which he tried to cover up with his cane.

Since his wife's death, Henry's routine at Alpine Brook Independent Living varied little. Between breakfast and lunch in his tiny bungalow, mornings found him in an armchair in the solarium of the main building, carefully reading the newspapers provided for print-addicted survivors of the last century. Afternoons found him in the computer room, scrolling through topic after topic. Twice a day he took one of the walking paths though the manicured grounds of the community, often accompanied by another resident or two. Following the evening meal in the communal dining room, Henry sat in an armchair in the parlor, quickly gathering a group of night owls and asking "Do you remember…?" Henry was an avid student of the past.

Almost every night Henry and his friends discussed past and present events: the housing bubble of 2008, the Korean War, the Three Mile Island accident, wind energy, NATO. Given his age, the evening staff wasn't sure how he remembered so many details, but he always sounded authoritative and no one contradicted him. The composition of the group changed nightly, with the same small core always present. *The regulars*, they called themselves, *Henry's regulars*. Then Oleg Lebed arrived.

A tall man, completely bald, with piercing hazel eyes, bushy gray eyebrows, and large ears, Oleg gave the appearance of eternal watchfulness. When he talked, his head leaned toward his listener and his hands punctuated his words. He spoke with a heavy accent, halfway between Russia and New Jersey. Although clean, his mismatched pants and shirts were often rumpled. Since his bungalow was near Henry's, they sometimes found themselves on the same path to the main building. Oleg talked, Henry listened.

Soon Oleg discovered Henry's nightly conversations. At first he only listened, but after a few nights he began to contradict Henry. Design flaws and human error were not the reasons for the Chernobyl nuclear disaster. Climate change was not real.

Hamilton was illegitimate, not so important in American history. The others complained that Oleg was dominating their talks, but he seemed impervious to criticism. As October faded into November, the group began to fracture, meeting only once or twice a week.

A few days before Thanksgiving, Henry arrived at the small evening gathering to find his usual chair occupied by Oleg. Shrugging, Henry took another seat and carefully removed a magazine from a manila envelope. He said, "Let me show you one of my most prized possessions." In the upper left corner in black and white was one word: *LIFE*; in the lower right, "November 29, 1963 25 cents." Bordered in black was a picture of the 35th President. Murmurs of recognition erupted. He tapped the cover. "The next issue showed Mrs. Kennedy with their two children. So tragic."

Oleg swung one leg over the arm of the chair. "Who cares? He was not so good. Look at his women friends - disgraceful."

"I care. I was there, you see, when he was shot." Henry looked down. "In Dallas, along the route of the motorcade. Such a promising young leader, cut down in his prime." He sent the magazine circulating around the group. Frowning, Oleg stood up and strode off.

Heads began nodding and questions popped up on every side. *Where was Henry standing?* In a single line of people near the Depository, taking photographs. *What could he see?* President Kennedy slumping in his back row seat in the Lincoln, Mrs. Kennedy in her pink suit reaching back toward the Secret Service agent climbing toward them. *What did he hear?* Three shots, then people shouting and police sirens. More questions followed, then everyone's memories of where they had been that day. A woman held up the open magazine, pointing to a photo, and started to speak; Henry shook his head at her.

On subsequent evenings Henry entertained the group with his experiences in Oklahoma City right after the 1995 bombing, in New York City just after 911, and in New Orleans during Hurricane Katrina in 2005. One night he described the camping trip he and his wife and son took to Mount St. Helens in 1980. His son was a geology major and wanted to see the restless mountain firsthand. They awoke the morning of May 18 to see a tremendous eruption. "We were 10 miles or so away from the summit, but Lev made us leave everything but the dog and drive south as fast as we could." Henry described the ash cloud and mud rain that covered the windshield and the roads blocked by mudflows and how they were terrified they wouldn't find a way out. He was so engrossed in his story that he failed to see Oleg standing behind a nearby column.

The crisis erupted in mid-December, when Oleg confronted Henry as they left the dining room. Brandishing an old magazine, Oleg snorted, "Think you're so smart, don'tcha? I got you all figured out. You read something online or in a magazine and make up a story that puts you right at the center." He stabbed his large fingers at Henry's chest. "I wrote to a collector friend of mine and he sent me this *National Geographic*, January 1981. You read this and made up a tall tale. Don't say you didn't!"

Henry stepped back out of range. A few residents collected nearby, ready to intervene. "I guess you got me," he smiled. "You figured me out. I do have that issue. The funny thing is that inside it is a camping permit and a few photos I took as we were leaving, plus I have a piece of pumice that Lev picked up at one of our stops."

Oleg stared. "I don't believe you."

"Walk over to my place now and I'll show you."

"I call your bluff on this one," Oleg snorted, noticing the on-lookers. "But if you don't have it, they all know you're a liar." Henry just raised his eyebrows.

Whatever occurred in Henry's bungalow that evening remained between the two. When Oleg left, his face was very sad.

Oleg stayed away until late January, when he took a seat on the outside of the group. As everyone settled in, he cleared his throat and said, "Henry says it is important to tell our stories, even ones we don't understand. So, today I tell you." He took a deep breath. "Exactly seventy years ago today, I was in a concentration camp, Auschwitz. I was young and very sick. Because the camp was liberated that day, I lived."

Ruth Senftleber

Ruth has been an avid reader since childhood and is now happy to create stories for others. Her background in foreign languages and science provides source material for many ideas. Born in Jacksonville, she will always be a Florida girl wherever she may travel. (Photo: Jan Michele Photography)

The Dry Season

Coquina shells crunched under Gretchen's sandals as she walked along the path by the sinkhole. Her stomach growled. Regular meals were less frequent since the death of her parents. Her once tight shirt now draped from her shoulders. She tried the campus food pantry yesterday, but the shelves were bare. She needed to find work.

Gretchen placed her easel and portfolio on the ground. She watched a small gator floating on the surface of the sinkhole amongst the duckweed. Sunlight reflected from the alligator's back in an array of colors. For the moment, she forgot about her hunger, and debated sketching the reptile.

A white heron landed near the sinkhole's edge. It was the dry season, and the water level lay several feet below normal. The bird waded around the edge, but the sinkhole offered mediocre prospects for breakfast. The heron flew off in search of a better place to dine. Gretchen empathized with the bird.

Her scholarship covered tuition and rent, but not necessities such as food. Maybe she should learn from the heron, quit school, and search for better conditions. Her stomach growled again urging her to move. She must sell some sketches if she expected to eat today.

Gretchen walked down the shell path until she came to a concrete bench near the restrooms and water fountain. The bench overlooked a dry lily pond. The lilies lay crumpled on top of the mud. She felt depressed for the desiccated and dying plants. Their purple buds unopened, a testament to unfulfilled life.

She erected the wooden easel, and placed her artwork around it. She put out a sign that advertised drawings for $10.00. She opened her sketchpad, sat on the bench, and began drawing the dying water lilies. The quality of her work disappointed her. Hunger hindered her concentration, and caused her hands to shake. She rubbed them together, and squeezed them. She would starve if her hands refused to work.

A breeze blew her hair, and she swiped at it with her hand. Her hair felt coarse. She could barely pay the rent so a professional haircut and conditioner were luxuries she couldn't afford. The smell of fried food wafted on the breeze. Once again, her stomach sent a reminder how long it had been since she ate.

She heard footsteps and looked up. Her friend Matt stood there holding a McDonald's bag. Her mouth began to salivate. She looked down and got her emotions under control. She didn't want him to sense her desperation.

Matt held up the bag. "Mickey Dee's special, two sausage, egg, and cheese sammies." He sat down on the bench next to her and opened the bag. He passed a sandwich to her.

It smelled great, but she didn't take it. "No, thank you. I'm not hungry." She almost choked on the words, but she didn't want to rely on handouts from friends. She could take care of herself. She didn't need help.

Matt shook his head. He placed the sandwich on the bench. "In case you get hungry later." He stood up. "See you in English class?" He turned and walked back in the direction of the sinkhole.

"Thank you," she yelled after him.

Matt looked back over his shoulder. "Don't worry about it. I'll save a seat for you."

She watched him walk along the path as she ate the sandwich. Grease and salt clung to her fingers. She licked them clean. Gretchen wiped away tears. Only babies cried. She turned to the next page of her sketchpad and began to sketch a portrait of Matt.

A shadow fell over Gretchen. Startled, she looked up. A tall, slender woman stood by the easel. Gretchen wondered how the woman crept up on her especially in those heels.

The woman looked through the artwork. She wore a broad-brimmed hat that shadowed her face. "I like these. You captured the soul of the swamp."

Gretchen stood up. "I grew up in Green Swamp, east of here. This time of year, we listened to the bull alligators bellow and frogs croak. I miss it."

The woman smiled. "I also spent my childhood in the swamp, but I don't have pleasant memories." She held her hand out to Gretchen. "My name is Jessica, but my friends call me Jess."

"Hi, I'm Gretchen." She shook the woman's hand. It felt rough and calloused. Gretchen didn't want to stare, but the woman's features seemed somewhat masculine.

The woman reached for Gretchen's hair. "May I?" She didn't wait for permission, and started to run her fingers through it.

Gretchen pulled her head back. "Excuse me. Stop!" She pushed Jessica's hand away. "I don't know you." She stepped back.

The woman looked at Gretchen. "What did you do to it? The fact that you come from the swamp doesn't mean your hair needs to look like Spanish moss," Jessica said.

"I cut it myself. What's it to you?" Gretchen couldn't believe the woman's audacity.

The woman took a business card out of her purse and twenty dollars. "Honey, it looks like you used a weed whacker on your hair." She handed Gretchen the card and money. "I'll take two of your drawings." She picked two from the easel. "Stop by my salon tonight, and bring these with you." She placed the drawings on the ground near Gretchen.

Gretchen read the card, The New Wave Salon. "I can't pay for a styling."

"Honey, you don't need to pay me. I want you to draw a portrait of me, but be nice. Make me look good." Jess ran her long fingers through her own wiry hair. "My only rule is no drugs."

Gretchen shook her head. Who was this person? She assumed a lot.

Jessica poked at Gretchen's stomach. "Skin and bones; you need to eat more. I need a person to sweep, and clean at closing time. Would you like a job? It's not much, but it might grow into something more."

Gretchen pushed Jess's hand away from her stomach. The woman had nerve.

Jess stood back. She scrutinized Gretchen's bleach-blond hair with its abundant black roots. "We need to work on your style before I let you touch anyone in my shop. I'll teach you."

Gretchen scuffed her shoe on the ground, and chewed on her lower lip. "Why should I work for you?" She twirled the card in her hand. This offer wasn't charity. It was helping herself, and she needed to eat.

Jess pointed at the card. "Come by the shop about seven tonight. I'll have Matt fix your hair so you don't look like a swamp creature. Gretchen, don't walk away when an opportunity presents itself."

"Matt works for you?" Gretchen asked.

Jess smiled. "That boy, he was supposed to talk to you about me. Everyone has trouble at some point, but it's his story to tell, not mine. I'll see you this evening." Jessica turned and walked away.

"I need to do this," Gretchen said out loud. She packed her portfolio. She had an English class to catch, and a friend to thank. A few drops of rain plopped on the dry bed of the lily pond.

Bruce G. Smith

Bruce G. Smith has published non-fiction pieces such as textbook chapters and Internet content. His work has appeared in the online magazines Technorati and Blog Critics as well as other online venues. His most recent publication appeared in *The Florida Writer* magazine, April 2017, "Hot Italian Grinders."

When Character Really Counts

Cancer is that scariest of diseases that can tear families apart, ruin dreams, inflict serious financial havoc, instill fear of horrible pain and suffering, and leave family members with a feeling of helplessness and hopelessness. When the diagnosis is given, it's like a punch in the gut as the realization of what's ahead sinks in. For Michael, that date was June 28, 2014 and the lung tumor was almost the size of a softball. While it seems unbelievable that it could grow undetected, Michael was already suffering from heart disease and led a very sedentary life. Had he been more active, he would certainly have been aware of shortness of breath and had an earlier x-ray.

After the requisite tests, it was confirmed that the tumor was inoperable. To stabilize and hope to shrink such a large tumor was a nearly impossible task, and a program of radiation and chemotherapy was quickly drawn up by two different oncologists who specialized in their respective fields. We knew the diagnosis was a death sentence, but we couldn't know when that would happen, so all we could do was fight together as best we could.

The first chemotherapy occurred on a Wednesday in August and that night at home, Michael suffered a heart attack. We didn't recognize it as such and thought it was a reaction to the chemo. The next morning, when we appeared for the first radiation treatment, the staff took one look at Michael and sent him to the ER, where the heart attack was confirmed. He spent four days in the hospital being poked and tested and having his medicines adjusted. Right after being sent home, he began the radiation treatments.

The radiation oncology office offered a comfortable waiting room consisting of padded chairs, a Keurig coffee machine, television and bookcases filled with magazines of all genres and dozens of boxes of jigsaw puzzles. In the center of the room was a large table where a puzzle was always in progress. Scheduling for radiation treatment was every day Monday through Friday for about 33 to 35 consecutive treatments. Patients were generally scheduled at approximately the same time of day, so we got to know those who were scheduled before and after Michael's appointment. The patients had to wait in this room and many of them became avid participants in the challenge of the jigsaw puzzle. Some would even come early to work on it, expanding the circle of patients we came to know. We met family members and in some cases, learned of others with lung cancer. I think the puzzle was a way of diverting attention away from the grimness of everyone's condition and offering a respite from the effects of the treatment.

Michael often did not feel well, especially as treatment progressed and the burning of the radiation affected his esophagus, which negatively affected his ability to eat and drink. But he was regularly telling jokes and engaging the other patients in the waiting room with funny stories. This got several others talking about their backgrounds and sharing in the stories. But it was the laughter that Michael found most important. Realizing his own mortality, he saw how uplifting it was for the others to smile, relax and find humor in anecdotes.

"They all know they're facing death, and they're depressed most of the time, so why not find something funny to laugh about and draw their thoughts away from their own problems, even just for a while?" was the way he explained his attitude during these visits.

They all ended their treatments within a week or so of each other and we exchanged addresses and phone numbers with some of them.

I was amazed at Michael's ability to engage these other patients and put them at ease at a time when they were enduring painful treatment, often without a lot of hope. But Michael's tumor did shrink some and remained so for several months. It took a while though, for him to be able to swallow food and big adjustments had to be made in his diet. Five months later, on Valentine's Day of 2015, he suffered his third heart attack due to a blockage in his left coronary artery. An emergency angioplasty put a stent in the offending artery (his fifth stent).

Later that year, on December 9, 2015, he fell in the house, breaking his ankle and the bottom of the tibia. He was diagnosed with atrial fibrillation, which might have caused a momentary blackout and a fall, but it was the radiation that had made his bones brittle and easy to break. It took six days in the hospital treating the a-fib before they could give him the anesthesia necessary to set the broken bones. As soon as that was done, he was released to a rehab facility where he would undergo extensive therapy before he'd be able to go home. He spent Christmas and New Year's in rehab, and it was particularly sad to see that several of the residents had no holiday visitors, as though they had just been 'dumped' there.

But again Michael became friendly with several of the other patients as well as the staff. He would go in his wheelchair to the dining room and cheer up many of the residents. Plus the therapists would talk and joke with him as he underwent daily classes in Occupational Therapy and Physical Therapy. Often I would find the instructors laughing with him as he pushed himself to do the exercises. Sometimes they would visit in his room to pass their free time before having to deal with some of the not-so-cooperative patients.

One day when I arrived, I could hear laughter while I was still in the hallway outside his room. There was Michael, holding court from his bed, with a doctor, the Occupational Therapist and two nurse's aides laughing as though at a party. As I walked in, I joked that I should have brought vodka.

Michael was there for 28 days, and the staff all came to say goodbye to him, as did some of the other residents. It was hard to maintain that level of camaraderie for the month he was there, with so much serious illness surrounding him, but he displayed a healthy sense of humor in front of all of them, from the doctors to the maintenance man, who also paid him regular visits.

Is that kind of character strength inside us all our lives, or does it rise to the surface only when we are faced with incredible challenges? Did Michael, ever the storyteller and joker, realize the positive effect he had on those who faced such dire challenges and really needed a lifting of the spirit?

Michael passed away on May 25, 2016 from a combination of his cancer and heart disease, twenty-three months from his original diagnosis. Most people remember him as the patient who had the ability to make the burdens lighter of all around him. I remember him as the man who showed incredible strength of character at a time when it was needed the most.

Judith Weber

Judy Weber is the Writers Group Leader of the Ancient City Chapter and has been published in five previous Collections. Her favorite pastime is writing murder mysteries, with occasional forays into short story creations. She lives in St. Augustine with her White German Shepherd Reggie.

Brings on the Anxiety

1982, Xenia, Ohio, as told by Miriam

There she is … waiting for me on her narrow front stoop like I knew she would be, seated on a precarious white plastic stool. From the street, I see her pursed lips and sense her irritation. I leap from the car, certain I am in for a scolding.

Purple is the dominant hue today. The wide-brimmed lavender straw hat with a flowered band sits atop her bouffant wig. The tent dress with puffed sleeves covers her bulging breasts and belly with bright shades of pink, white, and more purple. Somehow, she has managed to wedge her swollen feet into misshapen plastic purple flats.

It has been a decade since Rozilla labored over an ironing board as she did for our family for thirty years. Having outlived our parents, she is our only mama now. She doesn't drive—never owned a car. We four siblings find time in our busy lives to take her places, and occasionally slip her a ten or a twenty.

As I step carefully up the cement walk toward her, trying not to trip in the cracks, I think of the only time I have been inside her house. A newly begun project lay on a table. A multicolored crocheted blanket, it surely joined many of the others she had made through the years—donations to brighten the life of a hospitalized child or keep a frozen death away from a homeless man.

Bright by-the-numbers flower paintings shared walls with three framed portraits. President John F. Kennedy on the right. Martin Luther King Jr. on the left. Jesus of Nazareth in the middle, in that familiar depiction where he gazes into the distance, simultaneously serene and sad, perhaps anticipating his early death.

Each step I take crunches louder on the thickening clusters of empty peanut shells. When I reach the bottom stair, she cracks a shell with two thumbs, pulls it apart, and pops the contents into her mouth.

Still chewing, she greets me sternly in her slow drawl: "Y'all know how I hate to wait."

"I *say*, y'all know I hate waitin'," Rozilla repeats, apparently not willing to raise herself until she has received an apology. "Brings on the anxiety," she adds.

Rozilla may be an illiterate southern lady, but she understands all about hours and minutes. She has also adopted a northerner's sensitivity to time, along with the emphasis on punctuality.

"Sorry, Zilla," I begin as I take her elbow and tug her upward, off the stool. "An accident on the highway. Cars all backed up."

I slip my arm through hers, and we carefully make it down three steps to the walk, she balancing a sweet potato pie in one palm, a pecan pie in the other, while I hold her elbow. It may be *her* birthday, yet she insists on furnishing her pies.

As I help her inside the car and reach over her to fasten her seatbelt, we both giggle at the effort this task takes.

"Oh, give it up, girlie," she says, flipping the belt away. "You hit a rut, I bounce. I be fine."

Once we're on our way, I slip into her vernacular and ask, "Why you waitin' outside in the sun, Zilla? You coulda waited inside the house."

"When I realize you late, it take me five minutes t' get up, five minutes t' unlock the door, five t' set m'self down, another five t' get up again, and still another five t' relock that door. Ain't worth it. Know'd you'd come along sooner or later."

It doesn't take long before I get another reprimand.

"You had no business wearin' that outfit. What was you thinkin'?"

I try to imagine what she could be referring to. Is she reaching back into my adolescence? A too-short miniskirt, maybe? A low-cut summer top? Has she been harboring disgust all these years?

As if my crime were unbearable, she hangs her head and shakes it. "At your father's weddin'," she says, giving me a stern sidelong glance. "That long dress. You could see straight through it."

"It didn't occur to me that anyone could see through black," I say. "And I was wearing black panties under it."

"Thank the Lord for that. I know it was a summer day … and a hot one, but did you have to wear somethin' so flimsy? And on such an occasion?"

When I say nothing else to defend myself, she asks, "Do you know where ya goin'? You know how to get to Jamie's? Y'all know I hate gettin' lost more than anythin'. Brings on the anxiety."

"Sure, Zilla. I've been to my brother's new place three times already."

Apparently, my reassurance is not effective. I observe Zilla bend over and search in her purse for the comfort of a peanut, her bosom nearly smashing the pies in her lap.

After looking straight ahead for a few minutes and chewing with the few teeth she has left, she says in a near whisper, "Jeremiah. He dead, ya know."

"Yes, I know. I'm sorry. Quite a while ago."

Why, I wonder, *is she mentioning the death of her long-term companion now, when he's been gone for years?*

After a long pause, I hear words spoken slowly in a voice so quiet I hardly recognize it.

"Lost my boy too. My boy. My only chile. My Micky."

Zilla sighs, sounding more resigned than sorrowful, staring ahead.

"You mean you lost him when he was convicted, Zilla? He's still in prison, isn't he?"

"Micky dead too, girl. Jeremiah. Now Micky."

"Oh, Zilla, I didn't know. When? Are you sure? What happened?"

Five years in that hole. Five years for sellin' a little of ... what they call it? Pot? Never had no daddy. Needed cash. Jes a little of that weedy stuff. Lawyer keep sayin', 'We gettin' you outta here, boy. You may not have served your full sentence, but you done time enough.' But nothin' happen. Micky kep' on day after day—doin' time."

I reach over and cover Zilla's hand that's still gripping the pie tins.

"When a fight breaks out," she continues, "them guards in them towers? They don't hold back. They jes shoot. Got my Micky in the back. Died fast, they tell me. The other prisoners? Gathered 'round watchin' my boy's blood seep over the blacktop.

"Wanted to send me the body. I say, 'Ain't got no money to bury my boy. You killed him, you bury him. Me, I pray for him.' Long as God listens, I pray for my Micky."

"Zilla, I feel terrible."

"You my only babies now. You, ya sisters. Ya brother. You may have babies of ya own, but you my only babies now."

Zilla stares straight ahead. She must be out of peanuts.

We bump along the narrow dirt road leading to the party, me driving with one hand, my other hand still covering one of hers. I see Jamie's red barn in the distance, but it's all blurry. When my eyes are awash, I can't see through the car windshield. When I can't see where I'm going? Brings on the anxiety.

Judith K. White

Judith K. White's careers span linguist, educator, entrepreneur and fundraiser. She is the author of three novels that together comprise *Amsterdam Trilogy* plus a memoir written with her husband, Allen L. White, *Autumns of Our Joy: A Tale of Romance, Stem Cells and Rebirth.* She lives in Boston and St. Augustine.

My Medicine Man

I watch as he cradles the tube of mystery cream in one hand. The contents contain his secret potion of healing herbs. So much about him remains surreptitious. I'm not sure if the secrets are intentional or habitual. I think the latter. Natural healing remedies and recipes flood his mind forming a current reference database. Lists of local Chinese doctors, healing centers, stand on call when requests arise. My friend waits for any semblance of health to enter conversations; then strikes into the powers of body detox or weekly acupuncture, a dissertation of everything wrong with today's health care system, filtering views through his Libertarian ideology. Tom practices natural healing while pursuing his lifelong work of building and managing real estate; likewise, when fishing, boating, having fun with friends. He disperses his formulas and removes engaged fish hooks like an ER doctor might.

Tom believes in the cycles of nature, goes to bed as the sun finishes its decline, begins his day with seagull chatter, in the darkness before sunrise. My friend does not own a computer–has a tiny fifteen-year-old television set, but prefers easy listening FM or National Public Radio. Sticky salt spray coats his Jitterbug flip style cell phone. He uses it rarely. *Text* or *Tweet* do not enter his language. This man even frowns and stutters when questioning the word *Email*? His home phone answering machine screens his life. I'm drawn to this style in a man and suspicious at the same time. Exceptions to the norm in today's world mesmerize me but are danger signals in choosing a partner. My rocky relationship record acknowledges that fact.

Sitting on the small black futon inside the shingled dockside shelter he built five years prior, we chat, updating history as people do after being apart. He turns toward me, lifts my legs across his lap, balancing them upon his long, lean, tanned legs. I adore this seventy-five-year-old friend still sports L.L. Bean cotton khaki short-shorts and denim colored pocketed t-shirts. Tan lines frame his tall body in familiar places. I picture him water skiing, jumping a slalom, cutting a choppy wake; likewise, I recall adventurous stories of him skiing in Cypress Garden shows, 1960 timeframe. I remember with excitement his tanned arms covered with bleached blond hairs, his squinting light blue eyes, the ball cap indentation in his then curly blond hair, now sprinkled white. I recall his certainty in rigging a sailboat, his patience in teaching my two children to sail and ski. Thirty-five years had passed since we first loved.

His calming voice reassures me the potion would relieve the cramping in my calves, a side effect of walking barefoot in the soft mushy sand along the Florida east coast earlier that day. I am as certain a good stretch and Ben Gay would do the trick, but I let him try his magic---well, I offer one leg as an experiment. I'd compare the two legs in the morning, weigh differences, and report back to him, those exact words of instructions he professes, smiling then laughing, tons of new lines surrounding his mouth and nose. I like those too. With his right hand, opens the tube, squeezes some of the sandy colored cream into that palm and closes the cap all in one motion, with one hand. That type of dexterity in a man fascinates, lures me. Why? Maybe it signals flexibility? In this man, it signals physical flexibility; opinion flexibility not so much, particularly in areas of politics or treatment choices.

Positioned side by side on the futon, me sideways, with my aging, freckled, sunburned legs draped across his lap, he lifts my right leg with his left hand and rubs the lotion up and down the back of my leg. The mentholated scent of Vick's soars through memories. I've not thought about croup and vaporizers in years. I smile, but he doesn't know why. For a rugged outdoorsman, Tom touches with a gentleness. My body remembers his touch. Medicine Man cares more about healing than advancing his strokes---well, for the time being.

Maybe age does this to a man, I thought. My history with another man during the previous twenty years indicates such. But that's my only point of reference. At this moment, I'd like my Tom to reappear with a lusty surprise and leave Medicine Man in the shadows.

My friend continues to push the cream into the rebelling muscle, stopping every so often to ask, in a soothing whispering voice, if it tingles yet. It did, and I did. Each touch feels deliberate and soft, familiar. I relax to the faint thumping of waves against the hut signaling the approaching high tide, a reminder of the 8:50 p.m. tide change he quoted earlier in the afternoon. Tide cycles rule his life of river and ocean living.

"Remember, fish the changing tides," his crisp New England accent teaches while walking this morning along his fishing pier, searching pilings for Joe, a manatee winter visitor. I hadn't fished in years. Fishing consumes him, settling on a tiny village near Ketchikan, Alaska as his preferred spot. At summer's end, he and four fishing buddies retreat to Florida, frozen blocks of salmon and halibut for neighbors and friends in tow. Alaska Air Lines accommodates his treasures. Orlando baggage handlers recognize his wave and of course his heavy frozen luggage.

He invited my son, Pat, on this annual adventure ten years ago. That call surprised me, but then Tom always surprised me. The two men bonded on that Alaskan trip, but neither knew the significance of their connection to me. Tom and Pat represent the loves of my life, one chosen, one given.

Partners entered and exited our lives. We never interrupted those commitments, just complimented them with our ongoing love, elusive timing enemy to our union. I went to him for comfort today, unsure why he agreed to meet me again. But this wasn't the first time. He housed my destination when I tripped and fell, and several years might pass between spills. My dear friend knew my medical history of breast cancer. During chemotherapy and radiation four years prior, he filled my mail with books, CD's, DVD's of alternative healing methods, encouraging me to take his lead. Instructional certainty always dominates his voice. I received his volumes of information and appreciated it. But it was my diagnosis, not his. It's easier to suggest tea leaves when cancer invades someone else.

Mystery and secrets veil this man. His powerful sense of privacy frequently conceals his motives, privacy which adds distrust to a relationship, by word omission, not by a deliberate deception. This medicine man shares my heart, my destination of sanity, the place where I go for my changing seasons, my spills, the ones needing a loving friend's touch.

Later, driving west on the Beachline Expressway toward my small Winter Park apartment I reminisced, likewise wondering again as I have on other return journeys, *will we ever be together?* My seventy-year-old heart replied, *this is together.*

Nancy Jenkins Wise

Nancy Jenkins Wise – Writer of prose and essays. Currently compiling book of short stories and essays for publication in 2018. Resides in Winter Park, Florida. Graduate of Rollins College, Winter Park.

The Old Cracker

No doubt he had been handsome once. A sonorous, southern drawl rumbled from somewhere deep in his chest. He wore old-fashioned cowboy clothes. His deeply seamed face was tanned like old shoe leather from fifty years of working outside with cattle. Even now, at nearly ninety-years old, his dark eyes twinkled with humor.

My husband and I never knew if all the tales he told about his cracker cowboy days were true, but we loved to hear him spin a yarn. So, we frequently invited our elderly neighbor to share a home cooked meal.

One unusually cold Central Florida evening we lit a fire in the wood-burning fireplace after dinner and settled in with anticipation of a good story.

"Who was the most unusual cowboy you ever rode with?" My husband asked.

"Well…" He cocked his head to the side and smiled. "I guess that'd be Hymie Abramowitz. He came down in the 1930s from New York City, little bitty, Jewish guy, skinny as a rail. Why, a good strong wind 'ud blow him away. Unlikeliest cowboy I ever seen.

"Hell, poor son of a bitch couldn't even ride a horse. But the boy was game. We trained him up and took him on the trail drivin' the cattle from Arcadia to Fort Pierce."

He took his tobacco pouch out of his pocket. "Mind if I chew?"

"Hang on. I'll get you a spit cup." I went to the kitchen and came back with a red Solo and two paper towels folded together. "Here you go."

He held the cup between his hands. "Me and Slim, we kinda took Hymie under charge. We was all young and full of piss and vinegar back then. Ropin' and ridin' all week, then goin' to the juke joint on Saturday night. Slim and Hymie, they was the real ladies' men. Me, I was content with their leftovers, all the not so-good-lookin', tagalong girlfriends.… But they was still soft and purdy." He shook his head, chuckled deeply, and laugh lines crinkled around his eyes. "Boy howdy!" He spit a stream of nasty brown juice into the Solo, set the cup on the end table, and wiped his lips on the paper towels. "Them was the days.

"Hymie regaled us all with stories of the bright lights in New York City. Dem local cowgirls was mesmerized." He wiggled his fingers in the air as if casting a hoo-doo spell. "While Hymie dreamed of bein' a cowboy all his life, dem girls dreamed of seein' Broadway, the Empire State buildin', and the Statue of Liberty.

"Me, I never had the desire to go to New York City, but Slim, he had a hankerin'. One day we was doin' a re-ride, checkin' for cattle missed the first time through the pasture, when we spied a couple of dogies mired down in a bog."

"What exactly is a dogie?" I asked.

"A calf that's been taken off its mother. A lot of times we keep the breedin' cows and sell off their young. We was taken this bunch to market.

"Hymie got off his horse, and Slim followed. The two of 'em was gettin' the first calf out when a pissed-off wild boar come chargin' out'a the scrub. You never seed two cowboys run so fast. Slim took a flyin' leap and hoisted himself up a low hangin' branch of a live oak tree. Hymie climbed up a scraggly, young longleaf pine barely able ta hold his weight. I liked ta laughed my socks off! That tree was bowed over 'bout ta dump poor Hymie right there in front of that big old boar." He chuckled loudly, and spit again.

"Hymie screamed, 'Help me Slim! That son of a bitch is gonna get me!'

"'Hold still,' shouted Slim. 'I got a pistol here. I'll shoot him. You gotta promise me one thing though, or I ain't gonna do it. If you ever go back ta New York City you gotta take me with you.'

"'I'll do it, I'll do it! I promise I'll do it. First time I go. Now shoot the bastard!' Hymie called back.'

"That boar was snortin' and tearin' at the ground under the tree, and Hymie was screamin' like a banshee. Slim killed the boar, and Hymie fell out of the tree right on top of it. But we got the calves out of the muck."

"That's a good one." My husband laughed.

"I'm going to the kitchen and get a cup of coffee. You two want one?" I asked. My husband nodded.

"Yeah, but I'll take a shot er two of Wild Turkey in mine," said our guest.

"You got it." I came back with the coffee. "Whatever happened to the two of them?"

"We lost Slim three years later. There was a big lightnin' storm on the spring drive. He got trampled in a stampede just outside of Okeechobee."

"Oh, that's terrible. And Hymie?" I inquired.

He took a big swig of coffee and wiped his lips on the towel. "Well…" he drawled. "Now that's an entirely *different* story. Hymie never went back ta New York City. He loved it here. Said he never wanted ta see that dirty place again. He rode the trails for ten more years. In the end, he was throwed from his startled horse into a pit of rattlesnakes. We couldn't get near him, had ta throw in a lasso and drag him out. Though we shot most of 'em, several of dem bad boys got in a good lick. It was quick. We buried him somewhere between Arcadia and Lake Placid.

"I got the address for his mama from her letters in his bedroll and wrote ta her about it. About three weeks later I heard back from her. Seems Hymie's family had quite a bit of money, which I had no idea. They wanted me ta ship his body back ta New York City so it could be buried in the family cemetery."

"So, did you do it?" I asked.

He flushed red, stuck his fingers in his collar, twisted it uneasily, shook his head, and spit in the cup again.

"Well… me and a couple of the guys took my old pickup truck and headed west, back to Arcadia. It had come up a big storm, and try as we would we couldn't find where we buried Hymie. I mean we looked everywhere. We dug up muck in about ten different places. But, I'll be damned if we could find him."

He put his elbows on his knees and his face in his hands. "I was beside myself with grief. I did not want to disappoint his mama."

"So, what did you do?"

He looked up with a wry smile on his face. "Well… It was just about then I remembered his promise to Slim. So, off to Okeechobee we went. It was all done hush, hush, in the middle of the night, don't cha know. I prayed Hymie's family wouldn't open that casket and get a gander at the size of dem bones inside."

He raised his cup. "Here's to Slim. I hope he's enjoyin' New York City."

Christine Yarbour

Christine Yarbour, a retired accountant living in Venice, Florida is a member of the FWA, the Ridge Writers Critique Group. She is an RPLA winner in both, poetry and children's fiction. Christine also writes non-fiction and historical fiction. She is an award winning wild life artist.

Florida Youth Writers Program

What a Chracter!
Florida Writers Association Youth Collection,
Volume 4

FWA Youth Writers Age Group 9-13

1st Place: Just. Like. That.

"Oh, thank God, Tribeca!" Roger practically screamed into the phone, even though the circumstances required absolute silence. He was breathing heavily giving the conversation a moist feeling.

"Roger, I'm scared." The statement was so simple, so obvious, but I needed to let the words fall out of my mouth into a heap on the floor of the closet I was hiding in.

"It'll be okay, I promise. They're doing everything they can to get you all out," he paused trying to conjure up the words he knew I was thinking the entire time I'd been locked in the cramped broom closet.

"Where is Annabella?"

"I don't know, I- I assume she's still in biology," I replied without much confidence.

I prayed she was still in biology. I shouldn't have gone to get my book from my locker, I should have stayed with her, I should have....I should have done a lot of things. Annabella was everything to me, and I just left her there. I mean, I couldn't have known, I couldn't have known the teachers wouldn't let me in their rooms no matter how hard I pleaded. I couldn't have known this would be the closet I would wait with crippling agony to know the fate of my dear sweet friend, I couldn't have known today was the day John Stevens would choose to come to school with a gun.

"It'll be okay, I promise," Roger kept saying over and over like a record stuck on a loop, "It'll be okay." I wish I could have mustered the words to say it back to him because he clearly needed to hear them just as much as I did.

"Do you know if Annabella has her phone?" he finally blurted out.

"Even if she does, the ringer would be too loud."

"Okay, it'll be okay, I prom -" My phone died. I was alone with my thoughts and the cleaning supplies. I leaned my head against the wall with the hooks and old dustpans hanging from them. I thought about Annabella and the way her auburn hair fell from her pale features. I recalled a time when I looked at her crystal blue eyes and saw, everything, every moment, every laugh, every single little glance that had made up our friendship. I wish I could go back to that time and tell her what

I was thinking. I wish I could have been there when the shooter opened the door. I wish I could have held her hand and told her it would be okay.

***

I was in the middle of reassuring Tribeca that everything would be okay when the line went dead. "Tribeca?" Nothing. "Tribeca!" Nothing.

Tears started to well in my eyes. She was gone. My friend was gone. I fell to my knees as if begging to something, anything. I couldn't move. I remembered her eyes, her beautiful green-gold eyes. They always reminded me of her favorite poem. The first time she showed it to me I could feel each word. Each line was tied into my mind for days on end. I saw words in the gold, flaking ink at the top at the page, *Nothing Gold Can Stay.* Then I imagined her eyes again, now cold and dead, with her lavender hair red with blood.

I began to shake uncontrollably. An EMT took me to a cot and had me lie down. How is this fair? My friend whom I've been with for eleven years is just "poof" gone. All the heartbreak, all the mistakes I've made, all the awful thoughts I've pulled her through just so she could see it does get better, shattered with one single bullet. I thought of her poem again and I wished it was wrong. I wished the things so perfect in this messed up world lasted longer and didn't subside to nothingness. Even though I didn't lose Tribeca that day, the words were true and they still echo in my brain. *Nothing Gold Can Stay.*

***

I could hardly breathe. It had been three hours of me hiding in that closet waiting for it to be over, to be rescued. I thought of everything. How I left to get that book from my locker. How Roger had left campus for lunch. How the intercom announced we had to hide. How my first thought was of Annabella and how I could have run the other way, back to biology instead of the dreadful broom closet. I remembered how she looked walking into school that morning, how she was wearing a new dress yet no one had paid attention. I remembered the days before, the time when she had to say something but let everyone else talk until her voice became nothing. I had watched her deem her thoughts unimportant.

I had been sitting there regretting everything when I heard the intercom announce we were allowed to leave. I don't remember much after that point.

I later found out John had intended to target a single student in the class but he had been so driven by anger and controlled by rage that he lost all sense of humanity by the time he got to the classroom.

There were people everywhere. Some crying, some screaming, some were just sitting letting the waves of the event wash over them. I couldn't see anyone else's pain that day; one person lost their twin, and another was in the room when it happened and lost his legs. He hasn't been able to walk since. I didn't care then; I just wanted to see Annabella.

I couldn't hear, I couldn't figure out where I was; SWAT teams tried to get me to leave but I didn't care. I kept running. I saw a group of people filtering in and out of a room carrying people. I lost everything after that moment. I remember only one thing clearly from that day. I saw them taking her out. I remember the way her auburn hair brushed the floor and her pale features were smeared with red. Her new dress no longer a sunflower yellow, but deep garnet. I remember her eyes, which used to be crystal clear blue like a reflecting pond, looked empty. Empty of all the moments, laughs, and little glances that had made our friendship. Gone, just, gone. Like they never happened.

I began to cry then. I had been crying all day but those tears were the kind that made me shake and sweat with nervousness, but these…these tears were different. These were the tears that fall without any feeling, with hopelessness, and with an emptiness that says it's all over, you can't be saved from your own crippling despair.

Annabella can't be gone. I will have no reason to be in this world if she is gone. She was unnoticed and unimportant to everyone else in this world. She was another name on the list, just another statistic. To me, though, she was everything. But now she's nothing. Just. Like. That.

"Seek."

Indigo D. TenEyck

Indigo TenEyck is a person whom you will likely never meet, and if you're reading this you're wasting your time. She only likes a few things in this world and these are: religiously listening to the band *twenty-one pilots,* her friends Aliyah and Luci, and rolling down hills.

Youth Writers Program
Florida Writers Association

2nd Place: The Cave

It will not delay
To strip me
Of my control
First happy
Then dismal
I try
Hard not to
Cut what
I can mend

I lay
Scared
In the dark
As my demons
Find me
I slowly
Stand up
And make my way
Back the way
I came
And I
Soon see
A light at the end of the black cave

I emerge
From the entrance
With wet tears
New souvenirs
Add to the collection
I look back
At the entrance
And see
My depression
Chasing
After
Me

Aliyah Paris Garcia

Aliyah is obsessed with music, specifically the bands *Twenty-One Pilots* and *Black Veil Brides.* Without music, family, and two best friends, she might not be here to have written this story. She really doesn't like writing, but her parents and teacher encouraged her to enter this competition.

Youth Writers Program
Florida Writers Association

3rd Place: Mother

Mother can you hear me?
I hope that you still do
I hope that you don't fear me
For we are here because of you

It all started slowly, life started to form
Which is truly amazing and far removed from the norm
Adaptations came after, leading from water to land
Now walking upright and counting on you to lend your hand

You have always given your all
Plenty of fresh air, water, and trees that stand tall
Millions of years, you have been so strong
Spinning and changing, but here we all belong

All things living and dead
A circle of life, a needle being thread
But now there is a fray no doubt
An urgency being overlooked, a desperate cry with no clout

Population exploding and technology amazing all
But I fear that you are choking and we fail to hear your call
All the years until now have taken a nice and steady pace
Within the last two hundred, it's been nothing but a race

Through all these years, you have always been strong
In a relative second, a sickness has come along
They say you can be cured, I sure hope it's true
Because there is no future that does not include you

Samantha Leslie

Samantha Leslie is from Lakeland, FL and has always possessed a passion for storytelling. Her favorite hobbies include writing, soccer, piano, and martial arts. She loves traveling and spending time with her family, friends, and her dog, Biscuit.

Youth Writers Program
Florida Writers Association

Honorable Mention: 11/16/1986

I always get very nervous when I go to the doctor because nothing good ever happens. I keep telling myself the cheesy line, "It will all be okay." I feel like I am going into battle with myself, but I am going to lose this one. As I sit in the waiting room of the surgical wing in the hospital, my father tells me the story of when I was born like he always does and after a while I stop listening. My mind keeps contemplating what is going on with my mom, trying to put the pieces together, but it just does not add up. Finally, my head rises as I hear Dr. Harlem calling my name.

"Alright Amber, you know the drill," Dr. Harlem says as she brings out her stethoscope.

"I do; please tell me you have good news."

"We won't know until after your scans."

I prepare myself for the inevitable; I am going to die soon. Dr. Harlem's face reveals the results of the scans even before her words, "Unfortunately, I have bad news. Your heart is failing. We can't do anything until we find a donor."

"Oh my God," my father reacts to the news as his eyes start to tear up. I, on the other hand, am fine. I feel no emotion, I am relieved.

Two days ago, I saw my father bring home a bottle of anti-depression pills. After the long, silent, gloomy car ride home, I check the bottle in his medicine cabinet and it is half empty.

***

Walking home from school, the towering trees seem to close in on me, just like my feelings. Dad is home doing the dishes, complaining as usual about how the dishwasher doesn't close properly; I chuckle to myself as I drop my backpack next to the stairs. I can't help but notice the first bottle of pills is empty and there is a new bottle on the counter.

"So Ambie, did you have to see Principal Samento today?" dad asks.

"Twice," I mumble under my breath.

"Well, gosh darn, what are we going to do with you?"

"It's better than last week!" I try to sound cheerful. "Hey dad, where's mom?"

"Not sure, princess."

"That's weird. No call?"

"Nothing."

"Strange, I didn't see her this morning either," I reply worriedly. "She didn't even leave a note?!"

"She's probably added the graveyard shift to her normal shifts."

"Again?"

"Well, season is almost over and we need the money for hospital bills with your heart and all."

"But that doesn't make any sense, the graveyard shift doesn't start 'til eleven."

"Why don't you do your homework and I'll make dinner," dad says trying to change the subject.

"Okay," I reply but am very suspicious. Something isn't right, I just can't figure it out. Right now is the time I need a mom; right now is the time my dad needs a wife. At the time we need her by our side to keep us sane, she is gone.

***

I wake up and I glance at my calendar, it is November 16, 1986, a Sunday. I excitedly spring out of bed because mom is off on Sundays! I run downstairs and see a note from dad.

Amber,

Sorry I had to leave so early for work, but I have good news. Dr. Harlem called and told me they have a heart for you! She said you are extremely lucky to receive a heart so soon. We'll go to the hospital for tests after I get home from work.

See you soon, Dad

I want to share the good news with my mom so I frantically search the house looking for her but she isn't anywhere to be found. "It's Sunday, why isn't she here?" I keep thinking over and over, "Why, why, why?" I find a piece of crumpled paper in the corner of the hallway next to the side door. My judgment tells me not to waste my time, that it's probably nothing, but my curiosity tells me to look because I am so desperately worried. This is my only hope so I unravel the paper.

Dear Molly,

I miss you terribly and so do the children. I hope all is well with your daughter; I am sure they will be fine. Springfield is not the same without you. I will be on a business trip this week so please come to the house at night and stay with John and Lisa; they will feel so much better. The Nanny will reserve a key under the flower pot for you. I look forward to the wedding next month in Montana. I cannot contain my excitement!

Love, Daniel

I call my dad on the yellow phone bolted to the wall but he doesn't answer - the first fifteen times. On call number sixteen, he picks up the phone and I tell him everything – from coming home to finding the letter. Dad tells me to sit down and breathe, to calm down and not leave, while he hurries home.

As I'm sitting and waiting for dad, I ask myself over and over again, "Who is this Daniel guy?" I think to myself, "John and Lisa are awful names." Finally, in a fit of rage, I grab the lamp next to me and throw it at the television set as *Teenage Mutant Ninja Turtles* blares away inanely.

"Alright, I'm here," dad says, "let me see this letter."

"Here take it; I can't look at it anymore."

"I knew it!" My dad picks up the other lamp and throws it at the television. "Come on, get in the car."

Racing down Blair Drive, my dad doesn't tell me anything. I am very scared because I suspect my dad took way too many pills. His speech was slurred and he wasn't walking straight during our conversation at home. He is headed all the way to Springfield where Daniel lives.

After a while, my favorite song *I Can't Wait* by Nu Shooz comes on the radio and time seems to stand still as a strange calm comes over me. I notice the sky is completely clear with not a single cloud in the sky. To the right of me is a lush forest, green with a variety of tall trees. To my left is a cliff where you can hear the sound of rushing water from the river at the bottom. I look at my dad and am about to say how beautiful this view is and thank him for everything he's done for me when he passes out, loses control of the car, and we drift off the shoulder of the road toward the edge of the cliff.

Luci A. Blanco

Luci is just your average girl who is training to become a professional ballerina in a ballet company. She loves spending time with friends and family, listening to music, photography, and playing the piano and ukulele.

Youth Writers Program
Florida Writers Association

Honorable Mention: November

I love running. Cross-country, to be exact. The pitter-patter of my sneakers, the thump-thump of my heart, the whoosh of wind in my ears. I'm only thirteen years old, but I know that I want to go to the Olympics for track-and-field and become a legend that people will remember for years to come. That's me, November; that's my dream. But a few years ago I wasn't so sure about that. I'd never been too sure of anything. I was a coward. My family and friends tell me that's not true, but it is; that's the only way to put it in words. I was an escape artist, an expert at running away from my problems.

Take soccer for instance. I was nine then and psyched to try the sport—you know how little kids are, never expecting the worst. But at my first practice, I took a step to kick the ball and slipped, falling on my bottom. The other kids laughed at me and though they weren't trying to be mean, my cheeks burned with embarrassment. I sat out for the rest of practice, waiting for my mom to pick me up. Then I quit, not daring to go back there again in fear of making an even bigger fool of myself.

Three months after that, Mom signed me up for ballet to help me with my footwork. The thing was, she didn't tell me. She knows me too well; she knew that I would make up an excuse not to go. One day she said she'd take me out for ice cream and she dropped me off at ballet.

And let me just say ballet was not any better than soccer—I've never been good at dance-y stuff like that to begin with. If I tried to do a pirouette, I'd stumble and bump into another girl. If I tried to do a plié, I'd bend too low and I'd fall over. And the instructor knew I was her worst student, but she would not get off my back about it. "November, head held high!" she'd snap. "November, graceful arms! November, keep your behind in when you do your pliés! These are not squats!" November this, November that. I couldn't take her anymore and I quit after three weeks of ballet.

Then in sixth grade, my P.E. coach observed how fast I was on my feet and she asked my mom if I would be interested in cross-country. I wasn't sure at first, but Mom talked me into trying out one of the practices. I went and, well, that's how I fell in love with running. I thought I was where I belonged and the part of me that had been a coward, running away from my problems, had disappeared. But it hadn't.

This day, one of my first cross-country meets of the season, a 2K, is just the beginning of my dream to become an Olympic track athlete. We've been running on a dirt trail for almost fifteen minutes and I'm second-in-the-lead by a girl with a dark, glossy ponytail that doesn't move. *Glossy Girl,* I think to myself. We make a curve around the bend and I cut in front of her. First place. *Oh, yeah.* The finish line is on the horizon, ten yards away, and my heart skips a beat. This is it, make it or break it time. Adrenaline kicks in and I run with all my might. I have to win this. I'm ahead of Glossy Girl, but she might make a comeback; she has a chance. I approach the finish line, running faster than I've ever gone in my life. Glossy Girl and I are side-by-side and this can be anyone's game. *You can do this, November! Come on!* And Glossy Girl and I are just about to leap over the finish line when a blur of—what is it? A leg? A tree root? I can't tell and I don't have time to look down because whatever it is, I trip over it and fall down on the dirt trail. *Pop!* The world spins around like a pinwheel and before I can grasp what's happening, everything goes black.

***

A broken ankle. That's what that "pop" was. I tripped over a tree root and fell, hitting my head hard. The doctor took the X-ray when I was out; I have to wear a cast for six weeks. As for my head, she said I'd have a bad headache, but there was no concussion. Mom thinks this is great news, but it's not. A concussion doesn't change the fact that I can't run. Cross-country is everything to me. It's in me. It's a part of me. It is me. And I'm not letting a broken bone stand in the way of that.

With my hands, I push myself off the couch and stand up on my left leg, the one that doesn't have a cast. It's been three days since the accident. Mom's at the grocery and Dad's out of town for work so I'm home alone; the coast is clear. I look down at my cast. *Let's do this.* I take one step forward and fly backwards on the floor. My head bangs on the rug. *Owww.* I close my eyes tight, holding back tears.

Just then, I hear the lock on the front door jiggle. I open my eyes and there's Mom, walking in with the groceries. "Why are you lying on the floor?"

I wipe my eyes and act like nothing's happened. "Trying to walk."

She sighs, drops her things on the kitchen counter, then comes over and helps me up. "November, we've been through this before. The doctor said you shouldn't put any pressure on your foot. That's what your crutches are for."

"But Mom, I have to—"

Mom shakes her head and laughs a little. "You can't walk, November! You broke your ankle. You need to understand that you can't just run away from your problems. You have to accept the difficulties that life throws at you— no matter how tough they may get."

And that's when it hit me that I was as much of a coward as I was three years ago; I hadn't changed like I thought I had. My mom was right— I couldn't keep pretending there wasn't a problem, I had to be the brave person I was and face my adversities. Now that, I knew, was what the true me would do. What November would do. So that day I made the decision to no longer let my problems affect me for the rest of my life. Because doing that wouldn't be me. I am November, and that was exactly who I would be from here on out.

Mary Grace Galione

Mary is the second-oldest of five kids. She is a brown-with-black belt in karate and a student leader in her church's youth group. Even though she's been dancing and writing fiction most of her life, she wants to make dolphin training a career.

Youth Writers Program
Florida Writers Association

Honorable Mention: Monstrosity

During the first few weeks, Ivan's screaming was inopportune and frequent. Once Ivan started screaming, Thing would scream and there'd be no telling when it would stop. As unusual as it was, it provided an effective way to pass the time for both parties. The reason the screaming continued for hours was mostly because both man and creature were horrid to look at – Ivan with his natural ugliness and Thing with the deadly spikes and strange dents sprawled across his body.

Ivan hadn't designed Thing this way, but he'd always known he'd resemble something terrifying when the experiments ended. Every time he thought back to those times, he'd shake in rage and resentment remembering how his experiments had been cut short by government forces and his project was left unfinished. But the world would never know that because all it cared about was that the evil villain was captured and detained. Little did they know that Ivan was detained as well on a remote island with one of his test experiments.

Thing grunted in frustration, shaking Ivan from his thoughts. He walked over and found Thing struggling with a straw and juice box, one of the rations the two prisoners received. "Let me get that for you." He quickly poked the straw through the box, then handed it to Thing who gaped at him. "It's, uh… it's all in the wrist." Thing began downing the juice box's contents. Even when not provoked, Thing was bulky and dangerous-looking even though he wasn't much taller than Ivan.

Just then, Ivan noticed something amongst the week's rations: there was a note tucked in the boxes. He quickly tore it open and saw it was a letter from his daughter. Thing noticed tears dripping down Ivan's face, which was abnormal, so he trudged over to see what all the fuss was about. He grunted questioningly but Ivan was not in the mood to discuss his discovery.

"It's nothing. You can have my rations for tonight. Just get away." Thing grunted again, this time doubtfully. "Yeah, like you know what this is." Thing snatched the letter from Ivan, but he grabbed it back. After three months, he finally had a purpose. He needed to leave the island, but he had no idea how to do it.

***

"So I have to wait 'til next week's ration delivery and then jump into the basket. As soon as I get back to the mainland, I'll ask around for Jane Anders and maybe someone'll know where she is. It's foolproof!" Ivan tried to convince himself of the brilliance of his plan. But then he slumped down, defeated; it would never work. He had examined the box in which the rations were delivered before – it had weight sensors and an automated mini-gun attached to the box. If the weight limit was exceeded, the mini-gun would trigger and begin firing.

At first, escape had seemed obvious: just leave the building. However, their island prison had been designed to prevent any and all form of escape to civilization. Ivan's thoughts were interrupted by a groan from Thing. "What do you want?" Thing nodded towards the lamp that Ivan had received in one of the ration deliveries. "No, I'm keeping this on," Ivan pushed him away. Thing grunted. "You don't need to know why," Thing whimpered.

Ivan didn't intend to let Thing in on this. He just wanted to begin a normal life with his family; having a monster along with him wouldn't help with that. Thing threw a blanket over his face, attempting to block out the light. "Yeah, good luck with that," Ivan said sarcastically.

Then it came to him. He would put Thing in the ration box which would trigger the mini-gun. Then he would jump over him, disable the gun, and get rid of Thing's corpse. Ivan smiled to himself as he wrapped up in a blanket and fell asleep.

***

"Okay, so you're gonna go in first and then I'll follow you. I'll be home to Jane in no time and you can, uh… you can go back to the lab! 'cause that's where we've got those radiation biscuits you love so much." Thing growled. "Well, you have to go in first because…" Ivan searched for an explanation. "... because you'll need to fend off the military, of course. It's not like I can fight them off." This wasn't far from the truth, actually. Thing pondered this for a few moments, then grunted decisively. Ivan thought it good that the experiments had destroyed half of Thing's cranial capacity. Before the tests, Mike had above average intelligence, which was why Ivan had selected him. If he had selected an average person with average intelligence, he most likely would have ended up with the intelligence and emotional capacity of a rock. A prize volunteer.

"Alright, get ready. The next ration delivery happens tomorrow." Thing went back to his deep slumber. Ivan decided to follow suit.

***

Ivan couldn't do it. In the end, he just couldn't send Thing to his death. He had already ruined Mike's life beyond belief and now he was just going to kill him? Ivan still had his humanity. So now how was he going to do it? How was he going to disable the weight scale? Thing stared at Ivan as he chewed on these questions, and then he nudged him. With no solution, Ivan followed Thing to where he led him outside. Thing extended a spike and drew a crude box in the sand. Then he drew a stick figure, presumably Ivan, and a hunk with spikes on it, him, inside the box. Finally, he made the sound of an explosion.

"You can do that?" Thing nodded quickly, leapt a few feet away, and then he blew up. Except, not all of him, more like a layer of his skin. "Amazing! I guess it's settled, then. Come on, the ration delivery's coming soon!" Thing screeched in surprise. "What is it?" Thing gestured towards something behind Ivan. He turned his head slightly. "Oh, that's not good." The building had Gatling guns sticking out across its exterior.

"Please return to the building as quickly and efficiently as possible," the automated voice repeated five times before the guns began firing wildly. Ivan looked at Thing, hoping he would disable the guns, but he did more than that; he bashed and smashed every single one until all that was left was a small pile of scrap. He picked up Ivan and scrambled up to the window.

Ivan quickly got down and looked out the other window. As if on cue, the box floated over on the zip line and stopped at the window. The box had a few minutes before it returned to where it had come from. Thing leapt in and the weight difference immediately triggered the mini-gun. Thing zig-zagged across the box, slid under the gun, and exploded his outer skin. The gun was demolished and Ivan broke the weight scale lying on the floor of the box. They sat and waited. The box started to move. They were on their way back to humanity.

Elliot Julian

Wait, you're still here? Go read another story! Go! Alright, fine. Elliot is from Staten Island, NY, and loves reading and writing. Also fencing. There. Now go! What, you want more? Well, that's about all you need to know.

Youth Writers Program
Florida Writers Association

FWA Youth Writers Age Group 14-17

1st Place: Because the Fuhrer Told Him So

A swastika-marked Jeep opened its back and SS soldiers filed out. Their boots hit the dirt as their eyes hit a pile of corpses that lay 10 meters from them. Saliva drained from their mouths. Death wasn't a new concept to these soldiers, but somehow this pile seemed more vile, more sickening. More evil.

A tight anxiety gripped Gideon—one of the enlisted. His eyes tore away from the sinister mound and up to the gray solemn sky. The wrinkles around his eyes squeezed tight in closure. He sat in his head for a moment, trying desperately to arm his mind in preparation for the work he would perform now. He had been reassigned to this work camp due to injury, but to him it didn't feel like a work camp. Something here felt profoundly wrong.

"These people look like human beings, but they're Jews. Remember that," Wal's slinky voice whispered into Gideon's ear. Icy shudders exploded over Gideon's back.

The next day, the sky's strained blue dimmed the whole facility.

Gideon was standing behind a guard who was situated to give the prisoners their bread. He had been detailed to this location. Gideon had not yet set eyes on the prisoners. The horrid air flooded his senses.

A bell rang and Gideon's stomach leapt. The prisoners came rushing in. Every nerve in Gideon's body sucked in its breath.

Skeletons with flesh barely covering their bones tripped over one another. Loose rags draped their bodies. Bald heads topped their necks. It was difficult to tell at first, but Gideon soon began to realize these barebones were all women and children.

Hands snatched bread as if it were gold. Legs found a place on the bench to collapse. Broken teeth devoured the miserable ration. Gideon's eyes found the ground and his lungs grasped for dusty air.

He eventually dragged his eyelashes up to scan the other SS soldiers. Each one looked the same. A stiff back, a grimace, analytical eyes.

Wal strode up to Gideon and ordered, "Monitor the room."

Gideon gripped his rifle and began to pace the rows. He kept his eyes on the dirt.

He hated himself. He tasted it in his mouth.

He, only a week ago, felt proud of himself for how many Allied soldiers he had managed to murder. He, only a month ago, cried with happiness as crowds of Germans cheered him as he marched with his drafted brothers. He, only a year ago, had been told that joining the ranks was the greatest honor a German could have. He, only a year and a half ago, had turned his back on his best friend because of his religion. Because the Führer told him so.

Gideon suddenly felt frantic. What if Jamil and his family were here? What if his mother and sister were sitting amongst these lifeless creatures clutching onto their souls? What if the people he once considered family were piled in the mass graves under his feet?

Realization poured over Gideon like cold water. The whispers he never noticed, the posters he never questioned—all claiming the enemy was Them. Lies. He knew these suffering souls shuffling before him were not the enemy. He knew that if he brought his eyes to meet his own reflection, he'd be confronting the villain.

His Nazi-marked uniform no longer felt like a heroic costume, but a dirty, vile rag. He wanted to rip it off. He wanted to scrub the tattooed kisses of rallying German citizens off his cheeks.

He tried with arduous effort to keep himself composed. He felt heavy chains across his chest and steel cuffs on his ankles. The weight of it all was begging him to collapse. His chest heaved and his eyes filled. With every cell in his body, Gideon felt a horror and self-loathing never before warranted.

Gideon turned sharply and began to pace the third row. Through blurry vision, he watched as a piece of bread roll in front of him onto the dusty floor. A frail body threw itself over the scrap. His march halted. A girl, on her hands and knees, stared into his boots. He stared down at her bald head, frozen. The bread lay caught in the crossfire of the boots and the eyes.

The girl dragged her gaze up to meet his. She had bright brown eyes. Jewish eyes. Strikingly alive and heated, so different than her form, but yet they held a shadow of despair and weighted gloom. She dropped her eyes and the fire extinguished. Gideon, with a quivering hand, reached out and wrapped his scarred fingers around her bread.

Frantically, her eyes jumped from the floor to the bread to his eyes. Panic and horror glassed over her pupils. Gideon extended his arm and opened his palm. He didn't smile, but gave a sharp nod. She reached out her boney hand and snatched the bread.

Gideon turned on his heel and walked straight out of the hall. The brisk air washed over his face. He reached the back of the building with quick steps. Sobs escaped his chest and vomit accompanied it.

Carissa Clough

Carissa is a sophomore and co-president of the Creative Writing club. Carissa is also a competitive swimmer and a pianist. Through her community organization, Bringing Reading into Diverse Groups Everywhere (BRIDGE), Carissa installs Little Free Libraries in disadvantaged areas and organizes Proyecto Escribir, a preschool bilingual writing program.

Youth Writers Program
Florida Writers Association

2nd Place: The Special Snowflake that Wasn't Special Enough

It was the flyer posted on the old oak tree in the park that started it all. The flyer had been put by the director of the Deborah's Dancing Studio, Miss Deborah Danby herself. But this is not her story. This is the story of the twelve-year-old girl who stood beneath the old oak tree in the park on New Year's Eve and read the flyer.

Her name was Elizabeth Baker. Or, at least, that was the name mentioned in the short note that had been dropped off at the orphanage's door in the dead of night along with the sleeping baby girl. But Elizabeth's own name was nothing of consequence to her at that moment. The only name that mattered to her was the one on the flyer: Deborah Danby.

Elizabeth figured out what she wanted to do with her life when she was eight. During that summer, a school for dance opened two blocks down from the orphanage. It was called Deborah's Dancing Studio. From the moment Elizabeth looked through the window and into the class of dancers, she was enraptured.

Even though the orphanage director wanted Elizabeth's dream to be realized, no amount of kindness or belief in the aspirations of a young girl could pay that tuition. Elizabeth knew this well as she stared up at the flyer.

"A ballet competition," she said with a sigh.

Lost in dancing fantasies, Elizabeth drifted away from the flyer and into the cold streets. She reasoned that even if she couldn't participate in the competition, she could watch it. She could watch those graceful ballerinas glide across the stage the same way glimmering snowflakes glided through the air. She could watch and wish that someday she could join them.

That day came sooner than she thought.

As she made her way back to the orphanage, Elizabeth suddenly remembered an elegant melody she had once heard a street violinist play. It was such a beautiful tune with soothing low notes that stretched on so far, it made you want to grab onto them and let them take you far away. Before long, Elizabeth had taken her place among the fluttering snowflakes. She leaped and twirled across the sidewalk, imitating skills she watched the dancers perform.

Then a sound broke through her symphonious reverie and changed her life.

A single cough.

Elizabeth turned to see a tall woman with long ginger hair. She wore a heavy brown overcoat and a mischievous grin. Elizabeth gasped.

"I believe I've seen you before," Deborah said after a long stretch of silence. "You hang around my studio sometimes, but I've never seen you in class. So where did you learn to dance like that?"

Those next moments were magic for Elizabeth. All the time spent trying to learn ballet on her own finally seemed worth it as the moment Deborah Danby noticed her became realized.

Elizabeth told of about how she had watched the dancers. She told of all she had learned from staring at them from the window. She told of how she longed to join them.

"Why don't you?" Deborah asked.

Elizabeth shuffled her feet. "Mr. Wright says there's not enough money."

"Mr. Wright?"

"The orphanage director."

Deborah considered this for a moment before breaking into another mischievous grin.

"Well," she said, "with that talent of yours, *I* should be paying *you* to dance for me."

***

Deborah's Dancing Studio opened up for the first time since Christmas week on January 2nd. The ballet students were a bit surprised when they came back from the holiday to find a girl they had never seen before stretching.

Deborah came in with a CD player and her trademark grin. With the lesson started, no one paid much attention to Elizabeth. A couple of times, she noticed one of the boys nodding when she displayed a skill she was particularly good at. At the end of the lesson, she smiled to herself. She felt a bit out of place, but her dream was coming true.

"Hello?"

Elizabeth blinked. The boy who had been watching her earlier stood in front of her.

"Finally," he said with a laugh. "You were spaced out for a while there."

"O-Oh," Elizabeth stammered. "I'm sorry."

"It's okay," he replied. "I just wanted to tell you that you did well today. Where did you practice before coming here?"

"I taught myself some things from watching them done, but this is my first real lesson."

His eyes widened. "Really? I've been doing ballet my whole life, and you might be better than me. You're talented."

"Thank you," Elizabeth said, grinning.

"I'm Nathaniel, by the way," he said, holding out his hand. "Nathaniel Stone."

She took it. "Elizabeth Baker."

***

The weeks passed as excitement and snow piled up around Deborah's Dancing Studio. On the day of the competition, Elizabeth studied herself in the bathroom mirror. Elizabeth finally looked as she had so often imagined herself.

She stepped out of the bathroom and caught sight of a snowflake stuck on the window. It stared in at her, the way she used to stare in at the dancers.

"I'll dance beautifully," she told it, "for the both of us."

The snowflake seemed to wink before being carried off by the wind. It was like a good omen. A special snowflake, just like Elizabeth.

The competition started and Elizabeth's stomach felt knotted. Nathaniel assured her she would be fine before he walked out for his routine.

While the previous acts were nice, Nathaniel's routine was definitely the best thus far. Within seconds, the audience—and the judges—were enraptured. When it was over, everyone felt disappointed that such a beautiful dance had to come to an end.

Elizabeth took a deep breath. *It's not easy, having to follow up* that, *but this is my dream and following dreams was never meant to be easy.*

The next few minutes were a blur. As Elizabeth finished her dance and took her bow, she thought back to the old oak tree and the flyer. *Look at me now.*

After the last performance, Deborah took the stage with an envelope in her hand. She said some nice things about the performance and told a few jokes that fell flat before opening it up. Elizabeth looked at Nathaniel, and they both smiled. The excitement in the room was so thick, one could almost hold it.

"The winner of Deborah's Dancing Studio's first ballet competition is,"—she paused for dramatic effect—"*Nathaniel Stone!*"

Applause filled the room. Audience members stood and cheered. Once it was all over, Nathaniel ran to Elizabeth and hugged her.

"That was exciting!" he exclaimed. "But I think I need some water now."

"Congratulations," she said as he ran off.

"Hey," the voice of Deborah Danby reached Elizabeth's ears, something that would have thrilled her three weeks before. "Your friend won. That's pretty exciting."

"Yeah."

"You don't look excited."

"I want to be happy, but I can't. This has been my dream for years," she sighed. "I thought I had talent."

Deborah frowned. "You do. But Nathaniel has been doing this for years. You have something special, Elizabeth, but on its own, it's not special enough."

Alice Elysian

Ainsley loves to write and is happy to share her story. She hopes that all who read it enjoy it.

Youth Writers Program
Florida Writers Association

3rd Place: The Siege

"What kind of men are you! Put some back into it!" The commander's words barraged us as we readied the battering ram. We rolled it off the hill's peak, towards the large doors of the impressive bastion. "Move it! Scouts caught sight of enemy cavalry from the north. We don't have time for dawdling!"

We forced the ram past the archers; their arrows like a murder of crows flying towards a fresh feast of death. A major watched over his archers, ordering them to let loose their quarrels into the sky.

Beyond the bowmen were the shields and the poor souls behind them. The infantry shrouded themselves with the thick boards. They hung on for dear life, as it wasn't just our arrows clouding the skies. We passed the line of foot soldiers. They began to advance alongside us. We continued until we had finally approached the fortress wall.

The infantry pressed their bodies against the wall. Their shields faced the sky as rocks poured on top of them. A man on my right toppled over as a heavy stone crashed on top of his barrier. I wiped the sweat from my brow, brushing aside my hair in the process. The commander shouted, "Attack! Bring down that door!" In unison, our men began to take siege of the castle. We grabbed hold the ram's sturdy beam. It crashed against the castle's doors with astounding power. The entrance creaked and squealed as its swan song played, until it collapsed like a slain beast.

As we recoiled our mechanical monster, our troops stormed the inside of the stronghold and began to engage the combatants in the courtyard. The enemy archers that focused on us were eliminated by our marksmen. Footmen had advanced to a key position and gained the advantage in mere seconds. The commander rallied us and instructed us to join the infantry.

From the courtyard, we could hear the defenders inside the castle. A squad of men rushed us. Their steel armor was thicker than the boiled leather we had equipped. The swords they wielded were the size of a man. Wrapped around their breastplate was a purple sash, embroidered with golden flowers.

In his most authentic bravado, a lone warrior from our infantry rushed these iron men. His battle cry was silenced by the agile movement of steel.

Unlike the dead fool, the rest of us huddled close. The enemy, with his beautiful violet ribbon, lunged towards the group, eager to chop us all down. One comrade, as swift as a swallow, darted past his blade. Dodging his clunky movements, he sunk his spear into the back of the heavy foe. This young man was more successful than our dead ally. He turned and gazed on his kill, while he smiled with prideful pleasure.

In his hubris, he failed to notice the pack of metal men behind him. Their armor clinked and clanked as they ran towards the killer, who stood stationary. I bolted towards him, ripping him from Death's jaws. In that brief second, everyone on both sides had joined the skirmish.

In my haste, I had made a dangerous mistake. My footing was unstable, the ground too wet. I slipped while I held my ally's hand. We crashed into the mud. I got to my knees, lifting him simultaneously. With his arm around me, I began to guide him away from the battle.

"My leg, I think the brute got my leg." He grunted, and attempted to let go. "Leave me, I'm not becoming dead weight."

I stared at him, into his pleading eyes. "I won't leave you behind."

Even in this dire moment, the war continued around us. Our archers continued firing, the enemy bowmen were all finished, yet the arrows still flew. The projectiles assisted in the attack against the armored opponents. Allowing our allies to gain the advantage.

A dangerous echo filled the air, and an archer called out what could be translated as a condemnation. "Cavalry charge!" The archer's warning was accompanied by the now booming sound of hooves against earth. Knights rode on the pathway we used to enter. The archers were unable to hold a solid defense against the opposing reinforcements. Shouts continued until no more arrows flew. Mounted enemies entered through the demolished door and began charging our infantry. Men fell left and right, on both sides.

A knight charged towards me, his purple sash fluttered in the wind. My young companion, in a brazen move, pushed me away. I tumbled into the mixture of blood and mud. He fell next to me.

I escaped into a stable, dragging my friend by the arms. I swung the door closed. All the horses were either dead or absent. The smell was unbearable. I laid him on a bed of hay. With his back towards the thatch roof, I could fully see the red fissure along his back. He had tears in his eyes, his sobs muffled by straw.

Outside the stable, I looked through a crack in the door, our men were incapable of facing the incoming horsemen. This was becoming a massacre, not a battle.

The young soldier grasped my shoulder. He whispered to me, his voice was groggy. "I know..." He paused abruptly; before I could respond, he had collapsed for the final time.

With the passing of a late friend, a dismounted cavalier opened the stable door, and cleared the area. I quickly picked my comrade's discarded spear and aimed it at my opponents. I lunged towards him. The horseman dove at me in turn. We traded swipes. He had miscalculated his strike, merely grazing my helm, albeit enough to destroy it. Meanwhile, I had stopped him in his tracks with my attack. The spear pierced through his torso. I ripped off my damaged helm and stared at him, directly in his surprised eyes.

"You're… a… girl?..." He croaked, and then fainted. I stepped over him, sighed, and then walked back out into the war.

Matthew Scotney

Matthew enjoys exploring the world around himself! His hobbies include writing, reading, weightlifting, and video games. Some of his favorite books include "Going After Cacciato" by Tim O' Brien, "World War Z" by Max Brooks, and "The Stand" by Stephen King.

Youth Writers Program
Florida Writers Association

Honorable Mention: The Queen of Hearts

I watched the two of them from outside their window. I took note of the way the young woman shuddered every time the young man spoke; he threw back his hands as if defenestrating himself from the room, temples and throat veins bulging, eyes fractured with anger. Occasionally, I would hear surges of shouting loud enough to penetrate the apartment windows, and maybe even the mottled brick, and these would be followed by muffled sobbing on the woman's part. Her weakness bothered me the most, more so than the abusive way her male assailant spoke and raged.

It wasn't as if she were a frail little thing; she was sturdily built, with purportedly confident shoulders—assuming she wasn't withering and wailing as her present state suggested—and a considerable stature for a female. She appeared well-exercised, with a toned band of muscle around her stomach and tight calves that twitched when she staggered back at every vile, vitriolic verbal advance the man made.

The man wasn't monstrous by any measure, but the power of his words compensated for what his physique failed to accomplish.

My patience was growing short; I had the patience of a dynamite wick and I wasn't known to be one of the cultured, cultivated pansies championed by society. *Not by a milestone.*

The man let loose another assault—shouting, screaming, waving his sweat-speckled hands. The young woman cowered and I fought the urge to yell out and compromise my purposeful entrance into their apartment. Nevertheless, I couldn't help the diabolical twist in my stomach when I watched the pathetic creature struggle against her aggressor. If I weren't a slight advocate for feminism, I would have killed her as well.

When the woman wouldn't respond, the man unleashed his ultimatum. I wasn't sure of the precise wording, but I was sure of the disastrous effect, and I could very well predict the way the cowardly girl would crumble and crack and break. She fell with her hands over her face, covering tears that flowed like stampedes down her reddened, pathetic face. Mucous and snot and heated saliva coated her cheeks and arched down her chin; she was a condemned mess of a human being, and I briefly thought of conjuring a grain of sympathy for her, but then quickly dismissed it with a derisive snort once the thought occurred to me. She was so weak.

It was disgusting.

The man continued to scream at the woman, who had fallen prostrate on the ground, almost as if she were worshipping him through begging, supplicating tears. I thought I saw her reach for him from her position on the ground.

"We're done!" I heard him scream. The woman whimpered, broken further by the finality of his words. Was it possible to shatter her bones from all the shaking?

The perverse part of me hoped so.

I came closer to the apartment, keeping a curious eye on the window. The two individuals were too engrossed in the argument to notice the stranger approaching their unlocked door, which, in the end, would be the death of them.

"*Please.* Tell me what I did. I swear, Christopher, I'll make it up to you. *I promise.* Just tell me what it is, please tell me what it is!"

The man scoffed. He refused to meet her pleading eyes. "Like you deserve to know."

I rolled my eyes at the theatrics. It was time for me to enter.

I didn't bother with discreteness when I twisted the knob and walked into their living room. When I stepped into the adjoining hallway, the man's eyes traveled from the top of the woman's head, then to my boots, and finally locked on me. I took my time to smile, drawing out the wings of my mouth like one would draw out a weapon—slowly, deliberately, painstakingly. It made the outcome so much sweeter.

"Who are you?" The man's brow broke in the center, bowing like halves of a broken bridge over a sweaty forehead.

I took my time to answer, adding a supercilious sort of snort before replying. "I'd say your worst nightmare, but I'm afraid that's morosely overstated and relatively inaccurate; you've never seen me before, so you couldn't possibly pin me as anything remotely nightmarish." I picked at my nails. "But don't worry: I can assure you that by the time we're done, you can take comfort in coming to your own conclusions."

The man transitioned from his earlier bout of anger to confusion. I didn't see any signs of acknowledgement from the woman on the floor; perhaps her devastation had rendered her immobile in both brain and body. More reason to kill her out of disgust.

"I have a gun. I won't hesitate to shoot!" His voice shook—raising in volume—this time out of fear. I relished it.

"Darling, I'm sure you wouldn't hesitate to pull the trigger. But will you be able to hit me?"

I strode forward, excitement coursing through me when I saw the way he shook with each closing step. It was delicious to see power ripped from tyrants, and even more delicious to see them tremble as repulsively as their victims.

"Stay where you are! I'll call the police! I have a gun!"

I snickered. "All stated facts. But useless in your position."

I was now inches from the man; I could see every bead of sweat on his pale face, feel the quaking, petrified heat and torment pouring from his body. *A predator and her prey.*

"Please, whoever you are, stay—"

I thrust my hand into his chest, lengthening my fingers as they entered his body. The man bucked upon the initial surprise of my hand trespassing the inner cavity of his chest, and then a luscious swell of pain rearranged the symmetry of his face. He choked on words that would never come, and I nearly laughed out in pernicious delight when I pulled his heart from his chest and presented it to him.

The man gawked, and he could have died from fright and disbelief had I not held his beating, ragged heart for a moment longer. The young woman on the floor was looking up now; she was wickedly captivated in the heart I held in my hand, still pumping, still fighting. As if in anticipation of my next move, the man began to furiously shake his head. I smiled, drawing my fingers close as I crushed his heart.

His body crumpled onto the ground, falling next to the woman on the ground, who looked as lifeless as her once-living harasser.

"What did you do to him?"

I was surprised she was still able to talk, but answered regardless.

"He broke your heart, didn't he? I was only returning the favor."

Tears welled in her eyes. "I loved him."

"Even more reason to thank me," I said, collecting the dust of my kill from my hands and emptying it into a vial at my hip. I had done considerably well for a day's work. I turned to leave.

"You're a monster!" she screamed.

I turned back around and laughed. "Yes, yes I am."

Rachel Elisabeth

Rachel Elisabeth is an avid reader and writer. She has recently published her first novel, *Radioactive*, and is working on subsequent editions. In her free time, she enjoys lecturing, writing poetry, and listening to music.

Youth Writers Program
Florida Writers Association

Honorable Mention: A Writer's Crisis

One day, I decided to be an author. On that day, I apparently also decided that I'd be living the minimalist lifestyle; skirting along in life, with barely a paycheck to feed myself, nor exotic foods to consume. "I need something about... the moon... and rivers! Moons and rivers are the best ways to open up this kind of trash. It can fill up a good page or two, if I stall it out just right." I think out loud to preserve my own sanity. I'm alone. In high school, I was so busy trying to get into a good college that I forgot to make any friends. Now, I'm desperately writing my next book so I can pay off my student debt. I have written books in the past, but they haven't been very successful. I hate it when critics like your books but nobody buys them. It feels almost... unfair. So, instead of writing a good book that nobody will buy, I'll write a trashy book that everyone will read just to rag on. Then, it might make enough money and garner enough of a following for some people to MAYBE see my book after that.

The topic of the horror I'm writing is that there is a superhero named Jule with overwhelming powers who gets everything that he wants, at least, on a surface level. However, his real identity is dealing with a crumbling marriage on top of his extreme debt, and thus, is depressed. There are a few reasons why I chose this sort of topic. Firstly, a superhero who is perfect on a surface level but has deeper problems will always sell. The premise is a key selling feature of any book, and this one is a seller. Next, if I have a character who has good looks but is depressed, I have an excuse to make him sound edgy. That edge just KILLS the teenagers' emotional receptors, and then I have some guaranteed sales by means of angsty kids. On top of that, I have the inclusion of such adult problems as debt and marriage problems, and we have a possible sell there too. With all these elements combined, my book is going to sell so well that I can finally make a living off writing, pay my rent for once, and finally eat something other than ramen and cereal.

***

"So now, he's going to... uh... complain about his problems but act like they're not his fault. Yeah, yeah, that's some edgy, money-hungry dialogue we got here." Relatable for the kiddies, irritating for the oldies, money for me. I hate this. I'm ruining my consumer and publisher trust, I'm ruining my mindset for good writing, I'm destroying my confidence, I'm... just... making money. I'm making money. Not a book. Nothing that anyone will remember. I'm making money. This is not my legacy. This is money. I just need money.

And with that, I finished my book. I'm going through it tomorrow. I'm counting the money in my hand before I send it in. This money is mine. I'm making this money. No more will I be the poor boy who can't provide for himself, no longer will I be the guy who needs to get loans for money because I simply can't get a good job. No. Now I'm hiding behind Jule, my hero. Jule, the edgy, over-relatable, whiny superhero. Jule, the man with super strength and a messed-up marriage. Jule, the name of my new wallet.

I fell onto my bed regretting the scheme, while also slowly counting the money I would earn on my fingers. I got to around $204 and a lot of shame before I fell asleep.

I must fix this.

***

I woke up at around 9:30 AM, and immediately, I decided to change his superpower. Super-strength doesn't tell me much about him, so maybe… telekinesis might work. I could make it so that his marriage isn't working out so well because he can't read social cues very well, and him being telekinetic could be symbolic of his mind, and how he is intelligent, but just doesn't work with people that well. His mind is his greatest strength but his most glaring weakness. And at that point, I'll just place him on the autistic spectrum. I think that could work, I think as I open up my journal and note down my thoughts.

Next, his personality. He's too… whiny. Too whiny and standoffish and insufferable. No wonder he's depressed. If he were alive, next to me, and let his mouth run, I'd probably want to die too. Maybe I should make it so that, instead of being annoying, he's the opposite. Maybe I should make him be really quiet and thoughtful, easily flustered, and lacking in self-esteem. That's far more interesting. See, if he has overwhelming power in the form of telekinesis, but doesn't really show it in his demeanor, then he is lacking in confidence. He has the power to do so much more, but he doesn't think that he can, so he doesn't try at all. That also helps with the integrity of the character; as he gains more confidence in himself through the course of the story, his marriage slowly heals and his powers grow. I gleefully add even more notes into my journal.

My journal slowly fills to its end. As more and more ideas came up, I took the time to add a paragraph or two explaining why I chose to make the fixes that I made, and before you know it, I had filled up 150 pages of a loose-leaf notebook and was part way through a new one before I finally felt like I had fixed my monstrosity of a book. I began editing at 9:30 P.M.

***

A month had passed since I submitted my cleansed book to my publisher, and today, I got a letter telling me that they decided to publish my book. They liked the premise, enjoyed the characters, and thought my symbolism and irony was funny at first, but surprisingly deep.

It sold.

It sold so many delicious copies. I got nominated for some awards, some of which I won. I had so much money that I went on vacation. (Germany is truly a fascinating place) After I returned home, I started working on my next book, and decided early on to make it a good story over a good seller.

Marshall Bustamante

Marshall Bustamante is a real, authentic human being. If he wasn't... well, that'd be just silly, now wouldn't it. Haha! So silly. He attends St. Johns Country Day School and if you don't believe him, then that is very silly of you. Delightful.

Youth Writers Program
Florida Writers Association

Honorable Mention: Warped

Warped: to become bent or twisted out of shape. That's me and I have nothing to apologize for. My cape fluttered in the wind as it is harnessed to my body by a single thread. I don't know if I can do this much longer. *Boom.* Another explosive sounded in a distance. Would she ever stop?

I started for my car to get more supplies to capture her. I felt like I was being followed. I turned to my right and saw a figure. With a flip of my wrist, webs attacked the person and entangled them. I changed the direction I was going and moved towards the person.

"Wow! You're *the* Warp! The best-" I quickly clamped my hand over his mouth. The streets were deserted but I knew my enemy instilled cameras somewhere.

"Shh!" I whispered loudly. I combed my long brown hair using my fingers. "What do you want?"

"Can I follow you? You know, help you out?" He pleaded. His eyes were large like a puppy wanting a treat.

"Fine." I responded.

"Do you know who I am?" He asked with his arms draped on his slender figure. I noticed his attempt of a costume was made up of a matching T-shirt and pants the colors of a forest fire.

"Nope." I said with a popping sound.

"You really don't know who I-" I didn't want to hear him anymore. I'm sure anyone in my position would feel honored by this kind of attention but, I don't feel compassion. I hid that away a long time ago.

"You'd think the confused look and blank stare would give it away." I added cutting him off.

"I'm the Incredible Blaze here to make your acquaintance and partnership." He bowed. Blaze had something different about him.

"Great." I acknowledged sarcastically. Maybe it was a mistake letting him follow me.

"Awesome! I've got a plan as well." He added with a sense of pride.

"Well, what's your plan?" I turned towards him with a newfound interest. Maybe this kid won't be too bad.

"My plan was to follow your plan." He smiled shyly probably not expecting me to ask. With that, I slapped my hand on my face. My fingers touched the mask I wore to hide my identity. There was no way I wanted my foster parents to know this is what I did in my spare time instead of study. They would certainly insinuate this as a disturbance to 'my learning adventure.'

"Don't you have somewhere stupid to be?" I snapped.

"Not until four." I ignored him and made way for the car yet again. This time, Blaze followed without a sound towards my car. I put my hand on the logo and a beep noise sounded. The trunk split open to reveal weapons and plans I made prior. I grabbed a handful of items and tossed Blaze a handcuff. There was no way I was letting the kid hold a weapon of any sorts. He would probably hurt himself minutes after receiving it.

I beckoned him to follow me as we turned the corner to the area I last heard a sound. I had to get her tonight if it was the last thing I did.

"Okay, so you do your magic and I'll come up and watch your back." He told me.

"I've got my own back." I saw her in the air surveying the west. Signaling Blaze to stay out and hidden, I flew behind her and used my web to entangle her. She let out a sigh as loud as thunder. *It's working!*

Before I was able to use my Crampo, a machine to bottle any power or special ability, she began to glow. Her body shined with a blue light. The color distracted me as I became mesmerized by it. Before I knew it, her light exploded and I was on the ground with rubble all over me.

"Warp!" I heard a voice yell. I was in and out of fainting but, I had to get enough strength to beat her once and for all.

Blaze knelt next to me. "Get up." He pleaded. His voice soft and sweet. I looked at him as my pain seemed to be melting away. When I looked at my ankle, it was no longer burned and scraped.

"Did you, did you-" I began trying to formulate my words.

"Yeah. It's my healing mask. Now go up there and beat her. I know you can do it."

"How can you be so sure?" I was on the verge of tears at this point. All of my past came flooding at me as I remembered being deserted by my parents and everyone I felt was dear to my heart.

"I believe in you. You should believe in yourself. If you believed in Santa Clause for more than two years, I know you can believe in yourself for five minutes. Just do it for me and for you." His words came to me like rushing water from the Canal.

"Tell me. Why did you become the Warp? You need your motivation to help you find your strength." Blaze continued as he looked around for the girl.

"They told me I couldn't do, I had to prove them wrong." I whispered. Thoughts of my parents and my previous foster parents came to me. All the pain and sorrow I tried hiding away in my heart was unlocked by Blaze and I had feelings again. I didn't feel like heartless anymore. I felt something.

"Remember that as you go back up there to defeat Blue Wonder. And just know, a villain is a hero whose story hasn't been told. Tell everyone your story. Show them what Warp is made of. Make them pay."

I stood up with new confidence. *I will. I'll make them remember my name, Arden Jane. Not the name they gave me but the real me.*

Jade Browne

Jade Browne is a high school senior with aspirations to study English in college. She loves blogging, writing, and reading along with playing the piano and being with friends and family.

Youth Writers Program
Florida Writers Association

Where Does Your Muse Live?
Florida Writers Association Collection, Volume 10 and Florida Writers Association Youth Collection, Volume 5

The theme for our next book in FWA's Collection series is *Where Does Your Muse Live?* Florida Writers Association Collection, Volume 10, set to be published in the fall of 2018. It will include the youth collection contest, Volume 5, with the same theme.

Where does your muse live is all about from where the greatness of your writing comes. Who is your muse? Have you created a home for her/him? Is your muse a fantastical creature? Or a tiny faerie that flits about your mind? Fiction, nonfiction and poetry are all acceptable genres and how you define "your muse" is entirely up to you. Maybe you have a favorite character in your writing who has become your muse, or perhaps a friend who sparks your writing is actually your muse. It's a wide open theme this year so explore the possibilities.

These short story contests, sponsored by the Board of Directors of Florida Writers Association, and by Black Oyster Publishing, our Official FWA Publisher for Collections, was created to offer our members an opportunity to be published, and another way to grow their writing skills.

Each year, the contest has a theme. All writing must conform to that theme, and must be within the total word limitations as set forth in the guidelines.

The annual contests are fun—they give you the opportunity to submit two entries. They stretch you, giving you parameters and guidelines within which you previously may not have considered writing.

All judging is done on a blind basis. Stories are posted by only title and number for the adult collection contest and by only title, number and author age for the youth collection contest. The number is assigned consecutively as stories are received. In the adult collection contest, judges read each entry entirely and evaluate according to whether or not it was well written, was strongly on theme, and struck a chord with them. Because the youth collection contest separates the entries into two age groups, judges also consider the writing-skill sets for each age group along with the same criteria as the adult contest. As with any judging, there is some subjectivity to the process. However, the judges understand that each entry selected as a winner must be ready for printing, as no editing is done other than fixing minor typos that happen to be caught.

Next year is our second year for the Royal Palm Literary Award Competition Published Book of the Year winner as our Person of Renown for the collection book. This new concept is inspiring our members in their writing journeys and providing yet another way for members to become published authors.

As in the past, our Person of Renown will select their Top Ten Favorite entries out of the judges' top sixty only in the adult collection contest. The youth contest winners are determined by highest scoring judges' total...and we'll be off and running with another book for the Collection, and, another set of contests to look forward to for the following year.

76437097R00124

Made in the USA
Columbia, SC
09 September 2017